D1282608

# Wedding Cake and Big Mistakes

Center Point
Large Print

Also by Nancy Naigle and available from Center Point Large Print:

The Adams Grove Novels
  *Sweet Tea and Secrets*
  *Out of Focus*

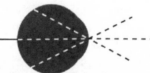

**This Large Print Book carries the Seal of Approval of N.A.V.H.**

# Wedding Cake
## and
# Big Mistakes

*An Adams Grove Novel*

# NANCY NAIGLE

CENTER POINT LARGE PRINT
THORNDIKE, MAINE

Library of Congress Cataloging-in-Publication Data

Names: Naigle, Nancy.
Title: Wedding cake and big mistakes : an Adams Grove novel / Nancy
Naigle.
Description: Center Point Large Print edition. | Thorndike, Maine :
Center Point Large Print, 2016. | ©2013
Identifiers: LCCN 2015042525 | ISBN 9781628998702
    (hardcover : alk. paper)
Subjects: LCSH: Weddings—Fiction. | Murder—Fiction. | Large type
books. | GSAFD: Love stories.
Classification: LCC PS3614.A545 W43 2016 | DDC 813/.6—dc23
LC record available at http://lccn.loc.gov/2015042525

# Dedication

To my cousin, Jenn, who left us way too soon.
You'll be in our hearts forever.

# Wedding Cake and Big Mistakes

# ❖ Chapter One ❖

Someone had apparently forgotten to give Jill Clemmons the dress-your-bridesmaids-tacky memo. Even in the wavy reflection, the gown Jill had picked out for Carolanne Baxter to wear in her wedding was not only stylish, but the color was perfect against Carolanne's redhead complexion. She twisted in front of the antique full-length mirror in her bedroom. It wasn't often that Carolanne embraced the softer side of things, and for a fleeting moment, in a dress as fancy as this, she could almost picture herself as a bride. She placed her hands in front of her as if holding a bouquet and paced slowly forward.

A wick of heated panic swam up her spine. *What am I thinking?* She shook the fake bouquet from her hands and lunged toward the bed to grab the matching shoes from their box. She stepped into the shoes and sucked in a steadying breath to push those thoughts from her mind. Then, she threw open the bedroom door and stepped into the living room to make her big entrance.

"What do you think?" Carolanne felt as awkward today as she had years ago back in Miss Bobbie's beginner ballet class.

Jill sprang to her feet. "You look beautiful."

The wrinkles in Milly's eighty-odd-year-old

face seemed to smooth away as her mouth spread into a grin. "Stunning. Absolutely stunning, dear." She crossed the room and rose on tiptoe to kiss Carolanne on the cheek.

Carolanne felt the waxy remains of Milly's signature color. She was infamous for leaving her red-orange lipstick tattoo behind.

Milly pulled her hands up on her hips. "I swear if I hadn't already seen Jill in her gown, I'd be worried to death you'd outshine the bride." She ran her hand along the delicate fabric—pinching and tugging to check the fit. "It's gorgeous."

"Too bad they shipped the wrong shoes." Carolanne extended her leg out to the side, showing off the sexy strappy rhinestone numbers they'd sent by accident instead of the platform peep-toe pump she'd picked out. "But I admit I do like these!"

"Me, too," Jill said. "And they aren't making us pay the difference. Happy accident, if you ask me. If that's the biggest catastrophe that I have in the wedding process, I'll be thrilled."

"The dress will need to be hemmed just a smidgen."

Milly tsked. "I can take care of that. It looks like a perfect fit otherwise." She took a step back and eyed Carolanne from head to toe. "You've never looked more beautiful."

Carolanne rolled her eyes. "With no makeup? I sure hope I've looked better."

"You never did need makeup," Milly said. "With your hair down like that, you look just like your momma. Teresa was such a beauty—inside and out."

A flash of loneliness stabbed at Carolanne. *I wish Mom were here today.*

Jill reached for Carolanne's hand. It was a bond they shared. They'd both lost their mothers at a young age. Jill's grandmother, Pearl, had been their guiding light, but now Pearl was gone and Carolanne was sure that's exactly what Jill was thinking about right now, too.

Milly placed her hand against Carolanne's cheek. "Your momma was a kindhearted gal. Everyone loved her. She'd have been so proud of you." She stood there with her hand on Carolanne's cheek for an awkwardly long moment.

Carolanne glanced over at Jill, but she was no help. Carolanne glared at her. Once they started laughing, they'd never stop. It had always been that way.

Then, like someone had squirted her with a dose of WD-40, Milly sprang into action, rustling through her flowered sewing box, whipping out old-fashioned hem clips and her pincushion, an old chubby tomato-shaped one. She shuffled over to the desk, grabbed the footstool, and dragged it to the center of the floor. "Can you step up on this in those shoes without breaking your neck?"

Carolanne lifted the dress as she walked toward

Milly and stepped up onto the stool. "I can."

"The dress, the color—it's all perfect," Jill said, clapping her hands.

Carolanne smoothed the skirt and spun, letting the fine layers of fabric swirl around her legs. "I love it."

Jill held her hands to her heart. "I couldn't have dreamed it more perfect."

Carolanne gave Jill a look. "You've had that giant binder of pictures and lists for your wedding since we were in junior high. Since before you had a groom. This perfection is *exactly* what you dreamed of."

Jill shrugged. "OK, OK. So it's just as I planned, but it's even better in real life."

Milly tucked pins between her lips and tugged on the dress. "Are you standing straight?"

"Yes, ma'am," Carolanne said.

"Hold still." Milly lifted the hem of the dress, letting it fall naturally.

"I feel seventeen again."

"Your prom dress wasn't near as lovely as this one, but I'll never forget how excited you were about going to that dance. You were so darn wiggly I liked to never have gotten that dress hemmed."

"Too bad I didn't get to go to the dance. All that time you spent on that dress—for nothing."

"It wasn't for nothing. I loved every minute of sewing that dress for you."

Even after all these years, Carolanne remembered every little detail of that night and how her father had ruined it for her by pulling one of his drunken stunts. *Why is it so easy to remember the bad things?*

"That was a long time ago. The future is much brighter. For you. Your dad. All of us," Milly said through the tight-lipped hold she had on the pins in her mouth.

Jill pretended to whisper to Carolanne. "Be glad she doesn't have to mark any more than your hem. I swear my heart couldn't take another hour of her nearly stabbing me or worrying about her swallowing those pins."

"My hearin' ain't gone yet." Milly's voice raised a notch in a slight tone of defiance. "Jill fussed the whole time I marked her dress. And I might remind you, missy, that it wouldn't have taken so long if you hadn't lost that weight, causing me to have to take in the gown a whole size. Not an easy task with all that beading, either."

"She looked like a catfish with all those pins hanging out of her mouth."

Milly raised a brow and aimed her question at Jill. "Have you ever heard of anyone swallowing pins?"

Jill set her chin in a stubborn line. "Well, no. But it could happen. Tell her, Carolanne. It could happen."

"Oh no," said Carolanne. "I'm not getting in the middle of this."

"I swear you are just like Pearl," Milly said to Jill.

Carolanne stifled a laugh.

"And I love you, in spite of that," Milly said. "You're just like your grandmother when it comes to bossing folks around and controlling every little detail. But I guess someone's got to do it."

"Speaking of details," Carolanne asked Jill, "are there any other maid of honor tasks I need to take care of for you before this weekend?"

Jill shook her head. "No. We're actually ahead of schedule. My 4-H girls volunteered to work on the tulle bags of lavender after the meeting, so you're off the hook for that."

"I like that." Carolanne made a quarter turn and a mental note that she should get involved with some of the groups in town like Jill had. It was something she'd meant to do, but here it was a year later and she'd yet to do it. "I like it even more that I didn't have to tie all those ribbons."

"See, if I weren't so good at organizing tasks, we'd be up to our armpits in last-minute to-dos." Jill pointed to Carolanne. "You'll be thanking me when I'm helping you plan your wedding."

The thought of a wedding of her own sent her pulse spinning like an ice-skater, and not in a good way. She'd never let her happiness revolve around someone else. Seeing the crushing blow disable her dad when Mom died still hurt, and that wasn't a risk she was willing to take. "Don't you be wishing that on me. You know how I feel about marriage." Carolanne could tell by the dreamy-eyed look on her best friend's face that Jill was ignoring every word she'd just said.

"When you find the right guy, you'll be dying to walk down that aisle. Mark my words."

*That'll be the day. If there's one thing I don't need, it's man troubles.* "I'm perfectly happy just the way I am."

The front door swung open, and Carolanne jumped. Both Milly and Jill turned to look.

Connor Buckham ambled into the apartment without ever looking up from the newspaper he carried in his hand. "What's fourteen letters for *neighborhood?* It starts with an *n* and has an *o* in the middle."

Milly shifted a knowing look in Jill's direction. "What? You just walk right in with no good morning?"

Carolanne knew exactly what they were thinking.

He lowered the newspaper, looking confused and a bit flustered. "Oh? Sorry." The fine starched sheen of his blue-and-white-striped shirt made his eyes look even bluer, if that were possible. "I didn't know you had plans—company—this morning. Sorry." He glanced at Milly. "Good morning, Miss Milly."

Connor nodded to Jill, but when his gaze landed on Carolanne, his mouth dropped wide open. "Wow. He-llo-oo, beautiful." He lowered himself into one of the chairs, never taking his eyes off her. "You didn't tell me you were in the fairy god-mother business, Milly. What have you done to my law partner?"

Carolanne raised her hands to her hips. "Ha-ha. Aren't you a funny guy?"

"Hey, if the shoe fits." Connor winked. "A little Cinderella humor for you."

"Not funny."

"No? Are lawyers even allowed to look that good?" He motioned to Jill and Milly for concurrence. "In fact, if you dressed like that in court, I bet you'd never lose a case."

"I'm warning you," Carolanne teased. "You better quit teasing me, or I'll have Milly stick you with those pins like a voodoo doll."

He pretended to back up in fear. "Well, seriously, I'm just saying that I've never seen you looking this pretty in the morning. It's nice."

"Just how often *do* you see her at this early hour?" Jill turned toward Carolanne. "And you, you've been holding out on me."

Carolanne shook her head, but before she could defend herself, Milly chimed in. "I thought Carolanne renting the apartment up here next to yours over y'all's office was just convenient until her house was done. No wonder she's been such a good sport about the delay."

"And I thought all along it was because she was my best friend," Jill added with an air of defiance.

Milly wagged a finger at the two of them. "This little early morning visit, it's a regular occurrence, isn't it? Maybe there's a little something you want to share with us?"

Carolanne felt the rush of heat flood her chest and cheeks. "You two can just stop right there. It's not what you think."

"No?" Milly raised a brow. "Are you saying Connor is some sort of pervert who just walks into apartments uninvited?"

Connor interjected. "She knew I was coming over."

Jill's mouth curved as if on the verge of laughter. "Seems like Pearl was right about you two, after all."

"Not that again." Connor held up his hand to silence her. "It's just coffee. The two of us get together for coffee. That's it."

"Sounds cozy," Jill said. "Even Garrett and I don't have coffee together *every* morning."

"You're not helping, Connor," Carolanne groaned.

Connor rolled the newspaper in his hands. "Well, you and Garrett don't work in the same office like we do. Besides, she makes great coffee."

"Isn't that thoughtful?" Milly arched a brow. "Carolanne would make a beautiful bride, wouldn't she, Connor?"

"Well, you do look real pretty." With a smile, he added, "And tall."

"I'm in heels and standing on a stool." She pulled the dress up high enough to expose her feet and the stool. She instantly regretted the movement when Connor's face lit up like a kid peering into the window of a candy store. She dropped the hem, wishing for closed-toe pumps instead of the sexy strappy shoes she was wearing.

"Your toes look pretty, too." He tilted his head slightly, like he was sizing her up, and that made Carolanne even more uncomfortable. "Your hair—it looks good like that. You never wear it down."

"Stop!" She ran her hand through her hair, wishing she'd pulled it up this morning. "Connor, you're just trying to egg on Jill and Milly now. You're not funny. Jill, would you tweak the thermostat? It's hot as heck in here."

"I wasn't being . . ." Connor's voice trailed.

Jill headed to the thermostat, muttering, "It's the sexual tension sparking up the heat in this place, if you ask me."

"Sounds like Pearl's magic is kickin' in." Milly pinned the hem of Carolanne's dress. "And it's about time. I'm not getting any younger, and neither are y'all."

Carolanne silently cursed Pearl for making that silly claim at the end of her video will about Connor being her perfect match. Doggone if Jill hadn't taken up where Pearl had left off, playing matchmaker of Adams Grove.

Carolanne let out a long breath, then almost too loudly said, "Neck of the woods."

"What?" Jill and Connor both said at the same time.

Carolanne rolled her eyes. "Your answer. The crossword. Fourteen letters. Another name for neighborhood. Neck of the woods."

Connor raised his paper and started plugging in the letters. "Damn, it fits. How do you *always* know these answers?"

"Lucky guess." Carolanne pivoted to the right at Milly's poke to her calf.

One more pin and Milly stood, still clenching at least five more between her thin lips. "All done, sweetie. Step down and let me see what we've got."

Connor jumped to his feet and held out his hand to help Carolanne down from the stool.

*What are you up to?* She hesitated, then placed her hand in his and stepped down.

"Isn't that sweet?" Milly tsked. "I didn't know you had that in ya, Connor."

Connor leaned toward Milly. "I didn't know Carolanne had *this* in her. Did you?"

Carolanne swatted his arm. "It's just a dress. Quit making such a big deal about it."

"Well, excuse me for noticing how pretty you look."

An awkward silence fell over the room.

Jill snapped her fingers. "I almost forgot. I have

another surprise for you, Carolanne. This one is even better than the dress." She crossed the room to Carolanne's side and took her hands in her own. "Garrett shifted both of his crews to your place. They'll be done with your house this week."

Carolanne squeezed Jill's hands. "Oh my goodness. That's almost a month sooner than he'd promised."

"I know. Isn't it great? You should be able to start moving your stuff in just a couple days. You'll be the first official resident of Bridle Path Estates."

Connor looked stunned. "So soon?"

"That's awesome news," Carolanne said. "I'll have to get some boxes. Get on the schedule for the truck. I'm not even ready. It doesn't matter. I'll get it done. I can't believe it. Finally!"

"I know. We'll practically be neighbors," Jill said. "You can do coffee with me at the artisan center. I can't wait."

"What about coffee with me? You're not going to miss me?" He held up his finger and thumb in a gesture of a tiny bit, and squinted. "Not even a little?"

"Maybe a little." She smiled playfully. "But you'll miss *me* like crazy."

Milly took the last pins from between her lips and poked them back into the pin cushion. "We're all set, sweetheart."

Carolanne gave her a hug. "Thank you so much for doing this for me."

"It's my wedding gift to Jill. Go, change, and I'll get out of your way."

"Don't rush on my account." Connor headed to the kitchen and filled his coffee mug. "I'll leave y'all to do your girly stuff." He sipped his coffee, calling out a good-bye as he closed the door behind him.

Carolanne rushed off to the bedroom to change, then came back with the dress in a garment bag. "Here you go," she said, handing it off to Milly.

Milly draped it over her arm. "Connor's smitten. Don't tell me you haven't noticed."

Carolanne squared her shoulders. "He is not."

"Yes. He most certainly is. Did you see the way his mouth hung open when he saw you in that dress?"

"It's the dress."

Jill folded her arms across her chest. "No. It was you. And what is this with him making himself all at home—coming and going from your place? Something hot is in y'all's future."

"Stop it. We're friends. Just like he is with every other girl who grew up in this town." Carolanne knew Connor lumbering into the apartment was going to fuel their romantic hearts. OK, well, he didn't really lumber. Why was it she still thought of him as the overweight kid from school? The only thing big about Connor Buckham these days was his lumberjack-size arms and tight abs. Oh, and that snoring. She could hear that from across the hall some nights.

"He's a great guy," Jill said, "and it's clear he's crazy about you. What's not to love?"

"Don't throw that L-word around so casually. Connor's a huge flirt. That's why we all loved him in school, even now, but not like *that*."

"Now he's a grown man—a fit, hot, and successful man—and he's not flirting with everybody. He's flirting with you. Flirting of that kind is very different." Jill hugged her arms across her chest. "Admit it. It's romantic."

"No. It's not romantic. *You're* romantic—a die-hard romantic." Carolanne knew she was venturing down a blind alley when it came to shaking Jill off this subject. When it came to love, Jill Clemmons was like a hound on a rabbit trail.

"Friendship's a great foundation for a relationship," said Milly. "Look at Jill and Garrett."

"That's different. We're not that kind of friends. It's business between us. He barely dates since his mom died, and you know I'm not going to be running down the path of sharing my life with someone else. I like making my own decisions and living by my own rules."

"You need to let that go," Milly warned. "That's your baggage talking. Leave the past where it is and move on."

"I have dealt with it. I've totally moved on,"

Carolanne said. *Why do I have to defend myself?*

"Well, you don't really deal with stuff, you kind of ignore it," Jill said. "I'm sure it was a coping mechanism as a little girl, but eventually, you do have to deal with this stuff."

"There's nothing to deal with. I'm fine." Carolanne wished sometimes that it was just that easy, but she knew better. "Besides, this isn't just about dad baggage. Some people just weren't meant to be a part of a couple—like me—and that's OK. Everyone thinks it's so easy to deal with the past. Well, it's not."

"You're the only one making it *not easy*—making every man pay for everything your daddy ever did wrong. It's not right, Carolanne. If your momma were here, she'd tell you so."

"If Momma were here, it never would've happened."

"Probably true." Milly's voice softened. "Your daddy loved your momma. When y'all lost her, he lost a piece of himself. He's not a bad man."

*And he stopped being a good father the day momma died, too.* "He was the town drunk."

"He wasn't a drunk. It was the reaction to your momma dying, and you know that. Everyone knew how much he loved your mother. He was a well-respected part of this town for years. Everyone still loved him, and he's made great progress. He hasn't slipped in a couple years now."

"Or he's just getting more discreet, which would've been nice when I was a kid. What's the difference?"

Jill moved closer to Carolanne and took her hand.

"That's not fair. I know it wasn't easy for you, but it wasn't easy for him, either. Don't discount the road he's traveled." Milly settled her gaze on Carolanne. "And more important, don't let it shortchange your own happiness."

"I'm happy just the way I am. I have a wonderful job. I'm getting ready to move into my dream house. I have great friends. What more could I want?"

"You know the answer to that question." Milly gathered her things. Her lips pulled into a tense line. "I know you wish I'd drop this, but I'm at the age now that I don't have time not to tell you what's on my mind. Honey, you need to take the past and throw a big ol' shovel of dirt over it and leave it be. Your future is in your hands. It's time you gave yourself the chance you deserve."

Carolanne started to say something, but Jill gave her a look that made her hold back. "Thanks, Milly," she forced.

Milly smiled, looking quite pleased with herself for winning that round. "I'll have this back to you in a jiffy, dear."

"I'll drive you home, Milly." Jill grabbed her keys and followed Milly toward the door.

"It's just a block or two. I can walk if you want to stay and visit."

"I have to get to the artisan center and get that inventory on the shelves for the grand opening." Jill hugged Carolanne. "Thanks for getting your butt up out of bed so early and being pleasant. I know how you hate mornings."

"You got that right, but that's what best friends do." Carolanne closed the door behind them. Milly's words replayed in her head. *Your future will be as good as you let it be.*

# ❖ Chapter Two ❖

Milly tapped her fingers on the door to Connor's apartment as she and Jill walked toward the stairs. "Good seeing you, Connor."

"Bye, beautiful," he called through the closed door.

"You say that to all the girls." Milly's voice trailed as she descended the stairs.

*I don't say that to all the girls.* Connor scrubbed his hand across his chin, remembering saying exactly that about Carolanne just a little while ago. *Maybe I do.*

But when he'd said it to Carolanne earlier, he'd meant it—*felt it.* She'd looked amazing standing there in that fancy dress. That put an appealing twist on their all-business relationship. Her deep-red hair, not reddish-blond like his own, had hung down her back in a tangle of curls that accentuated where her lower back curved into her tight little rear end—a perfect one he hadn't noticed before, one his hands were now eager to touch. *Off-limits. Not only would it be bad business, but it would be pretty weird to get serious with Carolanne since her dad and I became such good friends when Mom took sick.*

He tossed the newspaper aside, irritated by the thrilling current moving through him as he pictured his business partner in a little less—OK, a whole lot less—than that bridesmaid dress.

Trying to put the sexy image out of his mind, he dialed his voice mail and picked up his messages. He saved two of them that were business, wrote down the number from one, and deleted the rest, which were all from Katherine, whose voice poured like honey through the line.

*Horny. That explained his reaction to Carolanne.* He dialed Katherine's number, and she answered on the first ring.

"Got your message," Connor said.

"It's good to hear your voice. I've missed you," she cooed. "How've you been?"

"Busy. Good. You?"

"Don't you miss me? I've been thinking about you nonstop. Wondering if you'd completely forgotten about me up here, and that just makes Katherine sad."

*What is it that makes women think baby talk is sexy? And what's with that third person stuff?* "Nope. I won't forget you." There was more to a relationship than hot sex. Though sex with her was better than great, he'd also expected that she'd be there for him in other ways. Truth was, though, after the way she'd played that convenient disappearing act when Mom became so ill, he kind of wished he could.

She let out an exaggerated sigh across the line. "It's been over a month since we've even talked."

"Couldn't have been that long."

"Well, actually, I can tell you exactly how long it's been. It's been twenty-seven days since we talked and forty-one since you held me in those big arms of yours and made me wiggle out of control."

*Look who's counting now. It'd been nice if you'd been counting when Mom was sick. Could've used your support then. Instead, it was Carolanne at my side.*

"It's not like you to ignore me like this. I was thinking about coming down your way to visit. Feel like company?"

His hesitation left an awkward void. "It's not the best time."

"Don't tell me you're becoming all work and no play. You know that's no fun."

"Jill and Garrett's wedding is this weekend. I'm going to be tied up with that, then I'll be helping a friend move." The thought of Carolanne moving out hammered at him like a sucker punch. It shouldn't have come as a surprise. It had been the plan the whole time, but now that it was happening, he didn't relish the idea much.

"Don't need a date for the wedding?"

*Hell, she'd expect me to buy her a dress and fly her down. Been down this path before.* "I'm in it, and you're not the sit-by-yourself kind of girl. It's really not your kind of party, Katherine."

"Well, I guess you'd know."

"That I would." Katherine was a socialite from her highlighted tips to the fancy painted toes she shoves into those designer shoes, and as pretty as all that looked, she couldn't find any pleasure in anything that was just down-home good fun.

"All right. Well, I'll just be up here in Chicago thinking about you. Let's talk soon. OK?"

"Sure. Yeah, soon." He shoved the phone in his pocket. If all he needed was a good time, Katherine would sure fit the bill, but then, she required way too much energy on his part, and he wasn't up to exerting it or the price tag that went along with it.

Connor heard Carolanne's apartment door slam across the hall. He got up from the leather couch and listened to her heels click like a metronome down the hall. He stepped out onto the landing.

Carolanne descended the stairs in dark trousers and a white blouse. Her French braid hung neat and tidily down her back, like it did every day. Things were back to normal. It was like this morning had never happened. Only it had, and he wouldn't soon forget the sweet smell of her hair as she'd stepped down off that stool.

He fought for restraint not to call after her and ask her to come back up to his apartment. Until an hour ago, she'd been the freckle-faced friend who'd slung back beers with the best of them, kept his crushes a secret, and played wingman for him all through college.

*Who'll be my wingman to catch you?* The unexpected thought made him nervous.

He turned around and went back inside. It suddenly felt like a good time for a run. He changed into shorts and a T-shirt, took the stairs two at a time, then ran straight out the front door toward the park without a second look through the glass door of their office, which took up the whole first floor of the old bank building.

The familiar rhythm of his running shoes against the sidewalk gradually pushed all those awkward thoughts aside. He hoped that tight coil in his gut would release, too, because those thoughts about Carolanne were nothing but bad news. *No sense screwing up a good business relationship. Mixing business and pleasure—never a good idea.*

The day was warming up, as was typical for Virginia in late May. The temperature was only in the eighties, but the humidity hung heavy in the air, making it feel much hotter as he ran up the block.

He jogged in place until the one streetlight turned green and he could cross into the park. His shirt was already damp and sticking to his body. The jogging path was empty since most people were already at work by now. That was one of the best things about having his own law practice and answering to no one else. He could build in time for his workouts and extracurricular activities.

The same old questions pounded out againstthe

pavement. *Impossible relationships.* He always picked the girls who were taken or unattainable, and before, maybe that had been by design.

Things had been different since his mom had died. She'd always wanted to be a grandmother. That ship had sailed, but now that she was gone, he'd been thinking more about settling down and having that family and kids she'd always wished for him.

*If I'm ever going to settle down and have a family, I'm going to have to break that trend.*

An image of Carolanne on a blanket in the park—under the big magnolia—with a child on her lap and holding up a glass of sweet tea for him as he ran by made him pick up speed. *Right.* Hell, Carolanne was more against marriage than Katherine was. At least Katherine pretended that someday she'd want to get married, just not now. Carolanne had vowed she'd never get married, and she seemed pretty comfortable with that decision—and there was the law practice thing, too.

What would normally have been a good forty-five-minute run, he completed in just over thirty minutes. Sweaty and feeling more in control, Connor slowed to a walk on Main Street. Through the wide glass front window of Baxter and Buckham, he saw Carolanne greeting her first clients of the day. He still had time before his first meeting, so he headed up the block to Mac's

31

Bakery. He'd need the sugar rush to get him through the meeting with Mrs. Avery. Ever since Pearl Clemmons died and everyone heard about her video will, half the seniors in this town wanted to do the same thing to supplement their written wills.

At this rate, he'd be able to add producer and director to his résumé. It was a hassle, but the good boy whom his mom raised couldn't say no to the old folks that he'd respected all his life.

Connor sucked in a big whiff of the salty bacon coming from the diner, but he wasn't dressed for a sit-down breakfast, so he continued toward the sweet, sugary smells from Mac's Bakery just a few doors down. He nodded to a woman he recognized from the gym.

The planter boxes around each lamppost down the block overflowed with flowers. One type flaunted petals in a soft hue of color that reminded him of Carolanne's dress this morning. Good thing Milly and Jill had been there. If they hadn't been there, he probably would've really acted the fool. *If I'd gotten there before they had, she might not have been wearing that dress by the time they arrived.* He laughed aloud at the big-talk thought. *Wishful thinking, man.*

Giant candy-blue letters in an arch spelled out MAC'S BAKERY across the center of the store-front window. Connor's appetite grew as he pulled open the door and the smell of fresh bread and cinnamon wrapped around him. Glass cases filled with colorful cakes, cookies, and homemade bread baked fresh this morning filled the space.

He glanced at the corner display boasting Mac's achievements. Trophies and ribbons flanked pictures of him appearing on that cable television cook-off. Too bad it had ended in disaster when Mac's cake came up just a smidgen short in the height requirement.

Connor stood in line as Mac's son, Derek, passed white wax-lined bags of goodies over the counter to customer after customer.

Mac came out from the back of the store with a bear claw on a plate so fresh that Connor could see the steam and smell the buttery cinnamon wafting across the room. Mac served a woman sitting in one of the five bright-blue chairs that snugged up against the stainless steel counter, then leaned across the counter in conversation.

"Good morning, Mac," Connor called across the room. "Got any more of those fresh bear claws?"

Mac lifted his head with a smile. "Just finished a batch." He raised a finger in the air, then hustled through the small space. Pans clanked in the back room. He poked his head back around the corner. "Just one?"

"Make it two," Connor said with a thumbs-up. "I need a cup of coffee, too. Large."

"Coffee?"

"Yes, regular." Connor hesitated. "Don't most folks drink coffee with their pastries?"

"You haven't bought a cup of coffee from me in months. I figured you had something against my coffee."

*Geez. Is everyone keeping tabs on me now?* "No, man. Not that. Ever since Carolanne joined the practice, I've been having coffee there. She makes a mean pot of coffee—about the only thing she can cook—but this morning she had plans and I got shorted."

Mac walked back out and set the box and cup of coffee on the counter. "Coffee's on the house, then."

"Thanks. Looks like I'll be having coffee down here more often. She's getting ready to move into her new place." Connor tipped his head toward the kid behind the cash register. "How's that workin' out for you?"

"Derek? Great. He'd rather work nights and sleep all morning, but we're working that out."

"I'm sure you were the same way when you were in your early twenties."

"Oh yeah, and he's a much better baker at twenty-three than I was, but he's into all that fancy new-way stuff. You know me, I'm old school."

"Nothing wrong with old school," Connor said.

Mac exchanged a glance with the woman nibbling her pastry, then moved in closer to Connor and lowered his voice. "Hey, I need to talk to you about some legal business, too, when you have some time."

"Stop by the office. You know I can always make time for you."

"Great. I'll do that." Mac's attention shifted to the doorway as the buzzer welcomed another customer.

Sheriff Scott Calvin walked in, lifting his bright-red on-the-go travel mug in a friendly hello. "Connor. Good morning. Hey, Mac, can I get a quick refill?"

Mac snagged the mug and spun around to fill the cup. "In a hurry?"

"Hadn't planned to be, but I just got a call that those doggone kids have pulled the chain down over at the old Dixon farm again, and I'm short a deputy this morning."

Connor snickered. "Our legacy continues. All those wild times we had there—the next generation is just trying to top us. Remember when we got your Jeep stuck up to the axles after Hurricane Floyd? It was fun as heck four-wheelin' through that mud bog. Well, until we got caught."

"You weren't the sheriff's son. I caught hell for that from the old man." Scott whistled. "Now that I'm the one who has to resecure the land every time someone trespasses on it, it's not nearly as cool. Did I just say that? We're getting old, Buckham."

Connor gloried briefly in the shared memory.

"We sure had that down to a science back then. How about I go take a look and put the chain back up? That is, if they didn't completely cut it like they did that one time. It's my trustee, anyway. We've got the funds set aside. Maybe it's time we put up a pole gate rather than just a chain and save everyone a bunch of hassle."

"Yeah, Connor, that would be great if you could do that. Big help, in fact."

"Consider it done," Connor said.

Mac handed Scott the coffee cup.

"Thanks for the coffee, Mac." Scott tugged on his hat. "I'll catch y'all later."

"Hope you don't catch me with that radar gun," Mac teased.

"Just doing my part to keep this town's books in the black," Scott said over his shoulder.

"Well, I guess I better get my day started, too," Connor said.

Mac wiped his hands on his apron. "Me, too. I've got to finish up Garrett and Jill's wedding cake."

"I hear Jill put in a tall order." He regretted the pun as soon as it left his lips, but Mac didn't seem to notice.

"Yep. Took me nearly all day to match the flowers to her color swatches."

Connor could picture that soft-coral color in his mind with no problem.

"That wedding cake might be my best creation yet. The beaded design will match Jill's dress, and it's taken some doing, but I think she's going to love it."

The woman in the chair piped in. "All your creations are fabulous, but I think the cake you're designing for the grand opening of the artisan center is going to be *my* favorite." The woman smiled wide. "Hi there. Sorry, I couldn't help but overhear."

"No problem. I think we're all fans of Mac's work around here. Do I know you?"

Mac stepped closer to the woman. "Y'all haven't met? Sure you have. Anita's from up the road in Hale's Vineyard."

"I'm sorry. I'm not always good with names."

"I'm friends with Katherine. She was in my yoga class." The dark-haired woman smiled. "Nice to meet you again, Connor."

Anita looked like the yoga type. Graceful and at peace with herself. At first glance, he'd thought she was in her early thirties, but now, closer, the lines that accented her smile disclosed a few more years on her.

"I didn't realize Katherine had made any friends while she was in town. She's a sweet gal, but Adams Grove plucked the happy right out of her." *Just one more example of relationships destined to go nowhere from the start.*

Anita had been talking, but he'd missed most of what she'd said. "I was so sad when she went back to Chicago," Anita said. "I'm trying to get

37

Mac to do another one of those competitions. Katherine was telling me about one up in Chicago. I should call her." Anita put the fork down from her left hand and pulled a napkin in front of her. "Mac, honey, let me use your pen."

He pulled the pen from his coat pocket and handed it to her.

Anita jotted down her phone number. "When you talk to her again, tell her I have a new cell phone number. It's been too long since she and I have talked."

Connor took the napkin, and Anita kept right on talking. "Anyway, she was here with me the first time Mac ever baked his famous vanilla-almond layered cupcakes. Miniature wedding cakes—absolutely to die for. I swear, if they won't make two people fall in love, nothing will."

Mac was enjoying the ego massage Anita was giving, no doubt about that. "Well, both almond and vanilla are known to increase passion and lust in the ladies. The creamy marzipan filling is the magic." Mac winked at Connor. "I'm no magician, but I always keep a few on hand, if ya know what I mean."

*I think I do.* "And they say a way to a man's heart is through his stomach. Sounds like you're on to something here that'll work on the ladies, Mac. Toss a couple of those into a box for me, too." *Maybe those magical little cupcakes will cure what's ailing my mood today.*

# ❖ Chapter Three ❖

As Connor walked up the block and got closer to his office, he resisted the temptation to spin the stacked bakery boxes on his finger like a basketball. He'd been able to do that back in the day, but there was surely no good sense in potentially wasting Mac's famous bear claws, even if the five-second rule applied. That sixteen-year-old boy inside of him still often tried to take over. Even now, seeing the old bank building, he got the urge to press his nose to the window and daydream of the olden days—bank robberies or a withdrawal from the big vault to keep a family indiscretion secret. The abandoned building had always evoked a strange magnetism to him. Maybe it was because of the stories his grand-daddy had told him from back when he was the president of that bank.

Buying that old bank building was definitely one of Connor's proudest achievements to date. Once a grimy abandoned piece of history, the building still had good bones, and he'd been able to restore its place as one of the gems of Main Street's history.

Connor stepped between the solid columns that flanked the extra-tall doors and walked inside the office he now shared with Carolanne.

Across the long solid-wood counter that used to be the teller space, Carolanne stood with her back to him, filing.

He watched quietly for just a moment as the sunlight from the front window cast a gold-and-auburn shimmer through the tight braid in her hair—a contrast to the darker brown it had looked hanging down her back this morning.

"Got time for a snack break?" He raised the bakery box for her to see.

Her eyes seemed to survey his running gear, followed by one of those looks, the kind mothers usually dole out. "Are you not working today?"

He plopped the box down. "You need to ease up. You're not in New York City anymore, in case you've forgotten."

"How could I forget with you reminding me daily?"

He liked the familiar sparring with her. "Maybe these will sweeten your disposition." He pushed the box across the counter. "I had a few important things to take care of this morning, like picking these up from Mac's."

She walked closer, then paused. "You are so bad. Mac's bear claws? I can smell them from here." She took two quick steps to his side and lifted the top of the box. "What's the occasion?"

"It's not every day a guy meets Cinderella." He waved one of the pastries under her nose. "Pretend this is your glass slipper."

"Too many of these and it won't fit!" She eyed the pastry. "If this is what they're arming Prince Charming with these days, it's not fair . . . but I like it. Good thing I'm not in the market for a man or I'd be a goner."

"You could use a little more meat on those bones of yours."

"Lucky me." She leaned forward and took a bite of the pastry, and then took it from his hands. "Mmm, that's good. Thanks. What's in the other box?"

"Something for later." *Why did I even buy those cupcakes? One horny morning and I'm suddenly falling for sappy old wives' tales to get laid? Somehow, "Hey, baby, want a cupcake?" sounded a little perverted.*

"They're still warm." Carolanne wiped the sticky sugar from her fingers.

Connor took the other bear claw from the box, but hesitated before taking a bite. "Question for you. Have you met a brunette named Anita from Hale's Vineyard? She was in the bakery this morning."

"If it's the same one I'm thinking of, she teaches a mean hot yoga class. I heard she's going to be teaching here in town once they finish the renovation on the storefront down on the first block."

"That's one of Mac's buildings, isn't it?"

"You'd know better than me. I'd had no idea

he owned half the buildings on Main Street until you told me."

"Has to be the same lady. I think she and Mac are a couple. They seemed pretty chummy, but I'm surprised no one's been talking about it."

"I heard she was a widow. Good for Mac. She seems really sweet."

He bit into the bear claw. "I ran into Scott down at the bakery, too. Someone pulled the chain down at the Dixon farm again. I told him I'd go secure it and look into upgrading the entrance with a pole gate."

"The way that property is all grown up, I'm surprised anyone can even find it anymore."

He walked over to one of the locked filing cabinets and got the keys to the property gate. "Guess I'll go get that knocked out." Connor headed for the door. "I'll see you later," he said as he turned to go upstairs to change out of his running clothes.

Dressed for the day, he took the back stairs down to the alley. Teddy Hardy was carrying a box of clippings from the florist out to the dumpster.

Connor waved to Teddy, then opened the door to the storage shed behind the building. He grabbed a small toolbox, put it in the trunk of his car, then pulled his blue Mercedes onto Main Street.

He drove past the airport and Malloy's Construction, then pulled into the emergency lane to slow down for his turn. It was a little early in the year for trespassers on this land. *Must have been the hot days we've had.* Usually, it was a bigger summer problem, with kids wanting to hang out at the spring-fed pond. It was always a good way to cool off.

Connor pulled his car right up to where the chain had once blocked the entrance to Old Pond Road. The grass held the indentation showing someone had recently driven down the path, but the only thing back there was the abandoned farmstead and acres and acres of overgrown cropland and woods that led down to the huge pond. Too bad the trust dictated that the land remain inactive and the entry barricaded. This would be a prime piece of real estate if the remaining family would sell, not that anyone local would ever buy it. The old-timers in town still whispered about the drowning that had happened here, even though it was so long ago.

Thick gravel crunched beneath Connor's expensive leather loafers as he approached the old wooden post. Someone had pried out the staple that held the locked end of the cable. He went back to the car and got his hammer to pound the staple back into place. With a few swings, the cable was back in place. *Just like new.* He quickly took a measurement to see what size pole gate they'd need.

He'd have to come back when he was more

suitably dressed to do a once-over around the house. A review of the property, fencing, and land was due anyway. He put the tools back in the trunk, then headed back to his office in town.

Connor had just returned to the office when the bells clanked against the front door behind him again, and Mac walked in.

"If you're here surveying how we liked your bear claws, they were too good to resist," Carolanne said. "You're still the number one baker in this town."

"I was going to say I'm the only baker, but I guess now that Derek is here helping me out, that's not true, so I'll take that as a compliment." Mac's face turned a little pink against the white of his uniform. "I'm actually here to discuss some business with Connor." He looked apologetic. "Is this a bad time? Anita said she could watch the store for a little while."

"Not at all." Connor motioned for Mac to follow him down the narrow hall to his office. "Come on back."

Mac paused at the door. "Do you mind if I close this?"

Carolanne went back to her filing. When she'd first partnered with Connor, she'd tried to talk him into hiring someone to do this kind of work. He'd won the first round, and she had to admit that he'd been right. She had plenty of time to do it herself, plus she'd come to rather enjoy the smaller tasks that administrative help would've covered for them.

Sometimes it was still a challenge to feel like she'd put in a full day at the office with the slower pace of the small-town practice compared to New York—not that she missed that rat race.

She went back into her office to review the real estate closing she was handling in the afternoon. Several of the older farms in the county were being split up and sold. Too bad the younger generations were not carrying on the agriculture that had carried this town for so many years. It was sad to see so much of that land get broken up. As one generation died, the next was making decisions that would change this town, but on the flip side, it was nice to see the town growing enough to stay alive in the tough economic times. Almost every shop on Main Street stayed busy, and the few empty buildings were in the process of being revitalized. That was a good sign for Adams Grove.

Mac and Connor walked by, still talking all the way to the door.

When Connor closed the door behind Mac, he pulled his hands up on his hips and stood there shaking his head.

"What's the matter?" Carolanne called from her office. "You OK?"

Connor looked her way, then walked toward her

office with a serious look of concern on his face.

*I hope nothing is wrong with Mac.* "I heard the door close. Is everything OK? I mean, he's not sick, is he?"

"No. No. Nothing like that." He laughed. "I jumped to the same conclusion, though." Connor sat down in the chair across from her desk. "He was talking about how things may have been different with Derek if he hadn't grown up in New York with his ex. Water under the bridge. He wants to change his will. Again."

"Thank goodness he's OK. He can change his will a hundred times if he wants to pay for your time. Why would you care?"

"I shouldn't worry. He's a smart man, certainly capable of making his own decisions." His set face and clamped mouth told more than he was saying.

"Then why do you have that flustered look?"

Connor looked behind him, then spoke in hushed voice. "Remember I mentioned Anita this morning?"

"The lady at the bakery, yeah."

"Well, Mac wants me to rewrite his will so everything goes to her. He's going to let her administer stuff to Derek instead of it going directly to him."

"So? People do that all the time. I guess you were right about them being an item."

"Yeah. Only, this change doesn't sit well with

me. They couldn't have been together all that long, or else everyone would've already known. It would be different if they were married. I asked him if he had someone in his family he could ask instead."

"Not your place to make those decisions for him. You know that. If that relationship falls apart, he'll come back and change it again."

"Maybe I'll just let it sit for a week or two, give him a chance to think about it. I told him we could take care of a trust for him. Maybe he'll come to his senses." He pulled his ankle up to cross his knee. "Be different if they were engaged or something."

"You don't have to be married to someone to count on them, Connor."

"Well, it doesn't hurt."

She closed her file and leaned forward. "Since when did you get so opinionated?"

He pressed his fingers together. "I trust my gut, and I have a bad feeling about Mac's decision."

Trying to lighten the mood, she teased, "What, are you going to tell me you're psychic now? You're not going to whip out a crystal ball, are you? There's not a crop circle on the top of this building I don't know about, is there?"

Her reaction seemed to amuse him. "Oh, hell no."

She sat back in her chair and folded her arms. "Then you need to let it go. Our job is to advise and execute."

Connor got up. "If I stall, I bet he'll come to his senses."

"Helping them make good decisions is one thing, but stalling a request based on your own moral code . . . that's a whole other issue. And a problem when what you're pushing them toward actually benefits the practice."

"You know I'm not steering him to let us handle the trust to get his money."

"Just saying it's a fine line."

"I don't see the big deal. If he thinks he can trust this lady with his whole estate, then he'll still feel that way in a couple weeks. No harm, no foul. Or he ought to marry her and make it really official, and I'd shut up about it."

"Not everyone wants to get married."

"What do you have against marriage?"

"I just don't agree that marriage is the only way for two people to form a good partnership."

"It *is* telling, though. Seriously, if you trust someone enough to carry out your last dying wishes, there's more to it than friendship, so why not seal the deal?"

"If Garrett and Jill weren't getting married, would you have felt the same way about the changes we just made to Garrett's estate?"

Connor nodded. "Yeah. Absolutely."

"Well, that's stupid."

Connor jerked his head up, locking his line of sight on Carolanne. "Stupid?"

"Yeah. It's shortsighted and silly. Marriage is a piece of paper, and it does not mean that someone won't hurt or backstab you just as easily as if they were just in love."

He sat back down. "Are you seriously telling me that you still never want to be married?"

"This isn't about me."

"I'm asking."

"Why do you care? You have to agree that it's an odd tradition, especially for women. We give up the better part of ourselves, even our names, to melt into someone else's life."

"Well, when you put it that way, it sounds like hell, but that's not what marriage is. It's not giving up anything. It's sharing." He studied her for a moment. "I know you've said you have no interest in marriage, but people say that kind of thing all the time. I never thought you really meant it."

"I don't joke about that stuff."

"Fine." Connor rolled his eyes. "You being an old maid will work to my favor. I won't have to worry about you taking off time for a big wedding and honeymoon or maternity leave. That's fine by me."

"Good. I desperately needed your approval." She couldn't refrain from the sarcasm.

"Yeah. Well, back to Mac. I'd be less worried if he hadn't told me that Anita was pestering him to take care of it."

"And so you're still going to make them wait?"

"I'm busy." Connor got up and headed to his office. "I'll get to it as soon as I can."

"That's playing dirty," she called down the hall. "You're crossing the line."

His footsteps sounded closer rather than farther away.

She looked up just as he poked his head back in the door. "Sometimes people just need a little time to know what they really want."

*I hope that wasn't directed at me, because I know exactly what I want.*

# ❖ Chapter Four ❖

Connor tapped out a rhythm on the dry cleaner counter to the Southern rock competing with the loud drone of the equipment in the back of the shop. Didn't matter what time of year it was, this building was always hot, humid, and way too loud for his liking, but it sure beat doing laundry. His mom's words rang in his mind: *If you had a wife, you wouldn't have to worry about that.* But somehow he couldn't picture himself with a wife who stayed at home ironing, anyway. He dug the folded bills from his pocket.

A tiny blonde weaved between rows of clothes to the front and stretched to hook the heavy bundle on the telescoping pole next to the counter. "Here you go. Ten pieces and your black dress suit. Guess that's for Garrett and Jill's wedding this weekend."

"Sure is." The last time he'd worn it had only been a few months ago at his mother's funeral. Even freshly dry-cleaned, the memories still seemed to cling to the very fabric. His heart clenched.

"It's been a busy week with everyone getting their Sunday bests ready for the big wedding." She punched the numbers into the cash register and counted out Connor's change. Her eyes shifted toward the door.

At the sound of his name, Connor swung around to see Carolanne's dad walking through the door. "Hey, Ben, how've you been?"

"Great." He pointed to the suit hanging with Connor's dry cleaning. "I see you're getting ready for the big wedding, too. How've you been?"

"Good. Most of the time, anyway. That daughter of yours gives me a run for my money, but other than that, no complaints." Connor reached out and shook Ben's hand.

"Not like you didn't know she has an opinion or two," Ben said. "I'm so glad she's back in town. Jill says they've been spending a lot of time together. That's good for her. I know it was my fault that she left Adams Grove, but I worried about her up in New York."

"That's old news. She's back now, and I doubt she'll be going anywhere," Connor said. "She seems pretty happy. So, how's your new job?"

"Really good. I'm putting my master gardener certification to good use for more than just volunteer work. With Jill and Carolanne being so close, I wasn't sure if Jill'd be comfortable with me working for her. I'm grateful they gave me the chance."

"Jill is fair, and they needed some good help to transform that property into something presentable. It would have surprised me if she hadn't given you the chance."

"It's been a heckuva job to pull off, but I've

really enjoyed seeing it all come together," Ben said with a smile, but his face fell. "I hope Carolanne won't stay away from the artisan center because I'm there. I haven't seen much of her."

"That's because she still has that New York state of mind, and she's trying to make small-town work into big-city hours. I can't half talk her into taking a lunch break most days."

"That's my girl," Ben said. "Carolanne knows what she wants and, maybe more important, what she doesn't want. She never was one to let grass grow under her feet. We can thank Pearl for that. It was surely no thanks to me. I let her and Reggie down. My poor brother had his hands full trying to keep my stupid ass out of jail. I can't take it back, but Lord knows I wish I could."

"Don't be so hard on yourself. That was a long time ago, and Carolanne turned out just fine. Although, I swear New York carved an edge on her."

"May have, but trust me, she left Adams Grove with an edge."

Connor wasn't about to argue with the man about his daughter, and he was already dancing a fine line between the difficult past those two shared by being close friends with both Ben and Carolanne. "Enough about her. We need to get together for some golf. It's been too long. I guess since Mom passed."

"Yeah, it has. She was a good lady, your mom.

We all really miss her. How are you handling all of that?"

*Carolanne was an easier subject than Mom.* He needed more time to ease that pain. "It's hard. I miss her, but thanks for asking. Your friendship was special to Mom. Means a lot to me, too. Our friendship shouldn't wane now that she's gone. Stop by the office, we'll catch lunch."

"I'm not sure Carolanne would like me dropping in at the office. I'm trying to give her some space."

"She's my law partner, not my wife. You're welcome in my building anytime you please. Besides, she'll be moving into her house next week, so she'll only be around during working hours." His gut twisted again at the thought of her moving. He hoped his voice didn't carry the disappointment that he was feeling right now.

"You say that now, but don't push your luck. I seem to remember a little prediction by Pearl Clemmons about the two of you. There never was a match that Pearl decided that didn't work out."

"There's a first for everything. Besides, Carolanne has made it pretty clear that she's not getting married. I think Pearl's record ends with Jill and Garrett."

"I left my daughter with a lot of baggage, but I pray she'll come around."

"Well, that, my friend, is none of my business,

but beating you in a round of golf is, so let's plan to get together soon."

Ben handed his ticket to the girl at the counter. "I'll be pretty busy up until the grand opening of the artisan center, but after that I should be available just about any Tuesday. Let me know."

"Plan on it." Connor swept the twist-tied hangers off the rack. "I better get back to the office, or Carolanne is likely to dock my pay."

"Sounds like my girl."

# ❖ Chapter Five ❖

At four o'clock, Carolanne juggled a stack of books in her arms and headed for the door. "I'm going to run down and pay for the ad at the *Gazette* and then drop these books back at the library. Need anything while I'm out?"

"Nope. I'm good." Connor swung past her to open the door. "Here, I've got that. I'm right behind you, anyway." He spun the WELCOME sign to the BE RIGHT BACK side and followed Carolanne out to the street.

"Coming in late and leaving early?"

"Summer hours." He pulled the door tight. "And one of the many benefits of living and working in a small town."

"I don't know if I'm ever going to get used to this. Hunting season, festival closings, and now summer hours?" She wondered what time he'd start his day when she wasn't living there anymore.

Connor stepped out to the sidewalk. "You're earning a decent living. You just need to find something besides work to spend your time on."

"I'm not sure I know how to do anything but work. It's always been my go-to thing." Even the stack of novels hadn't been able to slow her down. She seemed to read them faster than the library could stock them.

"Maybe you can help Jill down at the artisan center."

"That might be fun." She laid the books down on the bench just outside the door. "I'll lock up. You go on."

"Good luck," Connor said with a wave as he headed to the courthouse.

She worked the key into the archaic lock of Baxter and Buckhams. Connor had seen her struggle with it enough times that he'd offered to have the turn-of-the-century hardware switched out, but there was no way she'd let him replace it. A shiny new state-of-the-art lock just wouldn't fit the essence of this place, and she loved this old building and everything about it. The smells from the diner and the bakery, the sounds from the train tracks, and even the fire station alarm— daily at noon no matter what and anytime there was an emergency.

With a shimmy of the key followed by an aggressive lift of the extra-tall wood-and-glass door like Connor had shown her, Carolanne twisted the lock and the mechanism dropped into place. Each time she locked that door, it was a personal victory. *Now that I'm moving, I figure out the method. Figures.* She kind of missed living here already, which was just silly since she hadn't even moved the first box yet and she'd still be working here every day, but somehow that wasn't reassuring.

Carolanne hitched her purse up on her shoulder and checked her reflection in the window glass. She ran her fingers through her auburn hair to tame the wisps back into submission. *Not that it'll do much good in this humidity.* She dug into her purse to retrieve a tissue to brush away the handiwork of a spider that spanned the width of the door right across her name. The leggy spider scurried aside, disappearing into a crack in the mortar. She could end this daily battle with the critter with one quick thumb, but she figured that spider had seniority. Besides, he might have a big brother upstairs, and that was somewhere she didn't want spiders.

She traced the tissue over the letters of her last name.

*Baxter and Buckham*
*Attorneys at Law*

Simple. The script she'd chosen for the Baxter and Buckham lettering was much more elegant than the stick-on white block lettering Connor had there before they'd decided to partner last year. The gold letters were like the perfect necklace that completes an outfit. A nice improvement, not unlike the upgrade in the lobby furnishings she'd sprung for. She ran her fingers across the hand-painted gold letters worthy of the career she'd built.

Carolanne walked to the corner, crossed Main Street, and entered the *County Gazette* office.

The aluminum blind slapped against the glass of the door as Carolanne walked inside.

A young woman dressed in all black with hair to match stood talking to Jack.

He lifted his chin, acknowledging Carolanne, but continued talking to the young lady. "We don't keep any of the archives here at the paper. The library has all of that. Good timing, though. Wasn't too long ago you'd have had to swirl through heaps of microfiche, but we got a grant and now everything is electronic. That ought to make things much easier for you."

"Thank you so much. How do I get to the library from here?" she asked.

Carolanne took a step toward them. "I'm getting ready to go to the library to return these books. You can walk down with me. It's not far."

"That'd be perfect," Jack said. "This is Carolanne. She'll show you the way."

The black-haired girl thanked Jack and stepped toward the door.

Carolanne handed Jack an envelope. "I just wanted to drop off the payment for our last ad, and Jill asked me to drop off this invitation to the grand opening."

"The whole town is buzzing about it."

"Sure hope so. Jill says thanks for the front-page article. The artisan center's been her dream as long as I've known her."

"And that's been forever." He turned to the young lady. "Carolanne grew up in this town. She might be able to help you with your research, too."

"Happy to help if I can," Carolanne said. "You ready to head to the library?"

"Yes. That would be great. Thanks for your help, sir."

"Jack. You can call me, Jack. Everyone does."

"Thanks, Jack." She turned to Carolanne. "I'm Gina."

"Let's go, Gina." Carolanne held the door and gave Jack a little shrug. She didn't look like the type of girl who would land in Adams Grove. Aside from the flashy shoulder bag that she clung to like a life-support system, there wasn't any color on her except a bright band of blue from a tattoo on her wrist.

Carolanne and Gina walked in silence up the first block.

"What brings you to Adams Grove?"

Gina ran a hand through her hair. "I live in Florida, but my mother grew up here." The sleeves of her black jacket lifted, exposing her eerily white skin and the bright-blue band of tiny butterflies around her wrist.

*For a Florida girl, she sure is pale. Maybe*

*the gothic look was intentional, but the playful butterflies sure don't seem to fit in with that.* "Well, everyone knows everyone around here, so you shouldn't have any problem finding what you're looking for. Where are you staying while you're in town?"

Gina's arm twitched, and she shrugged before answering. "I'm crashing at someone's house for a few days, you know, until I figure out how long I'll be here. I'm planning to head up to New York to look up my father, too. We've never met."

"So, you never lived here?"

She shook her head. "We lived down in Jacksonville my whole life." Gina chewed on her bottom lip. "My mom died. I just want to know some things about her childhood, get some answers."

Carolanne felt the familiar emptiness in her gut. "My mom died when I was little, too. It's something you never get over. I *still* miss her."

Gina's voice cracked. "It wasn't that long ago. She . . . It was suicide."

"I'm so sorry." Carolanne's heart tugged at the sadness in the demeanor of the young woman who walked beside her. "When you're ready, if there's anything I can do to help, you let me know. My office is on Main Street." Carolanne pulled a card out of her wallet and tucked it into Gina's pocket. "Really. Don't lose that."

"Thank you." Gina shook her head and swept a tear away. "I'm sorry."

"No. Don't be. It's my fault." Carolanne's heart broke a little at having caused the girl that emotional tug of war. "I always ask a million questions. Occupational hazard. I'm a lawyer, and I've been exactly where you are. Don't say another word. I get it."

Carolanne watched the girl make a visible effort to swallow and pull herself together. She thought about how her mother's death had completely broken her dad. Had Mom known that she'd die at such a young age, would she still have married Dad? Probably not if she'd known it would devastate him. "Do you worry your life will follow your mother's?"

"It's possible, don't you think?"

"I guess I hadn't ever really considered it." The landscape seemed to quake beneath Carolanne's shoes. If her life followed the path of her mother's, could she be nearing the end of her days? She still had things she wanted to do. *Mom wasn't much older than I am now when she died.* The lump in her throat suddenly felt like a lump in her breast—still her worst fear even now, after a clear mammogram.

Carolanne glanced over at the girl walking next to her. She looked younger. The bottom of her faded black jeans were frayed and dirty, as if she'd walked off the parts that were too long rather than getting them hemmed. She was thin—too thin, really—and that made her eyes look too big for her face. And those eyes, they looked sad.

"Do you need help? I mean, you said your mom, and well . . ."

"Oh. No, not like that. I'm mentally fine—just confused." She looked directly at Carolanne. "I just need to understand why she did it, understand her more. I'm not suicidal. I'm sorry if I scared you."

Carolanne breathed a sigh of relief. From her own past, she knew too well that the answers weren't always as easy to understand as they were to find.

They walked down the sloping sidewalk over to Peach Street in silence.

Out of habit, Carolanne paused and looked both ways before crossing the street, although the quiet was evidence that there was nary a car on it. The bookmobile was parked next to the library, restocking before heading to the outskirts of the county. The library building was well over a hundred years old. A wide handicap ramp had replaced the original stairs, but the front door was still original to the turn of the century and was so heavy Carolanne had to push her whole weight against it to get it open. Inside, the fourteen-foot ceilings still held the beauty of the original moldings.

Carolanne motioned Gina inside in front of her. The floor creaked beneath their feet, and they picked up speed as the floor slanted toward the back. Carolanne couldn't help but picture someone in a wheelchair sailing through the long space and straight out the back door, maybe grabbing a random book as they zoomed past the tightly filled shelves.

It was those things that made this library so charming to Carolanne, but she saw the look of doubt on Gina's face. "Don't let the size of this library fool you. I spent many an hour in this place growing up. They've got access to everything you could possibly want."

Carolanne placed her books on the counter. Mrs. Huckaby's head was just barely visible over the long row of short shelves across the room. "Good morning," Carolanne said loudly.

Like a meerkat, Mrs. Huckaby popped up and surveyed the space until her line of sight set on Carolanne and Gina. "Hello. I didn't hear you come in."

"No problem. I'm not in a hurry. I'm just going to look around for a few minutes. Did the book you ordered for me come in?"

"It sure did. Let me know when you're ready, and I'll be right there."

"I have someone here with me. She's looking for the newspaper archives. I told her this was the place to come."

Mrs. Huckaby whipped around the aisle and was standing next to them before Carolanne could even finish her thought.

"This is Gina," Carolanne said.

"You can call me Doris. Everybody does." She stuck out her hand. "How can I help you? Research? I've got the best tools in three counties." Doris was tugging Gina toward the computer terminals. "I tell you what, those federal grants are amazing once you know how to get them. I can set you up right over here. We'll have you knee-deep in information before your butt warms up the chair."

Carolanne watched the smile spread across Gina's face. "I think you're in good hands."

"Apparently." Gina waved, sank down into the wooden chair behind the monitor, and followed Mrs. Huckaby's directions.

Carolanne headed for the shelf where Mrs. Huckaby stored all the new inventory and loaners from other branches. She scanned the shelves, tugging one novel out after another to read the back copy, but her attention kept drifting back to the conversation between Gina and Doris.

"Nineteen seventy-four," Gina said. "I think that was the last summer Mom spent here."

A few clicks and Mrs. Huckaby had the girl all set. "You said she went to high school here. We'd be about the same age. I might've known her."

"She did. Lindsey Edwards. Well, Lindsey Dixon back then."

"My goodness. No wonder you looked familiar when you came in. Now that I know, yes, you look just like her. I see it now. I never knew she had a daughter."

"So, you really knew my mom?"

"I did. Everyone knows everyone around here." Her smile pushed her cheeks into rosy mounds that shifted up her glasses. "Nice to meet you, Gina. My husband and I both grew up here in Adams Grove—and we both knew your momma. Nicest gal. She lived over off Route 58 near Old Pond. Well, anyway . . . Yes, we knew her. Oh my word, you know the whole town is just still so sad about the accident. I guess a town never really does get over a tragedy like that. Goodness gracious, look at me." Doris swept at a tear.

Carolanne turned and saw the look on Gina's face, and Doris must have, too, because she went right into damage control. "I'm sorry. I shouldn't have even mentioned it. If it makes me that sad, no telling how you feel about it. He was your uncle. Oh goodness, I'm always saying too much. You just holler if you need me." Doris rushed back to her cart and started shelving books.

Carolanne slid the book she was looking at back on the shelf. She'd read nearly every book they had in this place over the past year. She walked past Gina, then stopped and turned back.

"I didn't mean to be eavesdropping," Carolanne said, "but I overheard you talking a minute ago. You're a Dixon?"

Gina nodded.

"You should've said so. You need to stop by my office and talk to my partner, Connor Buckham. The address is on the card I gave you. We hold the trust for the Dixon family farm."

"A trust?"

Carolanne slid into the chair next to Gina. "Yes. It means that the law office handles the care of the land for your family. I don't know any of the details—Connor is handling that—but you definitely need to talk to him."

Gina's heavily mascaraed lashes flew up, and when she spoke, her voice wavered. "The farm where my mom grew up?"

"Yes. In fact, we were just talking about that property the other day. Connor can go through all the details with you." She watched Gina take in the information like she was processing a bigger picture.

"I didn't know the farm was still even in our family." After a short pause, Gina switched gears. "Have you always lived here in Adams Grove?"

"No. I've been away for a long time. I moved to New York City straight from college. I just moved back this past year."

Gina's eyes sparkled with interest. "I've always wanted to live in a big city. Jacksonville is huge compared to Adams Grove, but I mean a *real* one. I've been thinking about moving to New York City." She looked Carolanne in the eye, pausing like she was looking for a reaction. "I can't imagine moving back to a little town like this on purpose. Do you like it here?"

"Yes. Believe it or not, I used to think the same as you, though. I couldn't wait to move to a big city. It had this whole, I don't know, mystique about it, and frankly, I liked the idea of being lost amid the masses," Carolanne admitted for the first time.

She recognized the dreamy look in Gina's eyes. She'd had those illusions once, too. "I guess sometimes you have to leave and come back to appreciate the real charm of a small town. New York is busier, faster, and more intense. It took me a while to retrain myself to the slower pace around here. Actually, I'm still kind of struggling with that, but I'll tell ya, between the two, I think I'm much happier here."

And it wasn't until those words came out of her mouth that Carolanne realized she actually believed them.

# ❖ Chapter Six ❖

After a nearly sleepless night, Carolanne had gotten out of bed early but was still running late when she heard the knock at her front door.

*Who would be knocking on my door at this hour?* Following a quick peek through the peephole, she opened the door. "Since when do you knock?" She leaned against the doorjamb. "Is this payback for the other day?"

"I'm being polite," Connor said with a serious look, but Carolanne caught the hint of playfulness in his voice.

She moved to the side so he could come in. "Oh, Lord. This *is* about the other day. You're a smarty-pants."

He thrust a cluster of coral begonia blooms in her direction. "And charming."

She couldn't control her burst of laughter. *They're so pretty, but . . .* She lifted a damp hand from the flowers and saw the fresh soil clinging to the bottom of them. "Connor Buckham. You pulled these flowers out of the planter in front of the office. That's not charming—that's a crime. Johnny Cash went to jail for that!"

"That's a rumor."

"Still. That's wrong, and you know it," she said.

"I know a good lawyer *and* the sheriff. Here,"

he said, shoving them in her direction again. "Put them in some water. Is it safe to come in for coffee this morning or not?"

"The garden club is going to have your head for disturbing their hard work, but yes, all's clear." She headed to the kitchen to float the contraband begonias in water.

Connor followed her. "Actually, I think your dad has that gig these days."

"The planters on Main Street?" She didn't know why she'd thought she'd be able to come back to Adams Grove and avoid her dad, but that wasn't something she wanted to deal with this morning. She slipped the flowers into a squat vase. "There."

"Yep, and now you're an accessory to my crime." Connor leaned on the counter and nodded toward the flowers.

"You are just full of yourself this morning. Wish I woke up all eager to go like you. I got a late start, but the coffee should be ready by now."

"Good. I need some," he said.

"You were probably already up and out jogging before I got out of bed. I don't know how you do that. I'd get bored running."

"You should come with me. I'll slow down. I won't even talk to you." Connor crossed his heart. "Promise."

"It would never work for us to run together. We're too competitive. We'd just end up racing."

"True, but it'll wake you up and free your mind."

"Free my mind? Oh no, that's not going to happen." She tapped the side of her head. "There's too much stuff happening up here."

"Now who's full of themselves?" Connor poured himself a cup of coffee. "Do you have a cup yet?"

"No. I'm just going in circles." She disappeared into her bedroom to finish getting ready.

He poured her a cup of coffee and added one sugar and a splash of cream to get it to the right tan, then walked to her bedroom doorway. "Here you go."

"Thanks, Connor." She took a sip. "It's perfect." The surprise in her voice made the statement sound like a question.

He gave her a smug look. "Some people would say I'm a pretty observant guy."

*Yeah, but since when did you become so observant of me?* "I guess I'll be one of those people now, too."

Connor slugged back his coffee and went to pour himself another cup. "I'll be in court this morning, but I'm going over to Hale's Vineyard for an estate auction in the afternoon. Want to join me?"

"I've never been to an auction. That sounds like it could be fun. What kind of stuff?"

"Antiques and collectibles. Mostly guns and jewelry, some furniture."

She flicked on her mascara and then turned. "Count me in."

"It's a date." Connor grabbed his briefcase and headed out of the room.

The door slammed behind him, and as she heard him clomp down the stairs like a horse galloping for the finish line, those words played an endless loop in her mind.

*It's a date? It's just an expression, so why do those words bother me so much?*

Carolanne's morning schedule was light. Thank goodness for that, because for some reason, ever since she'd met Gina yesterday, her mood had been as black as Gina's hair.

She'd barely been able to concentrate all day. Her mind swirled with questions about the past, the future, her purpose. Would she make a mark on this world that made any difference at all? If not, what a waste that would be.

*My work is important. I have a good life, don't I? Is that enough?*

She stood up and stretched out the hours of sitting behind her desk. *When that yoga studio opens up, maybe I'll sign up for that class. Until then, maybe the ritual of a morning walk would be a good start.*

She flipped the sign on the door to BE RIGHT BACK and set off for a stroll down Main. The naked spot in the planter made her smile as she thought of the flowers Connor had sprung on her. It wasn't unusual for Connor to be silly or playful, but those flowers were schoolboy sweet and there wasn't anything laughable about that.

A slight breeze sent delicate, paper-thin pink petals swirling around her like wads of tissue paper from the rows of flowering crepe myrtles lining Main Street. The weather had been so summerlike that the Southern magnolias in front of the bank were already displaying their large cream-white flowers as big and audacious as Kentucky Derby hats.

Down the next block, the front doors of the bright-orange storefront rumored to be the future home of the yoga classes was propped open with a big gray paint bucket.

Carolanne slowed down and poked her head inside. A woman stretched, balancing on one leg with the grace of an angel, then slowly transitioning into another pose. Mirrors reflected blue and pinkish lights in a soft, serene glow. Shiny hand-painted silver words in a flowing script adorned the walls like clouds of hope. Harmony. Balance. Love. Peace. Joy. Share.

The woman moved her slim body into the different positions without a single wobble or creak of the joints. Like a choreographed ballet, it grabbed Carolanne's attention and made her yearn to move like that.

Carolanne stretched up, standing a little taller

with each of the woman's stretches and wishing for the calm that seemed to exude from her as she carefully moved from position to position.

Suddenly, the woman dropped from the pose and skipped to the door. "I'm sorry. I didn't even hear you come in."

"No. I'm sorry. I'd heard you were going to be opening a yoga studio down here. I was walking by, and I saw you. Your movements—they captivated me. I just walked right in uninvited."

"Don't be silly. Welcome!" Anita laughed like a xylophone working its way up the scale. "The warrior poses. So basic, but I love them. I can go through all of those poses without even thinking anymore. They totally clear my mind. Have you ever done yoga before?"

"No. I was pretty athletic back in school, but nowadays, it's just work, work, work."

"Well, then you have to come to my class. Try a couple for free. I bet you'll love what yoga will do for you."

Carolanne grimaced. "I'm not very graceful."

"Oh, it's not about grace. It's so much more. A lifestyle, really. It'll change your life." Anita paused. "You look skeptical."

*Lifestyle? Next, this woman will want me to give up burgers. If I couldn't nail ballet after four years of classes, it's doubtful that in my thirties I'll move like her. What was I thinking?* "No. I mean . . . Well, I don't know much about it."

"Don't let me scare you away. I get a little over-enthusiastic about it sometimes, but I swear it's such a great workout and life balancer. A good thing these days."

"Life balance is something I'm not too good at."

A flash of recognition crossed Anita's face. "You're the lady lawyer working with Connor Buckham, aren't you?"

"That would be me." Carolanne extended her hand. "I'm Carolanne Baxter."

"I thought I recognized you from your picture in the *County Gazette* last month. It's nice to meet you. I'm Anita Foster."

"I know you from the paper, too. For a paper that only comes out twice a month, they sure do a good job of getting us all in it."

"Slow news days around here. Part of the charm of Adams Grove."

Carolanne thought about the number of times her dad had been in the news. She'd have given anything for them not to have had room to run those stories back then. *Charm? Depends on your vantage point.* "Somebody was just telling me I need to free my mind a little. They suggested I jog, but that's really not my thing. I thought maybe yoga would be a better fit for me." *At least, I did before I saw you doing it. Looks more like really slow dancing than exercise.*

"Running is hard on your joints. Yoga would be so much better. It's like a little gift to yourself.

You have to make time to relax. It's absolutely essential to a healthy life."

Carolanne pictured herself all twisted up like the bow on a package. She couldn't deny this lady's enthusiasm was a little contagious. "When are you going to start classes?"

"Not until August. I'm trying to talk Mac into entering a couple cake competitions this summer. He was so close to winning last time. Can you imagine what that would do for his business?"

Carolanne pasted fake enthusiasm on her face to match Anita's, because honestly, she didn't quite see how Mac winning a competition would really help his business at all, since his business was local and everyone around was already his customer.

"Anyway," Anita said, "that doesn't matter, because I could get you started on some basic moves. In fact, why don't you stop by Monday and I'll show you some stuff that you can do on your own until the classes start?"

Carolanne liked the thought of that. "You wouldn't mind? I'd pay you, of course."

"Oh, don't be silly. I'd enjoy it. I'll see you around four, if that works for you."

*She's so nice.* "Well, thanks. I'd say I'm sorry I interrupted your workout, but this seems to have worked out very well."

"I agree. I'll see you Monday."

"Thanks." Carolanne left, feeling a little more

relaxed just having talked to Anita. She could only imagine what the yoga might do for her.

Carolanne said hello to a couple walking down the street, then paused in front of Jacob's Diner. Every table was full, and all but two seats at the long Formica counter were, too. She turned to leave, then stopped on the sidewalk out front. *Why am I always in a hurry? I have time. Relax.* Besides, the smell of fresh local bacon and sausage was too yummy to resist. So she slipped inside and took one of the last seats at the counter. Several folks issued good mornings to her as she settled in.

She eyed the menu on the wall, but she knew what she was going to order. The clanking of the pans and loud murmur of the patrons reminded her of the feel of a New York diner on an early weekday, only friendlier.

The waitress, Lara, took her order, poured her a cup of coffee, then whisked by her to greet someone near the cash register. Lara gave the person's shirt a friendly tug, and when she stepped aside, Carolanne recognized Gina standing there.

Gina dug something out of her purse and handed it to Lara.

Lara wiped her hands on her apron and took it, then gave Gina a hug and rushed away, yelling over her shoulder for Gina to wait as she ran back to the kitchen, shouted out two orders, then reappeared from the back with two big brown grocery bags. "You said you wanted them all, right?"

Gina looked excited. "Yes! Oh my gosh, you just don't know how much I appreciate this. Thank you so much."

"No problem. This is the best kind of recycling I know of. Have fun."

"I will." Gina took the two brown paper bags and practically ran from the diner.

Lara slid Carolanne's breakfast in front of her, and Carolanne couldn't resist asking her about Gina. "I saw you talking to that girl. She's new around here, isn't she?"

"Oh yeah. Sweet girl. She's from out of town." Lara pulled the change purse from her apron pocket. "Look at what she made for me. It's made totally out of old candy wrappers. Is it absolutely adorable, or what?"

Carolanne took the handcrafted item from Lara and turned it over in her hands. "Did she make that purse she carries, too? Those things sell for hundreds of dollars in the city."

"She did. I'd never seen anything like it before. I mean, we used to turn gum wrappers into key chains in camp when I was a kid, but I never thought anyone ever made nothin' else from them. I've been saving potato chip bags for her. She's working on some project using potato chip bags with the foil inside."

Carolanne held up the change purse. "It's great.

I bet Jill would love to have these for sale in the artisan center."

Lara's eyes widened. "That would be great. I get the feeling Gina is a little short on cash. I'll tell her to contact Jill next time she stops by."

"Great. Or tell her to stop by and see me. I gave her my business card the other day. I met her at the *Gazette* and showed her to the library. She'll remember."

Lara tugged the towel from her waistband and swept an area of the counter clear. "I gotta run, girl. Eat up."

Carolanne finished her breakfast and then walked back down to the office, looking forward to the short day and the afternoon at the auction with Connor.

Once she cleared all the work from her desk, she sat there thinking about some of the things she needed to change in her life. She opened a new page in her notepad and wrote *balance* across the top. There was something to be said about life balance; she preached it to others all the time. Not that she practiced what she preached. Her whole life centered around her work.

*Maybe that's why I'm struggling with the slower pace. Maybe Connor's right about me needing other things in my life. But what? Work has always been enough.*

The words painted around the yoga studio played in her mind. She closed her eyes and thought about them and what she'd tell someone else about life balance.

Health. Family. Work. Play. Friends. Give.

She eyed the list and crossed out the words *family* and *play,* then reluctantly the word *give.* *I'm healthy.* But then, she knew *being* healthy and *living* healthy were not the same thing. She crossed that one out, too. Two out of six wasn't a winning combination.

Health. Family. Work. Play. Friends. Give.

*I've got work to do.*

She crumpled the piece of paper and tossed it in the trash can next to her desk. Then she leaned over and retrieved the wadded paper and smoothed it back out. *Health will be easy. I already have that time to meet with Anita on Monday for the yoga. I could do some walking.*

*Family.* Even looking at that word was hard.

*Harsh realities. Jill was right. I've never been good at dealing with them.*

Carolanne folded the piece of paper and stuck it in her front pocket, then Googled information on the estate auction in Hale's Vineyard. There were tons of items listed. She scrolled through some of them, then stopped and looked at the jewelry. Some of the pieces appeared to be quite old. She glanced at her watch. Connor would be back any time—why not close up early for the day?

# ❖ Chapter Seven ❖

Carolanne raised her number in the air for the fourth time in a row.

Connor nudged her. "Is that necklace worth that much money?"

"I have absolutely no idea." She threw her bidder number up again. "It's worth exactly what I'm willing to pay, right?" Carolanne leveled her stare on the bleached-blonde woman standing next to the fat guy who kept trying to outbid her on the antique pendant. "At this point, it's the principle!"

*Been there, done that.* Connor laughed. "All righty, then. Don't get swept up in the competition of it, or you could way overspend."

"Don't spoil my fun. I didn't spoil yours when you spent a fortune on that gun."

"But that wasn't just any gun, and it was still a steal." *She's tuning me out.*

"Well, I really like this piece. It's special." She thrust her number in the air again. "I've got to have it."

*I know how you feel.*

The couple at war with Carolanne over the necklace started muttering between themselves. That was a good sign they were nearing the end of their purse strings. "One more time," Connor encouraged Carolanne, "and don't drop your arm."

She threw her number in the air and didn't lower it.

The auctioneer scanned the crowd for last bidders. "All in. All done. Sold to the little red-head."

"It's mine? I got it?"

"You did," Connor said.

Carolanne pumped both fists in the air, then turned and hugged Connor. He could feel her heart pounding, and the scent of something mystically spicy and flowery all at the same time filled his head. "Thank you! I was getting ready to quit. You knew."

"Shhhh."

Carolanne shrank back, apologizing to the people sitting around them. "Sorry. I'm so excited." She leaned close to Connor and whispered, "What do we do now?"

He took her hand and led her out of the room as the auctioneer began a round of bidding on a piece of nineteenth-century artwork.

"That was practically dizzying." Carolanne could barely stand still.

"I've created a monster."

Joy bubbled in her laugh. "You might have. Who knew this would be so much fun? Battling with that couple over the necklace—now, that was cool."

"That's because you love to win."

"Guilty as charged," she said.

Since the auction was still in full swing, the line to check out was short. Connor settled his tab, and then Carolanne did the same.

They both stepped over to the second counter, where they traded paid receipts for their goods. Connor walked out to his car while Carolanne waited for her jewelry.

He placed his rifle in the back of the car, then turned and leaned on the trunk lid just as Carolanne came out of the building. She walked toward him, clutching a black velvet box like she was one of the three wise men offering up a gift.

"So, let me see this to-die-for necklace up close."

Carolanne snapped open the jewelry box and held it out in front of him. A diamond-crusted bow hung from the center of a delicate chain, and below that, a stunning teardrop-shaped emerald matched the color of Carolanne's eyes.

"White gold?" he asked.

"No. It's platinum." Carolanne's hands shook as she lifted the chain out of the box.

"No wonder it was so expensive."

She lifted the chain to put it on.

"Here. Let me." He took the necklace from her.

Carolanne spun around with her back to him.

He took the delicate clasp between his fingers and then raised his hands up and over her head. The pendant settled just right at her cleavage. He could feel her racing heart as he hooked the chain. Then he unhooked the barrette that held her hair back and slowly pushed his fingers through the loops of her braid, freeing her rich auburn waves.

She turned around, taking a deep breath and looking up at him. "What do you think?"

He stared for just a second. Something innocent —hopeful, maybe—seemed to dance in her eyes. *That you're the most beautiful girl I know.* He leaned forward and pulled her closer to press his lips to hers, then gently covered her mouth. He felt her shiver beneath his touch, and as he roused her passion, his own grew even stronger. Her response was undeniable, but she pulled away all of a sudden.

"Wait." She swept her hand across her mouth. "What was that?" She twisted from him and shoved the box into her purse as she made her way around to the passenger seat.

*I wish I knew.* He let out a sigh and got behind the wheel of the car. "It was just a kiss." *Well, almost a really good kiss.* He wanted to let it go, but she looked even prettier sitting there at a loss for words. It wasn't his imagination. He'd felt the attraction, and it wasn't one-sided.

She fondled the pendant hanging around her neck. "Why—"

"Don't ask. Don't analyze it. Just let it be." He kissed her again, on the cheek this time. "It's OK."

She mouthed the word *OK* and avoided eye contact as he started the car.

He squeezed her hand and smiled, hoping maybe she was feeling something. She hadn't gotten mad—well, not redhead mad—and that had to mean something. "It's all good."

They'd ridden in complete silence for more than ten minutes when Carolanne said, "Do you want to know why I wanted this necklace so badly?"

"Because you thought it was pretty?"

"No. It's more than that." She shifted in her seat. "I don't know if it's even remotely like it, but in my mind, the one piece of jewelry that my momma always treasured was a pendant that had been in the family for years. I remembered the bow of diamonds above the teardrop stone mostly. She lost it when I was a little girl. I remember her crying. She was so sad to have lost it and so scared to tell my dad."

"That sounds special."

Carolanne swept her hand underneath her nose, then pushed her hair behind her ears. "Dad wasn't mad, though. I remember how gentle he was with her. He never liked to see Momma sad."

"Ben loved her. Still does as much today as back then, I think. You should have heard the way he talked about your momma with my mom. That's the real deal right there."

"He loved her more than anything."

"Do you think that necklace belonged to her?"

"I don't know, but it sure hit those memories hard. I knew I had to have it. At whatever cost."

He brushed his thumb across her knuckles. "I'm glad you shared that with me."

She smiled. "I am, too. This has been a really special night. Perfect timing. Thank you, Connor."

"You're welcome. I enjoyed it, too," he said. "It's still early. Do you want to stop by your dad's and see what he thinks of the necklace?"

She involuntarily tensed under his grip, and he tugged his hand back from her.

"Oh, I don't know if I'm ready for that."

"He'd probably like to know you have good memories of your mom. He worries about you."

That kiss may have confused her, but her guard was clearly up again, and she managed a feeble answer. "I'm not ready to just pop in on him."

Connor knew his disappointment showed on his face. "One of you is going to have to make a move someday. Seems like this necklace is as good a reason as any for y'all to get together to talk."

She turned and stared out the window. "Not tonight. OK?"

He didn't want to push, but it was hard to understand how Carolanne could shut out her father. His own dad had walked out on them when he was just a kid—no hero, by any stretch of the imagination—but he'd never turned his back on his dad. Parents are parents—flaws and all. He'd give anything to have even five more minutes with his mother. He hoped Carolanne would never regret the time she didn't spend with her father.

When they got back home, Carolanne made a hasty retreat to her apartment—saying good night and slipping inside the safety of her apartment before Connor could corner her for a good night at the door.

Confused, she paced the room, then dropped down on the couch, hugging a throw pillow. "Don't overanalyze it," he'd said, but that was impossible.

*That kiss was a mistake.* But her heart refused to listen to what her mind was trying to tell her. There was no mistaking that when he'd kissed her, she'd felt something. Something different. A reckless abandon to the tenderness of his touch in a way she'd never felt before.

*How did that happen? Why in the good Lord's name did I like it so much?*

"This is nothing but trouble," she muttered to the dark room. "Not a good idea."

Carolanne had nothing against having fun, but Connor wasn't a have-some-fun-and-move-on kind of guy. Plus, she'd have to face him in the office, and that was already going to be awkward.

She ran her hand through her loose hair. When he'd pulled that barrette from her hair and run his fingers through it to loosen the tight braid, she'd felt his every pulse tweak her own into a double count that had almost made her hyper-ventilate. *Heck, I might hyperventilate just thinking about it.* She swung her legs around to lie flat out on the couch, then took in a deep breath and let it out slowly to a three-count. *Get it together.* The streetlight danced against the panes of the turn-of-the-century windows, sending a wavy stream of light against the ceiling.

The thought of how she'd gotten lost in those blue eyes forced her to take another deep breath, but the truth was, in that moment, it felt like the safest place on earth.

She laid her hand against the jewels that hung from her neck. *Is this you, Mom, sending me a message? Was this your necklace, or even anything like it? Or am I just wishing so hard for you to be here, to guide me, that I'm making all this up?*

Lying there in the quiet, Carolanne took a deep breath and tried to let the images go.

She jerked with a start at what sounded like the snarling of a wounded warthog, which made her sit up and start laughing. Just as she was thinking of Connor all sexy and romantic, his snoring blasted her perspective back right-side up.

She looked to heaven. "Mom, I know that was your doing. You always had the best timing."

# ❖ Chapter Eight ❖

Carolanne tossed and turned all night, thinking about the random kiss Connor had planted on her. She kicked the covers off. *I'm never going to figure that out. I wish I could talk to Jill but dumping this on her the day before her wedding isn't the best timing. It'd be selfish, if anything.*

She forced herself out of bed and got dressed in a black scoop-neck T-shirt and slacks, then put on the necklace even if it was a little fancy for the outfit. She brushed her hair without taking her eyes off the lovely pendant reflecting in the mirror. She could almost see her mother's image rather than her own, brushing with long strokes. There was something peaceful about feeling so close to her right now. *Mom, I wish you could give me some guidance, a sign, anything.*

Carolanne picked up her purse and headed for the door, but at the last minute, she went back and tucked a note under the edge of the coffeepot on the kitchen counter that simply read:

*Good morning.*
*Off to help Jill with wedding stuff.*
*Help yourself to the coffee.*
*See you tonight. C-*

Pulling the door closed, she left it unlocked so Connor could still get his coffee. He'd be shocked that she was already up and out at this hour. Comfortable with the time that note would buy her until the rehearsal dinner tonight, she hurried to leave before he woke up.

Carolanne felt like a criminal on the run the way her adrenaline was pushing her to rush to her car. A sense of relief washed over her once she backed away from the building. It was still too early for Jill to be at the artisan center, so she rode through the neighborhood, trying to waste a little time, and then took the long way to the artisan center, turning down Old Horseshoe Run Road toward the church. She pulled into the church parking lot and sat there, trying to understand the tangle of emotions she felt right now.

Years ago, she'd walked hand in hand between Mom and Dad every single Sunday up the long walkway to the front doors of this church. Even when Mom was really sick and had to wear a scarf over her bald head from the chemo, they'd never missed a service.

She'd been a daddy's girl up until Mom died. Everything changed then. She'd been shepherded along from neighbor to neighbor the first couple of weeks, and then Pearl had taken control. Almost a month passed, and she hadn't only lost Mom, but hadn't seen her dad, either. Carolanne remembered crying night after night wondering if Dad had died, too.

That sadness had long since been replaced by anger, and she wasn't sure how to start again without the weight of that negativity. She shoved the gearshift back in drive and headed to the artisan center.

Carolanne parked next to Jill's car, relieved that Dad's car wasn't there. She went inside. "Hello, anyone around?"

"Back here," Jill's voice came from somewhere toward the back of the building.

Carolanne followed the voice but didn't spot Jill until she looked down behind the counter. "There you are." Carolanne laughed at the sight of Jill on the floor surrounded by packing peanuts and Bubble Wrap. "Looks like you just popped out of that box. Are you practicing for Garrett's bachelor party tonight?"

"Oh no. Garrett already promised me that he and the guys will be having a calm evening." Jill stood up and tried to brush the peanuts off her pants, but the static kept reattaching the white nuggets to her legs. "Are you OK? You look awful."

The day before Jill's wedding was not the day to dump all of her drama on Jill. "I'm fine. Sinuses, probably the weather changing, and I didn't put any makeup on this morning."

"Or maybe it's just that you pale in comparison to that necklace. Get over here. How did I not notice that when you first walked in?" Jill stepped closer to Carolanne. "I love that. When did you get it?"

"Isn't it amazing? It's like one my mom had."

"Where'd you find it?"

"I went to an estate sale with Connor yesterday. It was so much fun." *Too much fun.* There was that tingle again. *Better change the subject or Jill will be matchmaking, and I can't take that right now.* "But tomorrow's your big day. Anything we need to do for tonight or in the morning?"

"No. Patsy's handling the rehearsal dinner. I swear I'm going to have the best in-laws in the world. She won't even let me help. I'm meeting Izzy in town in a little while to go over the limo stuff one last time."

Carolanne started scooping the packing trash into one of the boxes while they talked. "Only Izzy Markham could make a limo service work in Adams Grove. I still can't believe she married a mortician. Don't you think that's creepy?"

"I met him a couple times before they divorced. He seemed like a really nice guy."

"Until he turned into a cheater?"

"Yeah, until then. I don't know what would have made him think he could get away with something like that with Izzy. That's one girl who doesn't take any mess," Jill said.

"I know. I always thought I was tough, but Izzy makes me look tame."

"I wouldn't go that far," Jill said with teasing laughter in her eyes.

"Well, you know what I mean." Carolanne helped Jill put the items from the boxes on the shelves and price items until it was time for Jill to go to town to meet with Izzy.

"Want me to give you a lift?" Carolanne asked.

"No. Then you'd have to drive back out here before going back to your house for the dinner. That doesn't make any sense."

Out of excuses to stay away from the office, Carolanne figured she'd just have to face Connor, and if that kiss came up, she prayed for some quick thinking. She followed Jill all the way back to town. Carolanne waved when Jill turned off, and she headed to the office.

She knew what she'd felt when Connor kissed her, because every time she even thought about that kiss, it sent the same powerful zing through her veins again, but she wasn't sure she really *wanted* to feel that way. And she knew she didn't want to admit it to him.

It was about lunchtime, so with any luck he'd already be out of the office. She parked along the curb since she'd be heading out again in a little while anyway and scolded herself for feeling disappointed that the BE RIGHT BACK sign was not flipped.

*See? It's already awkward, and it was just one kiss. I can't dread going to my own office. This is crazy. That settles it. That kiss is not happening again. No matter how good it was.*

She walked inside with a renewed strength and a reminder that she was immune to his little tactics.

But when Connor's voice carried through the office space, she felt her immunity wane a little as an uncontrollable ripple of awareness coursed through her. It drove her nuts how he always spoke on speakerphone, mostly because she couldn't keep herself from eavesdropping.

She busied herself with opening the mail, then walked down the hall to give Connor his.

"I don't think so," said another voice. Then the unmistakable metal sounds of a rifle pushing ammo into its chamber sent her two quick steps backward. She turned blindly, stumbling into the oversize painting that hung on the wall.

Her heart pounded so hard she couldn't hear anything else.

Ben rushed into the hall, with Connor right behind him. They both looked alarmed.

After a long night of troubled soul-searching, her worst nightmare stood right in front of her. Both Dad *and* Connor. Just seeing her dad aroused old fears and uncertainties. She closed her eyes and prayed that when she opened them, she'd be back upstairs in her bed, with the morning sunrise just peeking through the plantation shutters, but no.

Instead, Connor and Ben both stood there staring at her like she owed them an explanation.

She shoved the mail in Connor's direction. "I heard the gun cock, and it caught me off guard."

Nervous laughter filled the hallway, breaking the tension.

Ben's eyes softened. "I bet we did scare you. Sorry about that. Connor said you were with Jill getting ready for the wedding."

"I thought we were alone. Sorry, Carolanne," Connor said.

Ben handed the rifle off to Connor. "I'd just come by to see his new gun, and . . ." Then his gaze dropped to her neckline, and his face went slack.

Her hand went to her neck in response to him staring at the necklace.

Connor was staring, too, and she regretted not pulling her hair back this morning. He'd think she'd worn it down for him. Well, maybe in some stupid way she had.

Ben blinked and finished his sentence. "Where'd you get that necklace?"

Connor interjected. "Your daughter was like a wild woman when that thing came up for auction last night. Same auction where I got the rifle. She refused to let anyone outbid her."

A smile trembled over her lips as she reached for the pendant. "You recognize it, too? Are you thinking the same thing? When I saw it—"

He stepped toward her. "It's just like the one she had."

"Mom's, right?"

He nodded slowly.

"When I saw this, it reminded me of Mom. I wondered if it was my imagination." She smiled hesitantly, then looked to Connor as her dad stepped forward and touched the necklace.

"It's not your imagination." Ben rubbed his hand across his mouth. "I never thought I'd see that again. We never did figure out what happened to it. She loved that necklace."

"I remember when she lost it."

"You were so little then."

"Mom was so upset."

A flash of sadness filled Ben's eyes. "Oh yeah. She was tore up about it. The timing was bad, too, because her best friend had come to stay with us, and it wasn't long after that it turned up missing."

"I bet that was awful for her."

"As bad as losing the necklace, I think. My great-grandfather's bride received it from his mother when they had their first child. It had been in my family for generations. My mother gave it to your mom the day you were born."

"Do you think it's the same necklace?"

"It almost has to be. I mean, there could have been more than one made, but it's not like they were mass-producing stuff like that back in the day." He reached out and touched the platinum chain, then dropped his hands and let out a sigh. "You look just like her. Always did."

*Is that why you could never look at me?*

Ben patted his hand across his heart. "I'm glad it found you. Your mom would be so happy to know you are wearing it."

*What about you?*

There was a gentle softness in Ben's voice. "I'm happy to know you have it. It's supposed to bring great luck and long-lasting love. Not that your mom and I ever needed any help in that area."

"I know," Carolanne said quietly. "I know how much you loved her."

He reached for her hand. "And you."

She drew her lips tight, as tight as her heart felt right that second. She glanced toward Connor, wishing he'd disappear.

"And, Carolanne, I let you down. I know I did, but I never stopped loving you. You were the best thing your mother and I ever did together."

"Don't . . ." *Are you reading my mind? Not now, Dad. If you're reading my mind, read this, too. Please, not now. I can't talk about this right now.*

"It's important to me that you know that I know I let you down. I take accountability for that. I can't fix the past. God knows I wish I could." His voice shook as he spoke.

She bit the inside of her cheek and stared past

him, trying not to break down herself. Connor staring wasn't making it any better.

"Carolanne, I love you, and I'm sorry . . . for everything. I'm not asking you to forget the past, but if we could just . . ."

She tried to hide her misery, but his words sliced the past like a new wound. *We're both broken.* "Dad, let's put it behind us, OK?"

"Yeah," Ben said, then shrugged. "OK."

She stepped back, needing the space. *It was long overdue, but now what? How do you end a moment like this?* She had more questions, but what if that made things worse? This was progress. *Let it be, Carolanne.* "I've got to run and get changed for the rehearsal dinner," she said. "I'll leave you guys to play with your guns. I'll see you later, Connor."

They were still standing in the hall when she walked out the door and ran upstairs.

As soon as she got to her apartment, she turned the dead bolt and ran to her bedroom. She lay across the bed, crying and wondering how she was going to push past so many years of built-up anger and hurt without it suffocating her in the process. As much as she knew she should put it behind her, the little girl inside her still hurt.

*Connor, how could you have put me in that position? I wasn't ready.*

# ❖ Chapter Nine ❖

Three cold washcloths and a double dose of eyedrops later, Carolanne arrived at the church for the rehearsal dinner. She walked from her car up the long walkway. As a little girl, she used to think the doors to this church were gigantic. Nothing big about them now—must have just been the feeling of something bigger inside.

She'd prayed for many things here over the years. She'd prayed so hard for Mom to be well and for everything to be OK, but it hadn't been enough. That hadn't shaken her faith, though. There wasn't a time she set foot in this church when she didn't feel close to Mom.

Inside, Jill and Garrett were already talking with Reverend Burke near the front of the sanctuary.

It wasn't going to be an elaborate ceremony, so there wasn't much to go over in as far as a rehearsal. But that was tradition, too, so here they all were, gathering to step through it one more time to make sure Saturday would go without a hitch.

Carolanne walked over to the Malloys. "Are they nervous?"

Patsy Malloy laughed. "Are you kidding? I think I'm the only one nervous, and that's just because I know I'm going to boohoo like a fool.

I do it at everyone's wedding, so I can just imagine how seeing my own son get married is going to affect me."

"She'll be a weeping willow." Mr. Malloy pulled a handkerchief out of his left pocket and then one out of his right. "It's going to be a two-hankie day. I guarantee it."

"He knows me so well," Patsy said to Carolanne.

"I should. We've been married more years than we haven't." He reached over and gave his wife a kiss on the cheek. "Best years of my life, too."

"Sit down," Patsy said, scooching over in the pew. "I think we're going to go ahead and put the ribbons on the pews tonight before dinner if we have time. Reverend Burke said there's nothing else scheduled before Jill and Garrett's ceremony, so we can. May as well get it out of the way."

"Sounds good." Carolanne watched as Chaz and Doris Huckaby wrangled their twins back into a pew. The six-year-old girls were going to be the flower girls. Scott Calvin, the sheriff, walked in the side door with his nephew Robbie, the ring bearer, on his hip. Everyone was accounted for, with the exception of Connor.

Patsy placed a hand on Carolanne's leg. "When are we going to see you walk down the aisle?"

"Oh goodness," Carolanne said. "Let's just get Jill and Garrett married before we think about doing this again too soon." She could see in

Patsy's reaction that her comment had sounded harsh. "It takes a lot of work to put together a wedding like this."

Connor leaned over her shoulder and whispered hello into her ear.

Carolanne wriggled away from him just as Milly shuffled in and slipped under Connor's arm. "You two looking cozy together again. I like that." She patted her chest. "Keeps my old heart full of hope."

"Are you two . . . ?" Patsy's eyes lit up.

"No. No, we are *not*," Carolanne said. Milly would have this whole town talking if she weren't careful.

"You don't have to make it sound so bad," Connor said.

"You would make a cute little couple," Patsy said. "Don't you think, honey?"

"You think everyone makes a cute couple, dear," Garrett's dad said.

Milly piped in. "But she's right this time. Pearl said so herself. You know Pearl was never wrong." Milly pointed to the front of the church. "Just like those two. Once Pearl says you're together, that's it."

"Or not," Carolanne muttered under her breath.

Connor nudged her.

Carolanne glared in his direction. *Don't push your luck with me, Connor. You're already on thin ice.*

Reverend Burke marched up the aisle. "All right, everyone. This will only take a couple minutes, but let's run through it once for good measure."

In fifteen minutes they'd already walked down the aisle twice and hummed the wedding march, while the organist had found a way to tell the kids to keep pace to the music that kept them from running down the aisle. It would be anybody's bet whether they'd remember that tomorrow, though.

Connor and Garrett went out to get the big box of ribbons from the back of the Malloys' car. It was the first chance Carolanne had had to breathe since Connor had gotten there. Just having him in the same room was enough to make her feel jumpy.

Once the guys dropped the box at the end of the aisle, they went back outside, leaving the girls to work on decorating the pews.

Carolanne handed Patsy a ribbon and then scooched the box with her foot. "Is there anything else we need to do tonight?"

Jill picked up another ribbon and fastened it on the opposite pew. "We're in good shape. We can come get ready here tomorrow since we're the first wedding. Patsy said she'd bring us breakfast and have coffee ready for us."

Carolanne felt a little useless, and she was quickly realizing that when Jill got married, it was going to change their relationship, and that made her sad. Or maybe it was just everything piling up on her at once.

"I'll make a breakfast casserole. You need something in your stomach in the morning, or the nerves will get to you." Patsy looked at Milly for confirmation.

"She's right, and her breakfast casserole is the best," Milly agreed.

They placed the last two ribbons on the pews, and then Mrs. Markham from the bed-and-breakfast up the road came in to announce that the dinner was ready to be served.

"Perfect timing," Patsy called out to her. "I'll get the gentlemen."

"Great. I'm starved," Jill said.

When Carolanne opened the door to the meeting room in the new wing of the church, she and Jill both paused to take it all in.

"It looks beautiful," Carolanne remarked.

Candle flames licked the air under glass globes, and the fine china and silver glistened in the candlelight.

Soft music played and the smells coming from the kitchen seemed five-star for sure.

Patsy Malloy led a parade of men and children into the room.

"Patsy, you've outdone yourself," Jill said.

Carolanne stepped out of the way as Patsy slid into the chair next to Jill that she'd started to sit in herself. Carolanne maneuvered to the far side of the table and tugged Milly by the hand to sit on her other side to keep Connor from sitting there. She wasn't ready to be that close to Connor in a nearly dark room.

She caught the look on Connor's face. He was clearly disappointed. Just as well. If he thought there was going to be anything long term between the two of them, then he was going to be disappointed eventually. She wasn't going to put herself at risk for the kind of breakdown her daddy had had. It just wasn't something she was willing to test. Distance was the best remedy for now.

As everyone finished their dinner, Connor stood up and cleared his throat. "I know we said we weren't going to do toasts and all that, but I do want us to raise a glass for Jill and Garrett."

Everyone lifted their glasses.

"First, thank you, Mr. and Mrs. Malloy, for a wonderful dinner. Garrett, I've known you since grade school, and even then, you were pinky-swearing with Jill under the monkey bars. I don't think it's a surprise to anyone in this town that the two of you are getting married. Love isn't just about gazing into each other's eyes day after day after day after day . . ."

Everyone laughed, and Connor continued. "Well, you get the idea. Real love is about looking outward together, toward your dreams, and working together to make them come true. You two are doing that."

Connor glanced in Carolanne's direction.

A flicker of apprehension coursed through her, and Connor's mouth pulled into a sly smile, like he could tell what effect he had on her.

He then nodded to Jill and Garrett. "I can only hope to have as lovely, graceful, and smart a woman as you do by my side someday. May your good luck rub off on us all. *Salut.*"

Garrett raised his glass. "Guess I know who'll be diving for the garter tomorrow!"

Jill raised her glass toward Carolanne and gave her a nod.

Carolanne wished her glass had been filled with something other than water—something that would knock her out. *What is this? A conspiracy?*

Everyone pushed back from the table, and Mrs. Markham whisked in to clear the dishes.

"Mrs. Markham, you outdid yourself. This was an amazing meal," Jill said. "Thank you so much."

Franny Markham beamed. "It was my pleasure, Jill. I appreciate y'all letting me live out my little fantasy of being a caterer. It was as fun as I thought it would be."

Carolanne said, "This was as nice as the five-star restaurants in New York City."

Everyone chimed in with appreciation, and the

hugs and good-byes ensued with a flurry of excitement about the big day tomorrow.

Carolanne couldn't wait to get home and crawl into bed. She went straight to her car and slid behind the steering wheel, but just as she went to close the door, Connor stiff-armed it. He stepped between the door and her seat, filling the space.

"Not even going to say good night?"

"We did," she said.

"I mean you—to me."

"Good night, Connor."

He stooped down. "Are you mad at me? You've barely said a word to me all night."

*Please. You don't know why I'm upset? Fine. We'll play games.* "Why would I be mad at you?"

Connor lolled his head back. "Oh no, you don't. Don't turn that back around on me."

"Fine. Then don't play coy with me." She pressed her lips together. "Yeah, I'm a little miffed."

"Is that like a little pregnant?"

"Hardly." She twisted the key in the ignition, but Connor didn't budge. "Look, I know you were close with your parents, and I know you don't get how I feel about my dad, but you can't just start dragging him into the office on some stupid pretense and throw him in my face, hoping for the best."

Connor stood quiet. "It did go pretty well."

"It's not your business."

106

"I'm sorry. I didn't think you were going to be in the office. Honestly, I wasn't trying to pull anything."

"Not. Your. Business." She pulled the lever into drive.

"I'm sorry. Believe me. But you're my friend and my business partner, and he's my friend, too. I think that makes it a little my business." Connor stood, put his arm on the roof of the car, and peered down toward her. "Tell me the truth. Is this about Ben, or is this about the kiss?"

She winced like he'd stuck her with a dart.

"I thought it was a pretty fine kiss. I'd do it again."

"Don't you dare." The heat she felt could be passion or fury, but either way, it wasn't his to take. "We're business partners, and that kiss was a mistake."

"It didn't feel like a mistake to me."

"I can't do that, Connor."

"I felt something. You felt something, too. I could tell," he said.

"Don't stick your nose in my business with my dad, and don't kiss me again. I didn't like it like that." *Not so,* her heart argued. "Let's do ourselves a favor and just pretend it didn't happen."

"Calm down," Connor said. "Come on. It's not as bad as you're making it."

"Don't." She raised a hand and pointed a finger at him. "Don't you tell me what I feel."

"Got it," he said, taking a step back. "As usual, you're just going to pretend everything is status quo. Is that it? Ignore the problems and they'll go away." He stepped back from the car and closed the door. Through the window, he said, "For the record, that never works. You can't ignore it away. You should know that by now."

"I know what I want, and it's not you." She clicked the lock button. *OK, that was a little dramatic, but doggone it, I wish locking you out of my business was that easy.*

In the red glow of her taillights, Connor stood there shaking his head.

Icy panic twisted around her heart as she realized she couldn't tear her eyes from the rear-view mirror and the lost look on his face.

*Why did I lie to you?*

Back at their building, she stomped up the stairs and slammed the door behind her. Connor hadn't been far behind her, although his entrance wasn't nearly as loud as hers had been.

She hadn't even bothered to turn on the lights. She sat on the couch and cried. She cried so much she didn't know how there could possibly be another tear in her body. Connor was snoring already. *Must be nice to be able to sleep.* She grabbed her keys from the top of her purse and headed down the stairwell with no regard to being quiet, since it was quite clear that Connor was sleeping like a log splitter.

The air smelled fresh, and thousands of stars sparkled across the clear night sky. She'd make a wish on one of them if she knew what the heck to wish for. *How about wishing I could forget that kiss?* She visualized the worry of what that kiss meant falling into the gutter, then slowed as she turned down Laurel Road. She'd grown up in the neighborhood that backed up to Main Street. When she was a kid, it was filled with so many families you could round up enough kids for a game of kickball just about any day of the week. Now it was a mix of more seniors than young families.

The sidewalk only stretched as far as the back end of the Main Street block, so she found a comfortable pace along the paved road. Fireflies lit the dense lines of red-tip shrubs that separated many of the properties. Childhood memories of the kids gathering at dusk to hunt down lightning bugs and trap them in clear jelly jars with the tops punctured by one of the dads filled her mind. It was a united effort until dark, when the kids divided into two camps. Jewelry and war paint. Most of the girls were in the jewelry camp, plucking the shining lights from the bugs to pretend they were diamonds. But she'd always ended up with the boys choosing to use the fluorescence as war paint, like the Indians who had settled in these parts so many years ago.

Not one car had passed by since she'd been

out. If New York was the city that never slept, Adams Grove was the town where everyone hugged a pillow at the same time every night.

She turned right at the next block. Dad lived on this block now. Not in the house she'd grown up in, which was two blocks over, but in one of the smaller homes. The lights were on in his kitchen. She knew this not because she knew the layout of his particular house so well, but because there were only so many floor plans in the neighbor-hood. If you knew one, you kind of knew them all.

She touched the necklace at her throat and considered stopping in to see him.

Connor's words echoed in the quiet. *One of you is going to have to make a move someday.*

*Dad made the first move. It's my turn.* But her heart galloped at the thought, leaving her feeling a little dizzy. She'd protected herself from being hurt by keeping that distance between them. She felt dangerously close to a point of no return.

Watching Connor mourn the loss of his mother had been heartrending, and she still missed her own mother every single day. Now, in her thirties, maybe it was time to put the past behind her and find a peaceful existence with Dad, even if it did scare her half to death. Yesterday had been a good step in the right direction. *I hope it gets easier.*

His old Pontiac sat parked in the driveway. She

stopped just behind it and stood there wrestling with herself over whether or not to approach him. *Just say hello. How hard can that be?* Squeezing her keys in the palm of her sweating hand, she took a steadying breath and headed toward the door.

As she stepped from the driveway to the sidewalk, the front porch light flipped on. Without an extra second to consider it, she leaped behind the tall spruce tree at the corner of the house. *Maybe it was a motion sensor.* She leaned against the brick, holding her breath. The rough brick picked at her shirt. If she'd thought explaining the visit was going to be difficult, how the heck was she going to explain hiding in the flower bed?

She pressed her fingers against her lips. *This is your fault, Connor. If you hadn't kissed me, I wouldn't be all screwed up tonight, and I wouldn't be right here, right now.*

Footsteps padded quickly down the sidewalk. Carolanne squeezed her eyes shut and slowly sank to the ground, praying she'd still be concealed when the headlights came on.

She held her breath, waiting for the engine to turn over, but it didn't.

The sound of a woman's voice surprised her. She could barely make out the words, but it was definitely not Dad's voice.

The spruce was itchy against her skin. The

thought of spiders and bugs crawling around just added insult to the predicament she'd gotten herself in, but there was no backing out of this plan now. Her breathing sounded so loud that she tried to hold her breath to stay hidden.

Carolanne heard a snippet of the conversation.

"I love you, too, Joey. Ben's been so nice to let me stay here. I never thought that I'd find so many answers right here in Adams Grove. Thank God I stopped here first. Soon. I hope. No. Don't call me back on this number, this is his phone."

*She's using Dad's phone?* None of it made sense, and who would be staying with him? She slowly leaned out to brave a peek. She leaned out carefully, and then she recognized why that voice had sounded vaguely familiar. It was Gina—the girl from the library.

Carolanne's composure was under attack. If Gina knew her father, surely she had to have known she was his daughter, and she hadn't said a word. The sound of the engine turning over sent Carolanne lunging back for cover just as the car eased out of the driveway.

The headlights swept across the front of the house as Gina turned onto the street and then disappeared down the road.

Carolanne stood from the cramped spot in the flower bed. Should she go to the door and demand answers? He'd just want to know what she was doing in his yard to begin with. Was it even any of her business? She'd practically written him off over the years. Did she even have a right to know, and if not, why the heck did it bother her so much?

With more questions than answers, Carolanne walked down the street.

*Why would Gina be staying with my father?*

A pang of jealousy turned her walk into a jog all the way back home. She pictured Gina at her dad's house, and that made her feel something unfamiliar. Not jealousy, but a terrible sense of bitterness that she wasn't proud of. She'd held that wedge tightly in place between her dad and herself over the years, and now someone else had swept right in and taken her place.

She didn't slow down until she approached the alley behind the office. She climbed the back stairs to her apartment, still winded, wondering if the creaking stairs or her breath was louder. Proof she wouldn't like running.

A roaring snore came from Connor's apartment. Carolanne gave up the attempt to be quiet and zipped down the hall, retreating to the safety of her apartment.

# ❖ Chapter Ten ❖

It was eight o'clock on the dot the morning of the wedding when Carolanne swung open her apartment door to greet Jill. "Good morning, Mrs. Clemmons-almost-Malloy."

"Thank you, most amazing maid of honor ever," Jill said as she came into the apartment.

"Why didn't I ever think to ask you if you were hyphenating or keeping your name?"

"Don't know, but I'm not doing either. I'll be a Malloy."

"Going completely traditional right down to the name. I don't know why I'm surprised. There's no way I'd ever do that."

"I knew that would make you cringe, but then, you say you'll never get married, either. So who knows?" Jill hugged Carolanne, then squealed with laughter laced with what sounded like a little hysteria. "It's my wedding day! Finally! I was so calm at dinner last night, but then I didn't sleep a wink."

*Me neither, and I can't wait to talk to you about all that's going on once we get through this wedding.* "Come on in. What's the matter? Nervous?" Carolanne caught the look on Jill's face. "Are you OK? You don't look like a girl who's ready to marry the man of her dreams."

"Just wishing Pearl were here." She walked into the living room and plopped down on the couch. "The what-ifs are killing me today. If only I'd followed this path two years ago, Pearl would've been here for the wedding. She'd have probably been a great-grandma by now. You know she'd have loved that."

Carolanne sat next to Jill on the couch. "She was so great to both us, and I wasn't even family."

"You are, too, family." She reached over and squeezed Carolanne's hand. "Better than family." Jill swept at a tear. "I'm crazy emotional this morning."

"I think that's normal."

"I'm getting married—not pregnant."

"It's kind of the same thing. Both are a huge commitment and change your life." Carolanne took another sip of coffee, wondering how she'd feel if she were getting married today. She'd probably be a hot mess, dry heaving, or maybe worse, a runaway bride. Just the thought of that depth of love scared her so much that she suddenly felt anxious to get out of the apartment and away from those thoughts.

Carolanne glanced up at the clock. "I have an idea. We have plenty of time. Want to head over to the cemetery for a quick visit with Pearl? There's no rule about us going early."

"Except that Izzy is supposed to pick us up here in a couple hours and take us to the church." She pulled her lips into a line. "We could be back by then, though. She's the one thing missing from this day. Thanks, you always have the best solutions."

"I live to bring you direction." *Only, this time I need the escape, too.*

Both girls grabbed their purses and clomped down the stairs.

"I'll drive," Jill said, leading the way out the front doors to her car. Other than the diner, Main Street was just starting to get moving this Saturday morning.

Jill gestured toward the sidewalk. "Pearl would love what they've done with the planters this year. The flower boxes look so pretty with the ivy, geraniums, and begonias. I don't think they've ever looked lovelier."

She wondered if Jill knew that her dad was responsible for their care. Probably. Funny no one had thought to mention it to her before. But then, she hadn't made herself too open to those conversations. She regretted the hard line she'd carried for so long. The whole town had probably been talking about her. The unforgiving daughter.

Carolanne's thoughts shifted to the begonias Connor had stolen. She found herself smiling at the memory and then pushed the memory aside. *Why do you keep invading my thoughts?*

Jill sped through town, like she always did, then turned onto Horseshoe Run Road, taking the curves a little too fast, like locals were known to do. She didn't slow down until she turned onto the gravel path that led to the church cemetery. She pulled the keys from the ignition and jumped out of the car, leading the way.

"Look. Teddy must've done that." Jill pointed to Pearl's headstone. "They match the flowers I'm carrying in my bouquet. That guy thinks of everything."

"You don't get that kind of personalized service in the city." Carolanne's focus shifted to about seven rows closer to the church. There was never one time that she'd visited her mom's gravesite that there hadn't been fresh flowers. From here, she could see the arrangement sitting astride the headstone, rising to the heavens. She didn't have to go over there to know what Dad would have made sure Teddy put in that arrangement. Alstroemeria. Not just any alstroemeria—or "I'll-still-marry-ya," as Dad would say—but the orangey-yellow ones. Mom's favorite.

Carolanne could picture Dad handing bouquets of the orange flowers to Mom, sometimes for no reason at all. Time after time, he'd say the same thing: "The perfect flower, for the perfect lady. That's why they named it 'I'll-still-marry-ya'— and I would."

He really was romantic. The things he'd do, say, for Mom. She hadn't thought about that in so long. Too long. A random breeze swept around her like a hug.

Carolanne walked over to where Jill stood. The fragrant flowers sweetened the air. Jill ran a finger across the carved rose in the granite. Around the rose were tiny raised circles meant to look like pearls—eighty-four of them, one for each year of Pearl's life.

A twig snapped nearby.

Carolanne and Jill both looked up as Garrett approached.

Jill jumped to her feet. "What are you doing here?"

"Same thing you are. I was feeling nostalgic and knew you would be, too."

Carolanne leapt in front of Jill, spreading her arms as if to block his view. "It's bad luck for you to see the bride."

Garrett shot her one of those *Are you crazy?* looks. "I thought that was just if she was in her wedding gown."

"Is that right?" Carolanne glanced over at Jill, who nodded. "I don't know. Who makes up all those rules? Who can keep them all straight? Do you want to take the chance?"

"I'm not afraid." Garrett reached a hand toward Jill and tugged her out from behind Carolanne's protection, and pulled her into his arms. "Bad luck couldn't ruin what we have. Pearl would never let that happen." He kissed Jill softly. "And I'd never let that happen. I'm the luckiest man in the world."

"I love you, Garrett." She kissed him once slowly and then two quick pecks.

Carolanne tried not to remark, but she couldn't hold it in. "Well, isn't that the cutest little kiss dance?"

"It's our tradition." Jill gave Carolanne the stink-eye. "Three kisses—one for the past, one for the present, and one for all the tomorrows to come."

"I might go into a diabetic coma with all the sugar y'all are pouring on." Carolanne stepped out of their romantic moment.

Garrett handed Jill the paper bag of flowers he'd been carrying. "For you. We'll be back in a minute, Carolanne."

"Take your time." Carolanne laid a hand on Pearl's headstone as Jill and Garrett walked away. "Pearl, you were so right about them. They *are* perfect." A ray of sunshine shifted through the trees. Carolanne mulled over the message Pearl had left for her about Connor. It had seemed so random at the time. But then, a year ago, Jill would've said the same thing about ending up with Garrett.

Carolanne closed her eyes and tried to picture a life with Connor outside of the office. It came easy, almost too easy, and that scared her a little—no, a lot.

Jill laid her hands on Carolanne's shoulders. "You ready?"

Carolanne jumped. "You scared me. I didn't hear you. I'm ready whenever you are." She stood to leave. "Are you OK?"

"I'm great. The luckiest girl in the whole world."

Carolanne wished she felt that lucky.


Connor took the stairs two at a time on his way out for his morning jog, passing Carolanne and Jill as they walked into the building.

"Good morning," they said in chorus.

"Ready for the big day?"

"You bet," Jill said.

"See you two at the church later. I'll be the one keeping the groom from escaping your evil clutches."

"Real funny," Jill called after him. "I'm not the least bit worried about him running off."

"You don't have to be. I've got your back," Connor shouted from the bottom of the stairs, then bolted out the door.

Running through this neighborhood was Connor's favorite weekend route. The smell of home-cooked breakfasts of bacon and sausage wafted from the homes. He liked the feeling of family that he still got here, even if it were his imagination creating the perfect scenarios within the old homes so carefully maintained in Adams Grove.

Connor kept up his pace until he turned the corner and saw Ben standing in his yard in front of his car with the hood up. He slowed to a walk to catch his breath, then turned up the driveway.

Ben leaned out from behind the hood and greeted him.

"Car trouble or maintenance?"

"Won't start. I think the battery finally died. Won't even make a click. No big deal, except for the timing. You know, with the wedding today and all."

Connor nodded. "If you don't mind going a little early, you can catch a ride with me to the wedding. I'm meeting Garrett at the church. I'm on my own, so there's plenty of room."

Ben reached up and slammed the hood. "I already called AAA. They'll be here shortly. Hopefully, she just needs a quick jump."

"Don't we all now and then?"

"You know that's right," Ben said.

"Speaking of getting jumped, did you know Mac had a girlfriend?"

"Hadn't heard about that. Good for him."

"Yeah. Maybe," Connor said. "I just thought it was kind of weird no one knew anything about it."

Ben's left eyebrow rose a fraction. "Well, I did hear the ladies at the Seniors Circle talking about Mac being taken advantage of by some younger woman. They didn't call her a girlfriend, but I imagine that might be who they were talking about."

*That's more like it. Nothing is ever that quiet in*

*this town. You just have to ask the right questions of the right people.* "Her name is Anita. I met her the other day. What'd they have to say?"

"One of them said that she'd talked him into letting her use that building on Main Street for free so she could start a health club or something. Another said that the woman had outlived a couple husbands already and that she'd probably give Mac a heart attack in less than ninety days."

"What a way to go." Connor couldn't help but laugh.

"I think they're just sour because they see the possibility of a man having a good time without the ties of marriage, and that makes them crazy. You know how women are about marriage."

"Most of them. Not your daughter."

"Well, you know my daughter can be a tough nut to crack. The other day, with the necklace, was the most we've talked in years. I can only hope we can move forward."

"I hope so, too, Ben. That's a big shift for her. That whole wedding thing seems like a helluva leap, too. You better enjoy her in the pretty dress today, because I don't think we'll see her walking down the aisle anytime soon."

"Carolanne might be the exception to the rule, but I wouldn't rule out marriage for her, either. Deep down, I think they all want to be married."

Connor wasn't so sure about that. "Well, look, I better get a move on if I'm going to get to the church on time. The best man can't be late. I'm sure there's some bad luck rule about that."

"I think as long as the groom shows up, no one cares."

"Good. I don't like having that much pressure on me." He turned to leave. "Well, if you end up needing a ride, just give me a call."

"Will do. Thanks," Ben said.

Connor turned and jogged to the end of the driveway, then headed up the street. Just as he got to Main Street, Izzy's blue limo cruised by. She tooted the horn, and Jill waved from the back-seat, with Carolanne next to her.

*Glad all I have to do is don some shiny shoes and a suit.*

He hoped the romantic mood of the wedding would ease Carolanne's anger. If it didn't, their little walk back down the aisle after Jill and Garrett's "I-dos" might be a little awkward, but then again, she could hardly make a scene with everyone watching. That might just play to his favor.

He took the long way around the block, hoping to pick up something from Mac's Bakery for breakfast, but the store was closed.

That was odd. It wasn't all that unusual for Mac to close the bakery when he'd worked it alone, but since Derek had come to town, Connor couldn't remember it ever being closed, especially on a Saturday. Funny after they'd just been talking about how responsible Derek was. Maybe Mac was right about not leaving everything to Derek, and maybe Carolanne was right that he should stay out of it.

They could have been busy with the wedding, and they wouldn't lose that much business, anyway, since most everyone would be headed to the wedding today.

On the other hand, if something had happened to Mac, God forbid—like Anita giving him that heart attack the old ladies were talking about—then at least the will was not in her name yet.

# ❖ Chapter Eleven ❖

Carolanne fussed with the back of Jill's gown, straightening the satin ribbon that hung from the corset at the small of her back. The tiny pearls that adorned the choker-style neck and bodice of Jill's dress shimmered like gemstones in the light. It felt like all those times they'd played dress-up in Pearl's attic through the years, only this time everything fit.

Carolanne mentally checked off the last details. Something old. Something new. Something borrowed. Something blue.

A simple strand of pearls that Milly had worn at her own wedding years ago laced Jill's wrist. *Something old and borrowed. Check.*

Pearl-and-sapphire earrings that Garrett had surprised Jill with at the rehearsal dinner completed the list. *Something new and blue. Check.*

"You've got all the 'somethings.' I think we're ready." Carolanne placed her hands on Jill's bare shoulders. "You look so pretty, and I'm so happy for you."

"Thank you for everything and for indulging me in all the tiny details."

There was no mistaking the look in Jill's eyes. Happiness wasn't big enough. Elation, maybe. *Will I ever feel that happy?* "It's perfect. Every single little task in that dictionary-size book of stuff you handed me as maid of honor has been checked and rechecked, and you're worth every single detail."

Jill laughed. "It wasn't that big."

"It wasn't that small, either."

"Guilty, but I wanted it to be perfect. You only get married once."

*Or not at all.* "Well, your marriage will be forever. You and Garrett were made for each other." Carolanne pinched a small section of Jill's bangs into her fingers and scattered them, then grabbed a small bottle of hair spray and spritzed them into place. "There you go. No humidity will penetrate this stuff."

"Thanks." Jill blew out a breath and twisted in the mirror. "I love this dress, but it kind of weighs a ton." She slumped and made a face.

"Small price to pay for living the dream. Besides, Garrett is going to be blown away when he sees you." Carolanne picked up the box of flowers Teddy had sent over for Jill's hair. "Spin around."

Carolanne tucked dainty blooms into Jill's updo, then checked it from the front and all sides. "This is it."

Jill took in a deep breath and let it out. "You ready?"

Carolanne nodded. "All I have to do is stand there and hold your flowers when you exchange rings. My job is easy."

"Then I guess we're ready."

Carolanne opened the door. The music from the main hall beckoned them to the big event. Carolanne watched as Jill knelt and gave words of encouragement to the twin flower girls and little Robbie. It probably wouldn't be long before she and Garrett had their own little ones. Carolanne felt the distance beginning to change their friendship already. Tears welled. Not girlie tears because of the wedding. No, these were tears of loneliness. A loneliness she hadn't prepared herself for.

She blinked back the tears and fixed a smile. "Here we go," Carolanne said as Ally Craddock began singing "Grow Old Along With Me"—the signal that was to kick everything off.

Carolanne stepped to the door and swept dog hair off little Robbie's suit from where he'd been petting Clyde, Jill and Garrett's Bernese mountain dog, who was wagging his tail and drooling, seeming pretty happy to be a part of the festivities as co–ring bearer. Satisfied, or maybe procrastinating, probably the latter, she swallowed, took a breath, and planted a smile on her face as she gave the nod for the doors to open and stepped into the aisle.

It seemed so easy last night, but today she knew exactly what those kids felt like last night when they went running down the aisle. It was all she could do not to break into a sprint to get it over with.

She smiled at neighbors and friends with each carefully paced step. Garrett looked a little nervous. His right leg was bouncing like he was going to break out into a chorus of "Hound Dog," and when her eyes met Connor's, her stomach did a flip.

Connor's smile made those little crinkles around his eyes. She saw him dressed in a suit all the time, but today he looked extra handsome.

Each step felt painfully slow, and her eyes kept connecting with Connor's. *Stop looking at me like that.* The way he looked at her made her feel like she was traipsing half-naked down the aisle. She glanced down just to be sure it was her imagination. She looked back up to see his smile again, and that made the butterflies in her stomach go crazy.

Carolanne finally made it to the altar and stepped into position. She turned to face all of the friends who had gathered for the joyous occasion. *Thank goodness I made it without a wobble or catastrophe, and now all eyes will be on Jill.*

Connor winked and nodded, just as an "aw" rose from the room.

Robbie marched like a little soldier with Clyde's leash in his hand, taking his role as ring bearer with serious intent. Clyde wore a black vest and bow tie, trotting to the beat of the music, and Robbie never faltered. Missy and Chrissy started down the aisle right behind Robbie. The pacing couldn't have been more perfect.

The doors closed behind Robbie and the girls. Carolanne wondered whether that was customary or if it was to keep those kids from darting back outside.

Missy clung to her basket like it was filled with golden Barbie dolls, with her lip stuck out so far it was a wonder she didn't trip over it. Chrissy tossed her rose petals, alternating from side to side, determined to make up for her sister's defiance. The girls ended up practically running down the aisle, and at one point, Chrissy tossed the petals so wildly that one landed right on Robbie's slicked side part.

When Clyde spotted Garrett at the other end of the aisle, he took off, and Robbie also hit an all-out sprint, trying to keep up. The faster Robbie moved, the faster the Huckaby twins moved to catch up to him, at one point almost passing him.

Once Robbie had reached the front of the church, he turned for reassurance from his Uncle Scott.

Scott gave him a thumbs-up. Everyone laughed as both Garrett and Connor slapped Robbie with a high five, T-ball style. Then Robbie joined Scott in the front pew, and Scott took Clyde's leash as the dog lay down in front of them, panting.

Missy and Chrissy did a U-turn and ran to sit in the second row between their mom and dad.

"I did good, didn't I?" Missy squealed from the top of her lungs as she wiggled into the pew.

Chrissy shushed her, then turned to watch for

Jill. "Here she comes," she squealed. "So pretty! Like a princess!"

The crowd rustled as everyone turned toward the back of the church to catch a glimpse of the bride.

First, the two large inside doors swung open; then two robed teens stepped in toward the outer doors and pulled them open. Jill moved like an angel into the ray of sunlight of the open doors, then right on cue took her first step down the aisle on the ninth beat.

Carolanne heard Garrett suck in an audible breath with Jill's first step, and although Carolanne had seen Jill in the gown all morning, it took her breath away, too. She tugged the handkerchief Milly had given her from the bouquet of flowers and dabbed at the unexpected tears.

Each of the flowers in Jill's bouquet meant something. Roses and miniature gardenias to represent love and joy, and daisies because they were Pearl's favorite. *Alstroemeria. I'd carry I'd-still-marry-ya's.* She'd once seen light-apricot ones with a little yellow center. *Perfect.*

"Finally," Garrett said in a hush but loud enough for Carolanne to hear.

Carolanne gave him a nod. She knew that the deal had been for Garrett to say the least amount of words allowed in a ceremony because, in his words, he just wanted to get on to the kissing part.

She stepped forward to take Jill's bouquet for the ring exchange. Her hands shook, and she prayed the fancy flowers wouldn't go tumbling down the stairs.

Before Carolanne had been able to shake the worry over dropping the flowers, Reverend Burke raised his hands to the congregation. "I now present to you, Mr. and Mrs. Garrett Malloy."

*That was fast. Garrett ought to be thrilled.*

The organ sent a joyous thunder through the space.

Jill and Garrett walked down the aisle, and everyone stood for the recessional. Since the ring bearer and flower girls had taken up residency with their parents, it was only Connor and Carolanne left before folks could begin leaving.

Connor moved to the center and stood with his hand out for Carolanne.

She stood there for a moment, hoping the dizziness she felt was just the excitement of seeing her best friend get married, and not fear ripping through her like a tidal wave, which was what it felt like. Connor dressed like that and standing there with his hand out felt somehow like committing.

She swallowed back the anxiety, but she couldn't move.

"Come on. I've got you," he said.

*That's what I'm afraid of.* She felt herself getting warmer, and when she looked up, it felt like all eyes were on her.

Connor took a step closer.

She smiled wider, hoping she'd convince herself she was OK. She clung to Connor's arm as he led her down the stairs to the aisle.

"Are you going to forgive me yet? You know I couldn't have known you were going to be in the office that day."

She nodded and kept smiling.

He hugged her hand in the crook of his arm. "Awesome." He patted her hand again and then stepped up behind Jill and Garrett. "Congratulations, man."

"Thanks, Connor," Garrett said with the biggest smile Carolanne had ever seen on his face.

She and Jill hugged, and they both started crying.

"Not before pictures," Carolanne said as she pulled her handkerchief back out. "Here, let me fix that."

The photographer snapped two more pictures, then shouted one last command. "Give me a head start. I want to be out front when you open the doors. So count to twenty before you start out, deal?"

"Deal." Garrett started counting backward. "Twenty, nineteen, eighteen . . ."

Carolanne nudged him. "I don't think she literally meant we had to count it off."

"Hey, I plan to be a good listener. I'm starting now."

Jill swatted him playfully. "I like that in a guy. You really might be a keeper."

"I better be," Garrett said, then gave her a quick kiss. "That's twenty. Open the doors."

Two young men opened the giant arched doors and Jill and Garrett made a dash for it.

Carolanne could see the crowd of friends in front of the church cheer and toss dried lavender as the bride and groom walked all the way to the curb to Izzy's navy blue stretch limo.

The lavender flew like so many snowflakes in the air around them. Garrett swept Jill up into his arms, just like in the old *An Officer and a Gentleman* movie, and made the last dash for the limo.

Carolanne rushed behind them to help Jill get into the car with all that dress to maneuver.

Jill gasped and sputtered as she climbed into the car. "Tossing lavender sounds neat, but it's kind of like running through a gnat storm. I should've gone with the bubbles."

Carolanne swept the fabric behind Jill like it was a pile of snow, and then Garrett slipped inside the back of the limo next to her.

They rode off as friends and family began to disperse to follow them to the reception.

Carolanne stepped back, feeling the love those two shared even from a distance, and that filled a spot in her heart that she thought had closed long ago.

# ❖ Chapter Twelve ❖

Connor hustled the wedding party over to Scott Calvin's restored 1940 Pontiac Woodie in the side parking lot, then jumped behind the wheel to lead the long line of cars that flowed like a stream of colorful floats in a parade from the church on Old Horseshoe Road out onto Holland Parkway to the brand-new Adams Grove Artisan Center. The wedding guests would get a sneak peek of the new building, which would host its grand opening on Memorial Day weekend, just a week away.

When they pulled in front of the artisan center, Connor took a twin in each hand. Carolanne followed alongside, holding Robbie's hand and Clyde's leash in the other. Jill and Garrett waved from the long country-style porch of the artisan center.

"Y'all look like one big happy family," Garrett said.

"Don't we, though?" Carolanne laughed at the thought. She'd never thought of herself as the marrying or mothering kind, but she seemed to be managing kids, man and beast just fine. She dropped the leash and let Clyde run to Garrett.

Carolanne caught up with Jill and they all went inside to get ready to greet the guests.

"Oh, Garrett. Look at the cake! It's gorgeous." Jill made a beeline toward the cake.

Carolanne darted in front of Jill. "No time for that, my friend. Folks are starting to head up the walk."

"That's the bad thing about being the bride— you don't get to see anything!"

Garrett walked up behind her and tugged her close. "You get me. I'm the prize."

"You're a prize, all right," she said in a mocking tone.

Carolanne rushed off to position their bouquets into the centerpiece on the wedding party table like Teddy had instructed her. Teddy had placed cards right where she was supposed to put them. *I could hardly screw this up.* She fussed with the greenery. Jill's smaller bouquet to toss later was sitting next to the large arrangement. It was almost as pretty as the one she'd carried down the aisle.

She stepped back from the table, still admiring Teddy's work, then backed right into someone. "I'm sorry."

Connor grabbed her by the shoulders to steady her.

"You're beginning to make this sneaking-up thing a habit. Quit scaring me."

"Didn't mean to scare you." He scanned the room. "This place looks amazing. I could see lots of people wanting to book it for events."

"That's the idea, but it wasn't me. Jill handled

all of that by herself. It does look pretty, doesn't it?"

"Pretty as you."

"You're such a flirt."

"It was a compliment. Why can't you just trust my intentions?" He leaned in, but Carolanne braced her arm between them.

*How can I answer that?* "You scare the heck out of me."

"We've known each other our whole lives. Why would you be afraid of me now?"

"Not scared of *you,* scared of what you're making me *feel.*"

"Well, that's different. That's good. It's time that razor wire fence you've piled up around your heart gave way."

"Not so fast. We're partners. We could ruin everything."

"We won't let that happen."

She crossed her arms. "You can't promise that."

He pulled her back to the corner of the room out of earshot of the other guests and leaned in close. "You liked that kiss the other night as much as I did, didn't you?"

She glanced across the room.

"No one's looking. All eyes are on the bride and the groom. Look at me. I'm talking to you."

"I hear you," she said.

"Admit it." He pulled her close and tickled her. "Say it."

"Fine. Yes. I admit it—the kiss was nice."

"Nice?"

"Really nice," she said with a smile.

"I can do better." He leaned in and kissed her neck.

"No!" She spun away from him. "Not today. This is Jill and Garrett's day, and we need to really think about this."

"Why do you always have to be so practical? What's the worst thing that could happen?"

"Well, we could start this thing and figure out that we're not a good couple."

"So?"

"So, it would make work really awkward."

"OK, so if that happens, we'll just dissolve the partnership, and you can work from another building. That's easy. What else could happen?"

"You could break my heart," she said.

He looked into her eyes and swept her bangs from her face. "Carolanne, I'll never hurt you."

"What if you do? What if I go crazy like my dad?"

He pulled her into a hug. "Is that what has you so afraid?"

She nodded into his chest, unable to even utter a word.

"We won't get you a straitjacket and put you away, and I promise if I break your heart and you go crazy, we'll find an answer. But that's not going to happen. I know it." He tapped his heart. "In here."

"But it could."

"It's highly unlikely. Besides, Jill and Garrett would kill me if I did that."

"True, and that *is* somewhat comforting."

He swatted her butt. "Come on. We have celebrating to do. Relax and have a good time." He kissed her shoulder. "OK?"

His touch sent a charge through her, unexpected, but not bad. "This might be a long day."

He winked and led her back to where Jill and Garrett were greeting the last stragglers.

Gifts were piled high on long tables near the entryway, and people gathered in clusters sharing stories and catching up, feeling extra relaxed and appreciative on this special day.

Connor stepped to the microphone. "May I have everyone's attention?"

The loud chatter dropped to just a hum.

"Let's invite Garrett and Jill to the dance floor for their first dance together as husband and wife. Friends, family, let's give them a round of applause."

Garrett led Jill to the dance floor.

"I asked the band to play a song that I think is pretty special and appropriate, seeing how long we've waited for these two to finally make it all official."

The band started playing the first chorus of Marvin Gaye's "Let's Get It On."

Carolanne shot him a warning look.

The crowd laughed and nodded. Someone in the back of the room let out a loud whoop.

Connor raised his hand, and the band stopped. "OK, OK. I thought that was a good pick, but it seems the couple had a different tune in mind." The band regrouped and started playing "(Everything I Do) I Do It For You" by Bryan Adams. "I present to you Mr. and Mrs. Garrett Malloy."

The music filled the room, and Connor stepped away from the microphone and joined Carolanne alongside the open space where Jill and Garrett shared their first dance.

"It's so romantic." Carolanne swallowed back tears. Between the wedding, the stress of the previous week, and Connor being so doggone sweet, she didn't know if she was coming or going. She spotted her dad across the room. He nodded and waved. She smiled and wiggled her fingers in a wave back. *Baby steps, but we're taking them.*

"Are you crying?" Connor asked.

"No." *Why do you notice everything? I thought men were supposed to be so oblivious to our feelings.*

"You are. I didn't know you were such a softy."

"I'm not. But I'm happy for Jill. And Garrett. I'm just happy."

He put his arm around her and tugged her to him, hip to hip. "Come on. We can join in now."

*On the dance or the happy?*

He led her to the dance floor.

"Come on, folks," Connor called out to the guests, "the dance floor is now open."

The dancing continued, and folks lined up to help themselves to the food that sprawled on long tables down the entire walkway through the building. Benches and café table toppers had been placed from one end to the other, making it feel like a river of people floating in with the tide.

Waiters in formal attire swept through with trays of appetizers and noshes, keeping everyone well fed between buffet visits.

Carolanne checked her watch and then gathered Jill and Garrett to cut the cake.

Jill leaned toward Carolanne. "Have you seen Mac? I wanted to thank him and get a picture of him with the cake before I cut into it."

"No, he's not here. He must have had another event after yours."

The cake was huge, and all five layers of the white fondant cake shimmered under the light. Mac must have spent hours placing each of the tiny translucent pearls. Delicate pink rosebuds looked so real that, for a moment, Carolanne thought maybe Mac had gotten them from Teddy, like the ones in Jill's hair, but upon closer inspection, she could see they were indeed edible creations.

Garrett picked up the champagne flute with the

little black tuxedo on it and tapped it with a fork. "Folks are coming around with champagne, or whatever beverage of your choice. Please join us in a toast and the cake cutting."

Everyone moved in closer to the cake table, and Carolanne took that opportunity to go grab some quiet time. She needed just a moment to catch her breath. So much was happening, and that made her feel a little out of control. Not something she was accustomed to or sure that she liked.

She knew she should be happy for Jill, but in a way it made her feel lonely. Surely there wouldn't be the dozens of sleepovers and girl weekends that they'd become spoiled with.

Carolanne saw Garrett stand on a chair, and everyone began cheering.

*What is he doing?* She walked back over. This wasn't part of the plan, and she knew how important Jill's plan was to her.

Garrett had everyone's attention. "So, for everyone who agrees this is the most beautiful wedding ever, you can give all that credit to Jill. The only thing I had anything to do with was the groom's cake, and I think it's pretty fan-tabulous."

Mr. Malloy wheeled a cart with a huge box on top of it into the room.

Garrett stepped down from the chair, and he and his dad started to lift the box to unveil the groom's cake. "Wait a second," Garrett said. "Jill, you might want to close your eyes. This doesn't match the wedding colors."

Jill pretended to fan herself.

Garrett and his dad lifted the box and set it to the side.

A huge cake in the shape of a bulldozer rose from a chocolate cake with a ganache pedestal that had *The Malloys* in cursive on each side. The bright-yellow cake was so realistic that, at first, some folks thought it was a toy. Then Mr. Malloy did the honors of pushing a button on the platform, and the bulldozer chugged and blew steam from an exhaust pipe. Then slowly, ever so slowly, the bucket rose, and when the bucket tipped forward, a flag with *Congratulations, Garrett and Jill* unfurled from it.

Everyone cheered.

"Now, that's man stuff!" Connor hollered and reached over to high-five his best friend.

Carolanne laughed as she watched Connor and Garrett enjoy the moment over the truck cake.

"And chocolate, to boot." Garrett smiled and accepted the pats on the back from the guys.

Jill stood to the side with her arms crossed. Carolanne knew that only true love could make Jill OK with someone veering from her plan, and her smile told just how much she loved the surprise.

Garrett walked over and led Jill to the cake table with a kiss.

The band started playing Tim McGraw's "My Best Friend." Garrett and Jill made the first cuts and fed each other a piece of cake in the most peaceful demonstration there'd ever been. Not a hint of frosting out of place.

Carolanne made sure the ladies had the cake distribution under control, then went back over to sit at the table with Milly.

Connor walked up to the table with two pieces of cake. "Here you go, ladies."

"No cake for you?" Milly took a piece and picked up her fork, seeming less than interested in waiting for his answer.

Connor raised his drink. "I'll get one to go. I'm too full from the buffet to eat cake now."

"Beautiful wedding, wasn't it?" Ben said as he walked up to the table.

They all nodded.

Connor asked, "Was it the battery?"

"Yes." Ben turned to Carolanne and Milly. "My car was broken down this morning." He turned the conversation back to Connor. "AAA gave me a jump, then I went and bought a new battery from Graham's Garage. Guy there said that it was the original one. I'd say I got my money's worth out of it."

"You sure did," Carolanne said. "Did you get some cake?"

"No. Thanks. I'm going to head out," Ben said.

"Already?" *He looks uncomfortable. Maybe he doesn't like weddings, either.*

"I just wanted to let y'all know I was leaving. It was a lovely day, and you looked beautiful, Carolanne."

"Thanks, Dad." She stood up and hugged him.

Jill walked up and grabbed Connor by the hands, then called over to Carolanne. "Time for your help."

"Maid of honor duty calls," Carolanne said as she let Jill drag her away. She waved good-bye to her dad. He lifted his chin in that way he did right before he smiled. Funny, she hadn't thought about that in years. Connor set his glass down on a table as he followed right behind them.

Garrett had a wicked grin on his face. "Time for the garter and flower toss. The two of you need to be front and center."

Nervous laughter filled the space in response to the exaggerated glance between Connor and Carolanne.

Once Garrett got the garter off Jill's leg, it wasn't even a contest to get the garter. It was as if it were planned because every other guy stepped back, and Connor was the only one trying to catch it.

Carolanne dropped her head back. "Y'all are killin' me with all this."

"Come on. It's my day. You have to do what I say." Jill rushed over to the open part of the room and grabbed the microphone. "Everyone gather around. Single gals, I need you over here. It's time for the bouquet toss!"

Giggles, claps, and protests filled the space.

*I'm going to kill you for this.* Carolanne glared at Jill and kept to the middle of the crowd.

Just as the bouquet left Jill's hands and flew through the air, there was a commotion at the back entrance to the gardens.

A little boy in a muddy black suit ran into the crowd. "Where's my dad?" he screamed to no one in particular as the bouquet beelined right into Carolanne's chest.

# ❖ Chapter Thirteen ❖

Carolanne grappled as the flowers accosted her like a drunken bird flying on a kamikaze mission. "I wasn't trying . . ."

Jill cheered, jumping up and down in her heavy beaded gown.

Carolanne shook the flowers and glared in Jill's direction.

Connor wished he could have seen an instant replay of that. Carolanne had done her best to avoid the bouquet, but it was like that bunch of flowers was on autopilot. She couldn't avoid it. Connor glanced back down at the muddy boy at his side.

The boy couldn't have been more than six or seven. He was huffing an almost silent pant, standing there wide-eyed, frozen in his spot.

"Whoa there, buddy." Connor scooped up the young boy into his arms. "What's the matter there?"

"There's a"—his blue eyes were wide and his cheeks flush—"a dead body!"

Connor headed toward the back door with the boy in his arms. "No. No. It's OK." He patted his back and tried to calm him down. Looked like one of the Johnson boys, only they had like six of them and he could never keep them straight.

Connor waved off the attention of the guests who were standing nearby. "Boys will be boys. What can you do? I got this. Y'all go on." Connor grabbed Scott by the arm to bring him outside with the boy.

Tina Johnson's maternal radar must've gone on alert, because she rushed toward Connor and Scott just as they slipped outside.

"What did he do now?" she said as she marched toward them.

Connor carried the boy to the edge of the courtyard, but when he tried to set him down, the boy clung to his neck like a clip-on monkey. "All right, then. You can stay there." The boy barely wobbled from his position. "Tell Sheriff Calvin what you just told me."

"There's a skinny, scary ghost lady floating in the pond." He sniffled. "Turtles are eating her. It's so gross!"

Tina sighed and reached for her son. "I'm sorry. His brothers are always torturing him. Why can't they behave for just one day?" Her head lolled back, and her whole demeanor drooped like someone had thrown a wet blanket over her.

Connor gladly handed the kid over.

"Mom! I saw it this time. For real. There's a dead lady, and they're poking a giant turtle with a stick. I told them it's not nice."

"JD. That's crazy. I asked you boys to behave today. Look at you—you're filthy." She turned to

Scott. "I'm sorry. His brothers are always putting crazy stuff in his head."

The little boy shook his head and tugged on his mom's collar. "Mom! It's real. I saw it. Come on. We have to go. Quick!"

"I'll settle this," Scott said. "He obviously saw something. Let me take him down there, and we'll put this to rest. You go back in and have fun. With six boys, you need a little!"

"You don't mind?"

"Heck no. Go on. Enjoy the festivities. We'll be right back."

"Thanks, Scott. Tell my boys to get their butts up here."

He gave her a wink. "I'll even flash my badge."

"Good. That ought to cure them for at least a week or two." She urged her son in Sheriff Calvin's direction.

"My pleasure. I'll let this little guy lead the way."

Carolanne stepped outside. "Hey, guys. Is everything OK?"

"Yeah, I think so. We're just going to go squash some rumors," Connor said.

"Good. Can you squash the one that I'm going to be the next to get married while you're at it?" Carolanne lifted the bunch of flowers. Most women would have thought it was a bonus.

"I caught the garter. That means you're all mine, baby." Connor laughed at how flummoxed she seemed by the whole idea, and he wondered if she might throw the flowers at him.

"I have a say in it." But she looked worried.

He jogged to catch up with Scott as he called back over his shoulder, "Sure you do. We'll be back in a few minutes."

The little boy grabbed Scott and Connor's hands and dragged them down the grade toward the pond, his face red and sweaty with determination.

It wasn't hard to see where the source of the excitement was. Even from fifty yards, Connor could make out five rear ends in a half circle around something at the pond's edge.

"What ya got there, boys?" Scott yelled in his scare-the-kids-straight tone.

The boys snapped to attention.

"I brought the sheriff to check out the crime scene. Sorry it took us so long. He was just locking up some boys for filing a false report. That's a crime, isn't it, Sheriff?"

"Oh yeah. They'll do hard time for that. Nothing but bread and water for those boys. No TV, andno computer games, either." Scott could barely hold back the laugh. But as the boys stepped back, the humor in Scott's voice disappeared. "Boys, you need to come over here beside Mr. Buckham."

"Holy sh—" Connor caught himself. "Sure is a dead girl."

All five boys stood and took a giant step backward.

"It's the biggest snappin' turtle ever!" the oldest boy said.

"He was walking right on top of that girl."

"He's going to eat her. Good thing we found her, or there wouldn't be anything but bones left by tomorrow."

"Maybe not even bones! Maybe just her clothes!"

"Eww."

"See," JD said, looking proud to prove his case to Connor and Scott.

"I see," Connor said.

The turtle didn't seem to even notice he was balancing on a dead girl's thigh. He seemed more intent on sunning. One of the boys splashed a stick in the water, hoping to egg the turtle on to whatever it was going to do.

"Come on, guys. Back it up and quit tormenting the turtle." Scott pulled his phone out of his pocket.

Connor edged closer. "Couldn't have been here long. Doesn't even stink." Other than the fact that the girl wasn't moving and had a snapping turtle balanced on her knee, the body wasn't in half-bad shape. "Come on, boys. Let's step back over here."

Scott tugged his phone off his hip. "Connor, take the boys back to their mother. Then grab Deputy Taylor and get him to give you some crime scene tape and stakes from the trunk of his car to bring back. He'll secure the building. No one leaves."

Connor rallied the boys and led them up the slope to the main building. He stopped at one of the garden spigots and made the boys get the mud off their shoes. *No sense in them getting in trouble on top of finding a dead body. That's probably enough punishment for one day.*

When he got back to the building with all six boys in tow, Carolanne was waiting for him.

Connor wasn't quite sure how to tell her that Jill's big day had just veered into the ditch—or the pond, in this case. "Can you deliver these boys back to Mrs. Johnson?"

"Sure. What's wrong?"

One of the boys piped in. "There's a dead girl gettin' eaten by a giant snapping turtle down there."

Carolanne laughed and gave Connor a *What's the real scoop?* look.

"He's right. Well, the turtle isn't a snapper, and it's not eating her, but there is a dead girl down there."

The color from Carolanne's face drained. "Oh. My. God."

"Yeah. I know. Have you seen Deputy Taylor?" He stepped past her.

She ran to catch up with him. "He was over there eating cake a minute ago."

"Thanks." Connor pushed through the group of chatting locals. He tried to look calm, but everyone was going to know the scoop in a minute, so he didn't know why he was bothering. Finally, he spotted Dan.

Connor excused himself into the conversation, then pulled Dan to the side and filled him in on the details.

Dan handed Connor the keys to his car. "The crime scene tape and stakes are in the trunk of my car. I'll handle the rest of it up here."

Connor took the keys and headed for the front door. He hated that this was happening on Jill and Garrett's special day, but there was one thing for sure. It wouldn't be a day anyone in this town would ever forget. Just as Connor hit the front door, he heard the deputy making the announcement over the microphone. A chorus of concern filled the room.

Connor raced outside and scanned the parking lot for the deputy's cruiser. With the supplies in hand, he headed back down to the pond.

Scott looked up from where he knelt next to the body at the edge of the pond.

Connor stared at the lifeless girl. She didn't even look real, with the black T-shirt floating around her like a cape. One foot was bare, the other clad in a tennis shoe. Her naked foot was stark white, the tissue almost translucent. Her bright-red painted toenails looked like drops of blood against her skin.

Scott jumped to his feet and staked the

perimeter, about every six feet in a wide arc around the body. "Wrap that tape around these poles. I guarantee we'll have people down here to see it now that Dan has made the announcement."

*That's kind of sick.* Connor wrapped and tied the bright-yellow tape around each post as Scott had directed. It was hard to keep his eyes off that girl. "I thought drowning victims were supposed to be facedown. Kind of weird to see one faceup."

"How many floaters have you seen?"

*Good point.* "None in person. Only on television."

Scott walked over to Connor. "I've honestly never seen one myself. I've got a call into the State boys. We just don't have the resources for this kind of investigation."

"Is that common? I mean, to call in help?" Connor knew it was wrong to keep looking, but he couldn't help himself. The turtle flailed in an attempt to turn or jump off, but the way he was balanced, his feet just swam in mid-air. With no success, the turtle opened and closed his mouth in a way that looked like he was saying, "Little help here, please."

"Sure," Scott said. "We do it all the time."

Three local sheriff cars and a state trooper pulled into the back lot of the artisan center.

"I'm going to get out of your way, Scott."

"Thanks for your help, man. Sure didn't expect

to be spending today like this." Scott slapped him on the shoulder as he walked by.

He gave Scott a nod as he headed back up to the building. *I'm sure this wasn't exactly how Jill and Garrett had the day planned, either.*

Carolanne sat next to Jill on one of the couches in the back of the room. She'd probably be here all night consoling her. He'd counted on the romance of a wedding to soften her up. It looked like his plans for a romantic evening were not going to get too far tonight. *Nothing like a dead body to bust a mood, and under the circumstances, I'm not much in the mood now, anyway.*

Scott's team split up and began taking statements from folks.

Jill and Garrett talked with Scott in the office, while Carolanne and Connor waited for their turn to talk with the officers. Even though the space was filled with people, it was eerily quiet.

Connor took Carolanne's hand in his and gave it a squeeze. "There really aren't any words for what is going on. Such conflicting events—the beginning of two people's lives together and the end of another. And tragically."

Carolanne leaned against his arm. "Looks like everyone else is feeling the same way."

When Garrett and Jill came out, they walked straight over to Carolanne and Connor.

"She's so young," Jill said.

Connor nodded. "I'd never seen her before. Might have just been someone traveling down Route 58."

Garrett took Jill's hand in his own. "They're trying to establish the timeline, I think. Jill told them that Ben would've been the last one working on the grounds last night. Is he still around?"

"No. He left a little while ago," Carolanne said.

"I guess Mac and his team were the last to come in through the back entrance. I gave them the access code so they could come in sometime this morning to set up," Jill said.

"We can check the alarm logs to get that information," Garrett said. "I'll make the call."

She sighed. "I still can't believe this is really happening."

Connor knew Jill would be worried about the grand opening, too. No one mentioned it, but when the news got hold of this story, they'd be as excited as weathermen in a hurricane. Either people would flock to the grand opening to get a peek at the crime scene or steer clear. He hoped for Jill and Garrett's sake that the news didn't pick up the story at all. They had so much money tied up in this project. This could really break them.

# ❖ Chapter Fourteen ❖

Sirens screamed down Route 58, adding to the gray mood that hung over what should have been a day of celebration. As guests finished answering the deputy's questions, they left and the artisan center was beginning to empty out.

Carolanne wished she had a change of clothes with her. Somehow, hanging out in a fancy gown felt very wrong under the circumstances, and it wasn't too easy to sit elegantly for this many hours, especially on a hand-crafted love seat made of reclaimed barn boards. She listened quietly as Garrett played the role of new husband and best friend, a role that had always been hers, to Jill. Garrett had always been in the picture, so she hadn't thought them getting married would change her relationship with Jill. *It's changing.* That stung.

Sheriff Scott Calvin walked in and sat down next to Carolanne.

"Tough day," Garrett said.

Scott nodded. "Getting tougher. There's also been an accident."

Carolanne leaned forward. "Is there something you need us to do here? Do you need to leave?"

He turned toward her. "Actually, you need to leave."

"Me?" *What did I do?*

Connor walked up behind Jill and Garrett. "What's up?"

"The sirens that just went by—there's been an accident. It's Ben. They're taking him to Regional."

Carolanne froze into blankness as she searched for a plausible explanation. "No. It can't be Dad. He left a little while ago, right?" She looked to Connor.

"He did," Connor said. "Maybe he didn't go straight home. Is it serious, Scott?"

"It's not good." Scott clamped his hands together. "Sorry."

Carolanne flinched at the tone in Scott's voice.

Scott pulled the keys from his pocket and flipped them to Connor. "Here. Take the Woodie. Y'all's cars are back at the church. I'll catch a ride with my guys."

Carolanne stood, looking to Jill, then Connor.

"He's got to be OK. I'll come with you," Jill said. "Garrett, you'll stay here?"

"No," Carolanne said. "No. You both stay here." She pulled her hand to her heart. "How can so much happen in one day?"

Connor reached for Carolanne's hand. "I've got this. I'll take her and we'll call you as soon as we know something."

Carolanne nodded and let Connor lead the way outside to the truck.

"This can't be happening." *Dad, we just made our first step. Please be all right. Please, please, God, let him be OK.*

Connor helped Carolanne into the passenger seat of the old Woodie, then ran around to get behind the wheel. He started the truck and revved the engine, speeding out of the parking lot and heading west on Route 58 toward the hospital.

"I hope he wasn't drinking." She hadn't realized she'd even said it aloud until Connor reached over and squeezed her hand.

His voice was comforting. "I don't think so. I didn't see him even take a sip of champagne."

"I hope he's OK." Carolanne closed her eyes, trying to silence the worry.

"Me, too."

She stared out the window. Then, just a couple of miles up the road, flashing lights lined the right side of the road.

"Is this where the . . . ?" She raised herself in her seat, trying to get a better look.

"This doesn't look good," Connor said.

A suffocating sensation tightened in her throat. *Please let it be a mistake. Don't let it be my dad.*

Connor slowed down behind the rest of the rubberneckers.

"It *is* his car!" It looked like the metal pole had been pile-driven down the middle of the mangled mess that used to be the hood of her dad's Pontiac. The windshield was cracked, and it sure didn't

158

look like there'd be any repairing that old car.

Carolanne stared at the heap of wreckage. She twisted in her seat, still looking as they drove past the accident. Not until they were well out of sight did she turn back and sit straight in her seat. "Sweet Jesus, don't take him."

Suddenly, the anger she'd clung to for so many years seemed even more trite and the time she'd wasted harboring it even more precious. They'd made a baby step toward repairing their relationship—but maybe there wasn't time for baby steps when it came to things like this. She swallowed hard and wrapped her arms across herself. *I'm so sorry, Dad.*

"It's going to be OK."

"You don't know that." She placed her hand in the palm of his. "You saw the wreck."

"You're right. I don't. But I know I'll be here with you through it no matter what. Don't give those negative thoughts any power. Have faith."

*Faith.* She nodded and tried to gather strength through his touch.

Connor pulled in front of the emergency room doors at the regional hospital and stomped on the brakes. "Go on in. I'll park and catch up with you."

She leapt from the vehicle, slammed the door, and ran inside.

The woman at the desk looked like she had been there a long time already. She glanced up and then tapped her finger on a clipboard. "Sign in, dear," she said with all the speed of a rowboat in a river of molasses.

"My father was brought in by ambulance. Ben Baxter."

The woman raised her head and paused.

That pause made Carolanne's heart hitch. "Can I see him? Is he OK?"

She tugged the glasses from her nose. "They just got here. I'll let you know as soon as they give me an update. You can take a seat in the waiting area."

*Nothing reassuring there.* Carolanne glanced at the clock. How long would it be before she'd at least know that he was OK?

She leaned against the seafoam-green cinder block wall. She was too antsy to sit. All she really wanted right now was to curl up in a little ball and cry. She raised her hands up over her eyes.

A strong hand skimmed her shoulder.

She turned right into Connor's arms and let the tears flow.

"What'd they say?" he whispered into her hair.

She shook her head. "Nothing yet."

"You're shaking." He pulled his suit jacket off and draped it around her shoulders. "Here." He rubbed his hands over the jacket and then tugged her back into his arms.

In his arms, with her face buried in the darkness of his coat, felt like the safest place she could be.

Connor stepped away and plucked a couple of tissues from a box on a nearby end table. "Here you go."

She took them and squeezed them into the palm of her hand.

"Come over here and sit down."

Carolanne took off her high heels and hitched up the long gown as she walked so as not to step on it. She followed him to the waiting area, sniffling back tears and gulping air. Connor helped her to a chair and then scooped the box of tissues up and set them in her lap.

"Calm down. They'll let us know something shortly, but if it were bad, you can rest assured we'd already know that."

She struggled to keep hope through the uncertainty.

They waited, hand in hand.

She leaned her head on Connor's shoulder and closed her eyes. She had to, else she'd watch that clock, and the hands were moving painfully slow. Every time the doors opened, her heart lurched.

Finally, a nurse in navy blue scrubs came out to the waiting room. "Are you with Mr. Baxter?"

Carolanne sprang from her seat. "Yes, we are."

"You can come back and see him," the nurse said with an expressionless face.

Carolanne grabbed her shoes in one hand and raced to catch up with the nurse. "Is he OK?"

The nurse smiled a tired half smile. "He's going to be fine. Sorry it took us so long. Your father was unconscious when the ambulance transported him. We did a CT scan to rule out a head bleed or hemorrhage. Things look OK, but we'll be watching for any signs of a concussion. He'll be here at least overnight. He has pretty bad gash on his noggin, but he's in good hands here."

Carolanne let out the breath she'd been holding. "Thank goodness."

Connor gave her hand a told-ya-so squeeze.

The nurse breezed down the hall like she had on roller skates.

Carolanne let go of Connor's hand and double-stepped to catch up with her. "Excuse me. Wait. Can you answer something else for me?"

The nurse stopped and turned to face her. "Sure. I'll try."

Carolanne bit down on her lower lip and then gathered the strength to ask the question. "Was alcohol a factor?"

"No."

Her answer was quick. That was a relief.

Then the nurse tilted her head slightly. "Well, not unless that dog he swerved to miss was drunk. But no, your father hadn't been drinking."

"Thank you." Relief washed over her. Guilt, too, for even having asked, but she'd needed to know.

The nurse smiled and then started walking down the hall again.

Carolanne cleared her throat. "Don't tell him I asked that, OK?"

The nurse turned slightly. "It's fine. I understand." The nurse's white clogs made a squishy whisper sound with each step. She stopped in front of Room 11 and placed the chart back in the door. "He's all yours."

Carolanne glanced at Connor for encouragement. "I'll be right here," he said.

"Thanks." She gave his hand one last squeeze, then walked in the room. She stepped around the corner toward the bed. "Hi, Dad." He looked like an old man, lying there in the hospital bed in the loose blue-and-white gown. The bruising on his head was already turning colors. If she hadn't known it was him, she might not have even recognized him. "Oh goodness. That's got to hurt."

Ben opened his eyes and raised a hand to the bulky bandage on his head. "I think I'm better than I look."

His nose had a bandage across it, too, and there was a supersize gash on the side of his face that looked like it had been laced up like a football.

Carolanne wasn't sure why she felt so relieved—he looked awful—but after seeing the car, she had feared the worst. She edged closer to the bed. "Dad, I was so afraid. Your car . . . it's . . . It has to be a total loss." She swallowed a sob that rose in her throat. "What happened?"

"My mind was somewhere else. I didn't see the dog on the side of the road until he ran into my lane. My knee-jerk reaction was to yank the wheel to the right to miss him—and yes, I know better, but you know how I love dogs. I couldn't hit him. Last I saw, the dog was racing across the traffic into the median, then wham! Next thing I knew, I was here."

"Thank God you're OK. You look pretty bad, but you still look better than your car. You could've been killed."

He patted her hand. "Don't be so dramatic. I'm going to be around a long time. Only the good die young and I've got lots to make up for. I hope that dog is OK."

She could see the kindness in the eyes of the man whom Momma had fallen in love with. "Thank goodness you're OK." She looked closer at the wound on his face. "How many stitches?"

"All of them," he said.

"Looks like a lot. Are there stitches under that bandage, too?"

"Several. They wanted to wait for a plastic surgeon, but I told them, at my age, that was just a waste." He reached for her hand. "Hey, your hands are shaking. I'm OK. Calm down, Carolanne."

"You gave me a heck of a scare." Even now, knowing he'd be OK, she couldn't shake that feeling.

"Quit staring at my head like that. You're making me feel weird."

"I'll try, but it's kind of hard not to look at it."

He chuckled, but it was clear it hurt when he did. "Let's talk about something happier, like how beautiful you looked today."

"Thank you, Daddy." She smiled and squeezed his hand. "It was a beautiful wedding."

"Garrett and Jill will have a good life together. They are good people."

"The best," Carolanne agreed.

"I hope I'll be around to see you walk down that aisle someday," he said.

The faraway look in his eyes made her think of the pictures that once graced the end table in the living room when she was growing up.

"You'll be a beautiful bride. Like your mother. I'll never forget the way she looked that day. One of the best days of my life." He smiled, and his green eyes, like her own, sparkled.

"I was surprised you left the reception so early." *If you hadn't, would you be here? Would you have nearly been . . .*

He lowered his eyes, then looked back up. "It was a hard day for me, Carolanne." He licked his dry lips. "You, looking beautiful, like your momma. The wedding. The open bar. It just didn't seem like a good place for me to be. I thought it was better I skedaddle before I made a mistake. See how that worked out for me?"

Her throat threatened to close completely. *How could I not have considered that before?* "I didn't even—"

"It's OK. It's not your problem to deal with. It was a happy occasion."

*But it is. I'm your daughter. If anyone should understand, it should've been me.*

"Wipe that look off your face—it might stick that way."

She smiled. He'd said that a million times when she was a little girl, and it always made her laugh.

Connor knocked on the doorjamb. "Do you mind if I join you?"

Ben lifted his chin. "Come on in, Connor. I didn't know you were out there."

"He drove me here," Carolanne said.

"He's another good man," Ben said softly.

*I know.*

"Good waste of a brand-new battery on the side of the road up on Route 58, I hear. Some people will do anything to get a new car."

"That Pontiac has been a good car. I don't have any plans on retiring her."

"Oh, it's a total. There's no way they'll ever be able to fix it," Carolanne said.

Ben looked disappointed. "That bad?" He looked to Connor for confirmation.

"Oh yeah," Connor nodded. "It's a total."

"I guess I'll have to call Glenn down at Farm Bureau. They'll give me a rental while we work it all out." Ben looked around the room. "Is there a phone in here? I should probably do that now."

Carolanne pulled her hands up on her hips. "Not in the ER. You're not even in a regular room yet, and I'd bet that you're not going to be going anywhere anytime soon to need a car, anyway. I'll call Glenn for you when I get home."

Connor said, "It's a small town. He's probably already heard and started the paperwork."

"True," Ben said. "But yes, Carolanne, if you'd call, that would be helpful."

"I'll take care of it. I'm a lot less worried about that car than I am about you."

"I'm fine. Really," he said.

"You always say that." She glanced over at Connor. "You men always say you're fine. You could have a limb severed and swear you were fine. It's OK to be sick or hurt, you know."

Ben looked to Connor, and they both rolled their eyes.

"Y'all can make fun of me if you want, but you know I'm right."

"They're going to put me in a room as soon as they have one ready. I told them as hardheaded as I am, there's nothing that can put me out of commission, but they wouldn't hear of sending me home tonight. At least I'll get a nice big breakfast in the morning that I don't have to cook."

"Better safe than sorry." Carolanne was relieved

they weren't sending him home, since he'd be alone—or would he? She wondered if Gina knew about the accident. There was that feeling again. *What else don't I know about you?*

The nurse in the navy blue scrubs walked in. "That's exactly how we feel about things around here. We'll err on the side of caution." She smiled. "Mr. Baxter, we've got your room ready."

Moving him into a room was another sign that her dad was going to be OK.

"Is there anything you need us to bring you from your house?"

"I could use . . ." Ben started, but then stopped and shook his adamantly. "No. Nothing. I'll be out of here tomorrow. I don't need a thing, except maybe a ride home tomorrow, if you don't mind."

*Afraid I'll bump into your friend, Dad? What's going on with that girl staying there?* "We don't mind running by your house if you need something. Are you sure?" *Will he tell me?*

"I'm positive. You two go do something nice in your dress-up clothes. I didn't mean to add so much excitement to your day."

Carolanne got ready to tell her Dad about the even bigger excitement of the day, but Connor must have read her mind, because he shook his head and gave her a wink. He was probably right. It was no time to tell Dad that his accident wasn't the biggest surprise of the day. That would only worry him, and he could hear about that tomorrow. She'd just have to wait until then to approach the subject of his houseguest, too.

"Call me when they let you know when they'll be releasing you. I'll come right over."

Ben's eyes seemed glassy with tears. "Yes, I'll call you. Thank you, honey."

She reached down and gave him a hug. She didn't want to let go. It may have been the first real hug she'd given him in years. "I love you, Dad."

"I love you, too, little one." He kissed her on the cheek, then looked up at Connor. "Take care of my little girl, Connor."

"Yes, sir." Connor walked out behind Carolanne.

As soon as they stepped out in the hall and past Ben's door, Carolanne sprinted toward the exit.

Connor rushed to catch up with her. "Are you OK?"

She nodded. "Yes," she managed through the tears. "Yes. I'm good. It's all good."

And Milly's words echoed in her mind. *Your future will be as good as you let it be.*

# ❖ Chapter Fifteen ❖

A restful night's sleep must not have been in the cards for her because Carolanne hadn't slept for more than an hour or two at a time before waking up to the image of her dad's car in a heap on the side of the road. *A girl can only take so many of those dreams. Nightmares, really.* So she'd given up trying, and by seven fifteen, she was whisking down the halls of the hospital, determined to see how Dad had fared through the night.

She took the elevator to the third floor. Asking Dad how he was would be just plain useless. She knew the answer she'd get. *Fine.*

At the nurse's station, she stopped to get the real story. "Good morning. I'm Carolanne Baxter. My dad—"

"Good morning. I've been Mr. Ben's nurse all night. I'm sure he'll be glad to see you. I'm Merry. He's been chomping at the bit to get out of here."

"Oh goodness, has he been a handful?"

The huge black nurse laughed in such a way that her stomach bounced, and it looked to Carolanne like the woman's shiny cheeks bounced, too. "Oh, he did a lot of bellyaching about me checking on him all night, but once I told him that torturing him was the favorite part of my job, we found a way to get along."

*Only took her one night to figure him out. Why has it taken me all these years?*

The nurse patted Carolanne's arm. "Your dad's feeling pretty good, though. I knew he was feeling better when I went through my normal 'What's your name? Who's the president?' lines to check his brain function and he tore into me about politics. I swear he'd sat up the hour prior just trying to come up with something to get my goat."

"I guess that's a good sign," she said, but really, she'd put so much distance between the two of them over the years she didn't even know his views on politics—or most other things.

"Doc already made his rounds, but we don't have the release papers yet."

"I know I'm a little early for visiting hours, but do you mind if I go on in?"

"You'll have to wait your turn. Someone's already visiting with him."

*Gina?* She tried to hide her annoyance. "Who?"

"The sheriff, but when he leaves, he's all yours."

*Why does the thought of that girl with my dad irk me so?* She tried to shake her attitude back into shape. "OK, thanks. I'll just wait outside until they're done." Carolanne walked across the hall and stood outside his room.

Scott's deep voice carried out into the quiet hallway as he asked her father questions. "You were at the artisan center until six o'clock on

Friday night, but you didn't work yesterday morning? Is that right?"

"No. Jill gave Mac the code to get in. He wasn't sure what time he was bringing the cake over, so that seemed easiest. Is something wrong?"

"You were at the wedding. I saw you there. Were you leaving the reception when you wrecked?"

Her dad said, "No, I'd left earlier. I went to Penny's Soda Shoppe to eat, then on my way home from there is when I wrecked."

"Who else was at Penny's?"

"Mac's kid. That couple who bought the old house at the end of Abbey Road. Some tourists. Is something wrong? Why all the questions? This isn't about my wreck, is it?"

She heard the rustle of papers and then Scott's voice. "Have you ever seen this girl before?"

There was a pause and then her dad's response. "Never seen her."

Carolanne leaned closer to the door.

Ben's voice shook. "What happened to her?"

"We found her in the pond behind the artisan center. She floated right up during the reception."

"That's awful. Carolanne was here last night. She didn't mention it."

She felt badly for not telling him herself, but it hadn't seemed like the right time. She sure hoped he'd understand.

"Yeah. Well, I'm sure she was more worried about you. Not much we can do for this girl now. No one seems to know her. I'm talking to everyone with any connections to the artisan center as we collect evidence to see what we can piece together."

"No one knows her? Maybe she was just passing through."

"Maybe. You didn't see anything odd last night at the artisan center? No one hanging around?"

"No. It was quiet."

"Do you check down near the pond as part of your daily rounds?"

"Sure do. I ride the whole perimeter at least once a day, checking for trash, fallen limbs, whatever. I didn't see anything out of the ordinary."

Scott's words sounded thoughtful. "She could've been a runaway. Someone has to be missing her. Well, let me know if you think of anything that might help."

"I'll do that."

She heard Scott get up and move toward the door. "Hope you feel better soon."

Carolanne stepped out from where she'd been eavesdropping and tried to look as if she'd just walked up. "Good morning, Scott."

"Here to pick up your dad?"

"Hope so. He gave me quite a scare." Carolanne slid between Scott and the door.

"I bet," Scott said. "When you get a chance, can

you stop by the station? I need to get your statement from yesterday."

"Absolutely," she said as he walked away. She hesitated only a moment before walking into her dad's room. He looked pale and more tired today than he had last night.

"How's your head feel this morning?" She squinted as she looked closer. "The skin is so tight around that goose egg it looks like you might hatch a baby ostrich."

"Feels that big, too."

"I hear the nurses gave you a run for your money last night."

He pushed the button to raise the bed a little more. "The squeak-squeak-squeak of those shoes they wear is about as annoying as a hound dog scratchin' fleas. Between that and them coming in to ask me if I knew who I was all night, I didn't get a lick of sleep. I can't wait to get home."

"The nurse said the doctor already made rounds. They're just waiting on your release papers."

The scowl on his face said it all. "They're probably just trying to get another day's pay from the insurance. It's all a racket."

"Your nurse was right. You are cranky!"

"I don't mean to be like that. I'm just tired." Ben repositioned the pillow under his neck. "What do they make these things out of—old tires? It's impossible to get comfortable." He ran his hand through his hair in an unsuccessful attempt to smooth it down.

She'd never seen his hair in such disarray. He normally had it so slicked in place with Brylcreem that it didn't move. This morning it was sticking up in six directions. He looked a little like Jack Nicholson in *The Shining*. That was a little disturbing—and funny, at the same time. She sat down in the chair next to his bed and tried to think of something to talk about that might lift his mood.

"I barely slept a wink. It's like they waited in the hall for me to drift off before barging in to check on me. They probably have a points system. Extra points for being a real pain in the—"

"Watch your mouth." Miss Merry strolled in as Ben complained. "I heard that, Mr. Ben."

"You're not going to deny it, are you?"

"Oh, heavens no, and I've got good news." Miss Merry tapped her clipboard with her long bright purple fingernails. "I've got the release form right here, plus a long list of all the stuff you need to do and shouldn't do. A couple prescriptions to get filled, too. Maybe your sweet daughter will take care of that for you. I'll get you to sign that I delivered this message because I won't be held responsible for your hardheadedness when you don't follow these guidelines and you land back in here."

"I won't be back." Ben scribbled his name at the bottom of the page.

"I'll help him." She watched her dad for a reaction. "I mean, unless you've got folks from the Senior Circle or church whom you'd rather have help you."

He looked up, paused, then said, "No, no. I appreciate your help. Thanks."

"OK, well, then let's get you out of here." Carolanne jumped up from the chair. "Where's your stuff?"

"In the paper bag in that drawer," Ben grumbled.

She pulled his clothes out of the bag. The pants were fine, but his white dress shirt was caked in dried blood. "Dad, you can't wear this. It's a biohazard." She held it between two fingers and dropped it back into the bag.

Miss Merry shook her head. "Lord no, people would think right poorly of us if we sent you out of here looking like that. You can just slip on your pants and wear that hospital gown home. They gonna charge you a fortune for it anyway."

"Problem solved." Ben shifted to get out of bed.

Miss Merry threw an arm out toward him. "You take it slow there, mister."

Ben wobbled.

"See? Told you. You'll be having Bambi legs for a little bit. You take your time, and you'll be just fine. Don't fall, or you'll be back here on my floor again, and I'll be taking big joy in messing with you."

Ben steadied himself and muttered, "There's incentive to follow orders."

She smiled a toothy white smile. "That's me. Full of helpful tips. You holler if you need us."

Carolanne walked out into the hall and waited for Ben to get dressed while Miss Merry went to get a wheelchair to take him downstairs.

Ben grumbled the whole time Miss Merry helped him into the wheelchair and then all the way down the hall. Carolanne wondered how much of his crankiness was due to the secret he was keeping from her.

When Miss Merry stopped at the front desk to sign out, Carolanne whisked by them. "I'll go get the car and pull it around."

By the time she had driven up to the front doors, Miss Merry was helping Ben stand up. He slowly negotiated the shift from wheelchair to her car.

Miss Merry buckled him in before waving good-bye.

Carolanne waved back. "She's sweet."

"You only say that because she wasn't waking you up all night."

*I didn't have a picnic of a night's sleep, either.* "I'll take you straight home, and then I'll go get your prescriptions and anything else you need."

"Or we could stop by the pharmacy on the way."

*Was that a little panic in his voice?* "I wouldn't want you to have to wait in the car. You need to get some rest."

"Well, if you don't mind," he said, "I would like to lie down."

Carolanne pulled her car into his empty driveway and then ran to the passenger side to help her dad get out of the car.

He pushed himself up and steadied himself against the door. "I can walk. Just give me a second."

She held her arm out like a spotter with a gymnast. "Do you have your keys?"

He stopped mid-step. "Nope. I guess they're with the car at the impound lot."

"Do you have a hide-a-key?"

Ben shook his head. "No, but I think we can get in through the patio door."

"You left your patio door open?"

"No." Ben moved slowly through the yard with Carolanne at his heels.

When they got to the patio, Ben lifted up on the sliding glass door, and it pulled right open.

"How'd you know how to do that?"

"A friend told me." He looked pretty surprised that it had worked. "I never tried it before now. Works like a charm, though."

*A friend?* "Handy if you're a criminal. I'd suggest you replace those old doors with some secure French doors sometime soon."

"Not a bad idea." Ben walked in and surveyed the room.

He seemed to be disoriented, the way he stood there looking around.

*Is he looking for Gina? Anything out of place that might let me know that someone else has been staying here?* She scanned the room, too. "Dad? Are you OK?"

"Yeah, sorry, I'm just trying to get my sea legs here. Come on in."

Carolanne walked in behind him. "Are you going to rest in bed or out here on the couch?"

"I think I'll just lie on the couch."

She went into the kitchen and came back with a plastic bag of ice. "Here. Put this on your head. It should keep the swelling down."

He laid back, wincing as he placed the bag of ice on his head.

She winced right along with him. Just looking at the knot on his head made hers hurt. "I'm going to go get your prescriptions."

Ben balanced the ice on his head, kicked off his shoes, and then closed his eyes. "Just leave the front door unlocked. I don't know where my spare keys are."

"OK. While I'm out, is there anything else I can pick up from the store for you?"

"If I need anything, I'll call your uncle Reggie and have him get Mary Claire to run something over from the market. Really, I'm fine." He reached for her hand. "Thank you for being here for me."

"I'm glad to do it." And she really felt that way. Better memories pulled forward, replacing the harsh thoughts she'd carried for so long. She let go of his hands and wrapped her arms around him.

She'd hugged him more in the past week than she had in the last fifteen years total. He had to have a good explanation for Gina being here the other night.

"I love you." He patted her on the back.

"I'll be right back," she said.

"Hey, before you go, I just remembered Connor telling me that you're moving into your house this week."

"Yes. I can hardly believe it. I've never in my life heard of a builder delivering early."

Ben shifted the ice bag. "That Garrett, he's a hard working son of a gun, just like his pop. Let me know when you're planning to get started. I'd be glad to help you move."

"Dad, you just got out of the hospital. I'm thinking helping me move is the last thing you need to be worrying about."

"Don't be silly." He threw a dismissive hand in the air. "I'll be back at work by Monday. You helped me. I'll help you. That's the way it works."

"Back to work tomorrow? Don't push your luck."

"We open the center on Saturday. I've got a lot to do."

"Don't you worry about that. I know Scott told you what happened during the reception. With all that going on, I'm not even sure if they'll be allowed to have the grand opening."

"Don't say that. Garrett and Jill have worked so hard to keep that timeline on schedule."

"I know. I don't wish it on them. I'm just being realistic, but even if they do, Jill will not expect you back at work tomorrow. You know we'll all pitch in to be sure everything gets done. You need to just plan to take it easy." She glared at him. "You promise me."

"I hear you. We'll play it by ear."

It was probably the best she'd get out of him. Carolanne started to walk back toward the door but paused at the dining room table. The big family photo album sat on the edge of the table. "I didn't know you even still had this."

"What?" Ben couldn't see her from the couch.

She cleared her throat. "Our big family album. It's here on the table." She picked up the book and a bright-yellow-and-white potato chip bag folded like an accordion fluttered to the ground. She knelt to pick it up.

"I haven't looked through it in years myself."

"Then why was it on the table?"

He didn't answer at first. "I was just using it to hold something down."

"A potato chip bag?"

"No. Don't be silly. That's just trash."

*No, it's not. That's those bags Gina was collecting. Don't lie to me, Dad.* She placed the photo album back on his bookshelf. "You know . . ."

"What?"

"Um . . ."

*I can't. Not now. I'm not even sure I want to know. What if part of Gina's past is linked to Dad? What if my dad is Gina's dad? Did he cheat on Mom while she was so ill?* Her stomach turned. *Impossible. He loved Mom, or maybe that was the crushing blow, that he'd cheated and let me down?* She forced her curiosity to the side.

"You know, Doris said she has some new mysteries in. I'll pick a couple up for you."

"Thanks. That would be good. Sitting around here isn't going to be much fun."

"It won't kill you to take it easy for at least a couple days," she said as she pulled the door closed behind her. As she got into her car, she glanced at the tall shrub where she'd hunkered down the other night while Gina used her dad's phone and drove off in his car.

It's a wonder Gina hadn't seen her. That shrub didn't offer much coverage. Why hadn't she just confronted Gina? She had more right than that girl to be there in the first place.

She glanced at the note she'd written to herself to call Farm Bureau for her dad. *No sense bothering Glenn on Sunday.* Besides, if she could stall them on the rental car, Dad wouldn't have a way to go back to work too soon.

*Connor must be rubbing off on me. It might be manipulative, but it sure would be convenient in this case.*

She drove around the corner and parked behind the pharmacy, wondering who would take care of her if she was in an accident.

# ❖ Chapter Sixteen ❖

Early Monday morning, Carolanne stopped by her dad's house unannounced. It was a dirty trick. There'd been no sign of Gina, but she couldn't resist the drop-in just to see if she was still hanging around. She called from the driveway. Dad was already awake, and when she went inside he looked like he felt better, and there was no sign of Gina. A relief on both accounts. *If he wants to help out an old school friend's daughter, it really isn't any business of mine.*

She left feeling bad about doubting him, but better just the same. A quick trip to the Walmart to pick up boxes completed the chores on her morning checklist, so she'd gone straight home and started readying for her big move. She'd been at it for nearly an hour—folding in corners, then using her handy-dandy tape gun to secure the bottoms of the cardboard boxes. The room was filling up fast with empty boxes, but she was on a roll.

It was exciting to think that later this week these boxes would be filled with her stuff, and she'd be moving into her new house. And it was a whole lot more house than anything she'd have ever been able to afford up in New York.

*Swish-chick.* There was something powerful about wielding that tape gun.

She pretended to shoot a bullet from it and blew on the end, then spun around when she heard the front door to her apartment open.

"Good morning," she said with a smile.

"What's got you all sunshine and rainbows?" Connor strolled into the room with his crossword puzzle in hand.

She shrugged. "I don't know. Slept great. Feel good. Turning a new leaf. Already went over and checked on my dad. He's doing good, too."

"I was going to stop by and see how he's doing today."

"Good. He'd probably like the company, and it'll save me the worry." She put her tape gun down and folded another box. "He's already antsy to go back to work."

"You're like a little tornado in here this morning. Did you consume my portion of the coffee, too?"

"Real funny, wise guy." She marched over to the coffeepot, which was now hidden behind a teetering tower of boxes, and poured him a cup.

He was right behind her when she turned to take it to him. She let him sweeten and lighten it himself.

"Good thing you saved me some." His tone was gruff and playful at the same time.

She picked up the tape gun again. "You better be nice to me, or I'll wrap you up in tape with this gizmo."

"That sounds like it could be fun."

"Don't tease me. I seriously think I'm in love with this thing. I might quit my job and become a full-time box taper."

"That *would* solve the working-together problem you're so worried about."

"And that is the kind of statement," she said, pointing the tape gun at him, "that'll get your mouth taped shut."

"You're full of yourself today."

"I must have gotten that from you. Oh, and I'm taking the day off work today, too."

"You're what? I've never known you to take a day off work"—he shook his head—"like ever."

As their eyes met, she felt a shock run through her. "Well, I am today. I'm going to pack up and get ready for my big move."

"Want me to help?"

She placed an open box on the kitchen counter. "Not with packing. But I could use your help getting all this furniture moved."

"It took three of us to get that couch up these stairs."

She remembered that day. It hadn't been too pretty. Maneuvering up the narrow and steep stairs had been a real challenge. "Hopefully, going down will be easier."

"I better solicit some help. When do you want to move the furniture?"

"Will Wednesday or Thursday work for you?"

"Wednesday's good."

"Great." She pulled off the cap on a thick black marker and sniffed. Then she waved it under his nose. "Doesn't that smell yummy?"

"If you like black licorice."

"I do." She wrote KITCHEN in big capital letters, then capped the marker and looked across the stacks of boxes. "I thought I'd get all the boxes packed today and moved tomorrow. Then if y'all can move the big stuff on Wednesday, it'll be mostly done."

"That'll work. I'll borrow Garrett's trailer," Connor said.

"Excellent. Let me see what you've done on the crossword today." She took the newspaper from him and sat down.

He flipped his pen to her, and she snagged it midair.

"Nice catch," he said.

"I've got skills." She started filling in blanks without hesitation.

"You *could* make it look a little more challenging."

"I would—if it were," she said, holding back a smile. Sometimes she wrote over words he already had just to torture him.

"You always put me to shame on that thing. Why do I bother?"

"Because it makes me feel smart, and you like letting me have my way." Carolanne set the paper back down. "You only left me a couple slots today."

"I must've had a feeling you were too busy for me."

She knew he was teasing, but the truth was, she'd been too busy for way too many things lately. That was about to change. "Aw, I'm never too busy for you."

"Well, one of us has to get downstairs to the office and keep the legal wheels spinning here in Adams Grove. Just holler if you need me to lift anything heavy for you." He flexed a muscle and gave her a flirty grin.

She put her hand on his muscle as a joke, but he squeezed her hand into a hostage position between his bicep and forearm.

"I think I like you in this mood," he said.

"Thanks. I think *I* like me in this mood." She pulled away as he moved closer. *Were you going to kiss me? Slow down, lawyer boy. I'm not sure I'm in that good of a mood.* "Get, or I won't get anything done." She tugged her hand free.

"I wish," he said as he walked out the door.

Connor sat in his office, unable to focus on anything but the clomping around upstairs. She hadn't even moved out yet, and he knew it was going to be far too quiet once she was gone. He enjoyed morning coffee and word games together.

The front door creaked.

Connor added WD-40 to the list on his desk pad. *One more thing to fix.* Upkeep on the bank building was an ongoing job, but he enjoyed being owner, resident lawyer, and handyman. He walked out of his office to greet the client. Only, it wasn't a client; it was Doris Huckaby.

"Doris, good to see you. How are things down at the library?"

The short librarian scurried through the door and walked in with a big smile. "I'm fine, and so is the library. I just got another grant to get some e-readers. I'm getting good at that grant stuff."

"That's terrific."

"I was just heading over to the library, but I wanted to chat with Carolanne. Is she not in this morning?"

"She's packing for her big move later this week."

Doris's eyes went wide. "She's got to be so excited. Chaz took me over to Bridle Path Estates the other day. The house is gorgeous."

"It's very nice." *I'll miss having her here, though.*

The librarian's smile faded. "Would you ask her to give me a call later? I want to ask her about something that occurred to me this morning, and it's driving me crazy."

"Like a song that gets in your mind and won't let go?"

"Something like that," Doris said, though she looked more serious than that. "Only, not in a pleasant way," she mumbled. "Well, I need to scoot if I'm going to open the library on time. You take care, now."

"I'll do that."

Just as Doris went to grab the door, Carolanne walked through it.

"Oh. Hi, Doris."

"I was just looking for you," Doris said.

"Here I am. What's up?" She leaned in and gave Doris a hug. "You look worried. You OK? Would you like to sit down?"

Doris turned and went back inside, taking a seat near the window. "I wanted to talk to you about that girl. The one that . . . you know, the one in the pond."

Connor and Carolanne sat down across from her.

"I know. It's just awful," Carolanne said.

"It was so upsetting. I'm sure it was even worse for Jill and Garrett. When I saw the picture, I was quite certain I didn't know her—but this morning it struck me."

Carolanne leaned in. "What?"

Doris pressed her lips in a tight line. "Did you recognize her?"

"I haven't seen the pictures yet," Carolanne said.

Connor interjected. "We left before Carolanne got to talk to Scott. Ben was in an accident."

"That's right, Carolanne. I'm so sorry. I heard about that. Chaz was talking to a couple people from the hospital at church Sunday morning. He's OK, right?"

"He's home recuperating."

"Good." Doris pulled her purse up tighter on her lap. "Remember when you came to the library and you had that young girl with you the other day?"

"Yes." Carolanne's fingers tensed in her lap. "Gina."

Doris nodded. "Lindsey Dixon's daughter."

Connor leaned forward. "Doris, are you saying the girl in the pond was the Dixon girl?"

"I think so."

Connor's mood dropped. *That family has been through so much.* "Wow. Can you imagine? Another tragedy for the Dixon family involving a drowning? I hope you're wrong. That somehow seems like just too much bad luck for one family."

Carolanne stammered. "I sure hope it wasn't her."

Doris wrung her hands. "Not that it's any better if it were a stranger, but you're right, Connor. It would be so sad. I was going to talk to Scott about it, but then I thought I'd check with you, Carolanne, to be sure I wasn't just plain crazy."

Carolanne leaned back in her chair. Her voice was soft. "She was so sad. Her mom committed suicide recently, you know."

"That family has had so much tragedy over the years," Connor said.

Carolanne said, "I told her she needed to come talk to you about the trust. I wasn't sure what the details were, but I figured it was worth looking into."

Doris looked at her watch and got up. "I've got to open the library. Would you mind grabbing Scott and bringing him over to the library so we can talk to him about it?"

"I can do that. I was supposed to go talk to him today anyway. No problem."

Carolanne's mood had deflated. Connor watched the dark cloud wash over her movements and even her voice. He wanted to hold her and promise her that things would always be OK.

Doris tugged on the bottom of her shirt and started toward the door. "Tell Scott that I'd sent that little girl down to Mac's Bakery that morning, too. He might want to stop there and talk to Mac on his way down."

"I'll tell him." Carolanne walked Doris to the door.

Connor watched Carolanne stand there processing what she'd just heard. He wondered if it was dawning on her that her new house was only a football field away from where that girl had died. He wasn't about to be the one to mention it. Although, if it kept her here, under his roof, that would suit him just fine.

Carolanne's eyes had lost the sparkle they'd held just a little while ago.

"I'd made you breakfast. It's why I came downstairs," she said over her shoulder. "I was going to surprise you."

"Really?" He smiled, but at the same time his stomach twisted. The last time he'd eaten her cooking, he'd eaten half a bottle of antacids and still couldn't get relief.

# ❖ Chapter Seventeen ❖

Connor watched Carolanne walk down the block. Her step was quick. It seemed to have hit her hard that the girl in the pond may have been someone she'd known, even if briefly.

He went back and checked his calendar for the day. He owed that write-up to Mac, but that could wait. He didn't know if his stomach was ready for what Carolanne was dishing up for breakfast, but he remembered his mom's words. *It's the thought that counts.*

When he walked into Carolanne's apartment, the boxes made his heart sink.

On the table, there were two plates of pancakes and chocolate milk. *My favorite.*

This was a big step for Carolanne Baxter. He wasn't sure what had broken the ice for her, but something had changed. The chair groaned as he slid it across the solid-oak floor to sit down.

He took a bite of the pancakes and almost choked. *Thank goodness she's not here.* He spit the doughy, grainy mess out on the plate and drank the whole glass of milk just to get the taste out of his mouth. *How do you mess up pancakes?* He didn't know how she'd done it, but she had.

Mom had always made the best pancakes. So light you felt like you had to hurry and top them with sticky syrup to keep them from floating away. *I miss you, Mom. Wish you could've shared some of your cooking skills with Carolanne before you left this earth.*

Since Mom died, cooking had become like therapy. He'd made his way to the middle of her favorite cookbook—*Pass the Plate. If Carolanne would just follow a recipe, maybe her cooking would be edible.*

Heading to the kitchen, he stopped mid-scrape by the trash can. Instead, he grabbed a plastic bag from the counter and scraped both plates of food, if you could call it that, into the bag. He washed the dishes and stacked them in the drainer. He'd throw the evidence away in his apartment, and she'd never be the wiser. No sense hurting her feelings. It had been a nice gesture, after all.

He stopped at the door of her apartment and turned back. It was going to be odd with this place empty, but he couldn't imagine renting it out to anyone else.

In his apartment, he opened the cabinets under the sink to throw away the plastic bag with the disaster of a breakfast in it. When he spotted the hammer and screwdriver he stored there, a thought struck him about the Dixon farm trust.

Carolanne walked into the sheriff station praying Doris was wrong. Gina seemed like a nice girl, although Carolanne would admit that ever since she'd seen her coming out of her dad's house, she'd had less-than-amicable feelings toward her—for no real good reason. That just made it worse if something had happened to her.

The deputy working at the front desk sent Carolanne down the hall.

She knocked on Scott's door. "They said I could come on back. You busy?"

"Come on in. What's up?"

"I owed you a visit about the thing on Saturday anyway, but this morning, Doris Huckaby stopped by the office. She thinks we might know who that girl was who drowned."

"Oh? Well, come on in. Sit. How's your dad?"

"He's good. They released him yesterday."

"Glad to hear it. So tell me what you know about our mystery girl."

Carolanne cleared her throat and started from the beginning, telling him about how she'd met Gina and the girls' connection with the Dixon farm. "Doris said she realized this morning that the girl who died might be the same girl—Gina."

"Well, let's see what you think." Scott turned around and grabbed a folder from the stack on his credenza. He flipped through some pages and then pulled out a color image. He slid it across the desk.

She lifted the picture and held it closer. *It's her.* Nausea swept over her, and she was glad she hadn't eaten breakfast before coming down here, else she may have lost it right here and now. "It's Gina. She told me her last name. I can't remember—it'll come to me." Carolanne stared at the picture. "It wasn't a suicide, was it?"

"Why would you ask that?"

Carolanne stared into the eyes of the girl in the picture, wishing she could ask her. "She's not much younger than me, I don't think. We talked that day I took her down to the library. Her mom had recently committed suicide. She was looking for answers. She'd said something like she didn't want her mother's past to be her future. Something like that. Anyway, I asked her if she needed help, and she said she wasn't suicidal." *I didn't catch the connection before, but it makes sense now why I was so drawn to her. Our fears—they're really the same.*

"I doubt this was what she was looking for," Scott said. "Sad story, but no, it wasn't a suicide."

"Good, I guess." Carolanne nodded as she stared into those eyes. They haunted her and hung on her heart. *What were you looking for? Did you find it? Why were you with my dad?* She tried to remember the conversation she'd overheard snippets of that night, but all that consumed her whole mind was the picture of Gina, dead.

"So, we have a name." Scott wrote it down on the front of the folder. "Maybe now we can weave the rest of this together. No one else has been able to shed any light at all."

"She had a tattoo on her wrist. Did you see that?"

"Butterflies," he said.

"Yes. Bright-blue butterflies. Doris spent some time with her that day. She may know more. Oh, and Doris said she'd sent Gina down to talk to Mac that day." *I should tell him about her being at Dad's house. Oh, Dad, what the . . . ? I'm going to have to tell him.* "She said something about looking for her dad, too."

Carolanne sucked in a steadying breath, forging the courage to tell Scott about the last time she'd seen Gina. "And—"

A uniformed deputy swept into the office. "Need you, Boss. We've got a problem. They've pulled over a guy up the road, and he's got a pile of automatics in the trunk, and—"

Scott jumped up from his desk. "Thanks for the information. Tell Doris I'll check in with her later."

Carolanne sat there collecting her thoughts as the two men ran down the hall. She leaned over the desk and looked inside the folder from which Scott had pulled the picture. She knew more than they did at this point.

She backed out of the office and forced herself to walk down the hallway. Once outside, she bent over and tried to gather her composure. She felt ill, and her breath was coming in shallow, quick gasps. The same question played over and over in her mind about her dad. *Did you have anything to do with that girl winding up dead? Please let me be wrong.*

Her legs felt like noodles. She darted behind the building to take the alley back to the office. There was no way she could smile and make small talk with folks on Main Street right now. It was bad enough that a young girl was dead, but knowing her dad had lied, that was way too close to home.

She'd heard him tell Scott he didn't recognize Gina from the picture, but that picture was clearly Gina. It was easy to identify. That couldn't have been a mistake.

Carolanne racewalked her way down the alley. Small sheds hugged most of the Main Street businesses, containing excess inventory and seasonal decorations. Tuesday was trash day, so trash bins dotted a path down the left side of the street. A minivan sat right behind the bakery, but it wasn't Mac's. Maybe Mac had finally broken down and bought a second truck for deliveries.

The sugary-sweet smells from the bakery were usually a comfort, but today her stomach couldn't take the heavy aroma. Carolanne stopped and leaned against the extra-tall wooden shed that hugged the brick bakery building. The blue stain on the shed had faded to a bluish-gray, but the glossy logo glistened in the morning sun.

She knelt down for just a minute, hoping she'd

feel better. Something bright yellow and silver reflected in the sunlight, like a deflated Mylar balloon had blown into the corner between the building and the shed.

Carolanne walked over and tugged it from the crevice. Larger than a balloon, it only took her a moment to realize what she was holding. The extra-large tote bag had been fashioned out of potato chip bags. The same technique that Gina had used to weave bags from trash to treasure. The same brand of bag that she'd seen on Dad's kitchen table.

*Please don't send these clues my way.* She was trying so hard to put the past behind her, but the world just didn't seem to want her to have a happy ending.

Carolanne patted the bag. At first she thought it was empty, but she felt something inside. She opened the bag. There wasn't much in there. Only gum wrappers and one of those free address book calendars you get at the card store. She looked at the printed address on the front of the calendar. This one had come from a Hallmark shop down in Jacksonville, Florida.

Papers fell from the address book. She gathered them up quickly and clutched the bag to her chest. *This is evidence. Take it back to the station.* But no matter how many times she repeated that to herself, her feet kept moving toward the old bank building.

She ran inside, went straight to her office, and closed the door. With the bag on the desk, she stared at it and then the phone. She could leave a message for Scott that she'd found it. Rubbing her neck, she felt the tension crawl into her shoulders. *What am I doing? What am I even looking for? This is not my job.*

She stood behind her desk for a long moment, not sure what to do. She slid her hand inside the bag and pulled out the address book. She tipped the stack of papers tucked inside out onto the desk. With a sweeping motion, she spread all the receipts, cards, and papers across the desk like a blackjack dealer breaking out a new deck of cards.

Each piece might tell her more about what Gina had been up to and ultimately what had happened to her. Some of the receipts were from almost two weeks ago. *How did she stay under the radar so long?* In a town this size, that wasn't easy. Carolanne's hand hovered over the Florida driver's license. *Regina Lee Edwards. Edwards— that was her last name.* This picture showed a happier Gina. At least this would give Scott not only her name, but an address, too. There was also a pawn ticket from Billy's Pawn Shop in Jacksonville, a bus ticket, a coupon for a free cupcake from Mac's Bakery, a business card from Mac's Bakery with Derek's name and a cell phone number scribbled on the back, and the

Baxter and Buckham business card she'd given her the day they'd met. *Was she staying at Dad's all that time? She said she was staying at a friend's house, but if Dad was the friend, wouldn't Gina have known I was his daughter?*

Carolanne flipped through the calendar. The handwriting was neat, but most of the notes on the address pages were just random thoughts. She must've been using it as a notepad. Some pages had numbers listed, others tasks. About midway through, under the MNO header, there was an address in Brooklyn, New York, but no name was listed. Maybe whoever lived on Flatbush Avenue in Brooklyn could tell Scott more about what was on Gina's mind.

*Is this where you were headed? Please let this guy in New York be your dad.* The thought of her own father having had a child with another woman would be more than she could take.

As much as Carolanne wanted to stay out of this whole mess, especially if there was any chance her dad was involved, she knew she couldn't. She felt the need to clear any suspicion that her dad was involved. Plus, she felt a connection to Gina, and if looking into her mother's past had landed her dead, she sure didn't deserve that. Someone needed to pay. *I just pray it's not you, Dad.*

Connor hit the door with a double knock and opened it, startling her. "What are you doing here? I thought you'd still be down talking to Scott."

"I just got back," she said.

"Thanks for the breakfast. That was a nice thought."

"Glad you liked it," she said.

"So, was it the Dixon girl?"

Carolanne couldn't even speak. She just nodded.

His expression was tight. "I was just thinking about that trust. If her mom is dead, that means Gina would have been the sole heir to that property. Truth is, I'd always been under the impression that Lindsey Dixon was the last living member of that family. She never mentioned a daughter, and I'd checked in with her several times over the years."

"That day in the library, Gina seemed either unaware of her uncle's drowning accident, or she really just didn't want to talk about it. That could be the reason."

"The Dixon farm is a nice piece of land. I wonder if she had anything to do with that chain being down the other day."

"Don't know. Could be. She was definitely on a hunt for information."

"Deadly information."

"Don't say that. It creeps me out."

"But it's true. Maybe she's not related to the Dixons, or maybe someone else was more interested in that land than Gina was." He stepped inside her office. "What's all that mess?"

"I found it in the alley on my way back. It's a tote bag—Gina's tote bag."

He gave her a warning look. "You should have left it right where it was and called Scott."

"He got called out on a bust while I was there." She eyed the bag. Were these answers to some bigger puzzle? "I was walking back through the alley, and it caught my eye. It was tucked next to the shed out back of Mac's bakery."

Connor picked up Mac's business card off Carolanne's desk. "Derek's name is written on the back of this. Looks like a cell phone number."

"I saw that. There's an address in the little book there from up in New York. That's where Derek is from, isn't it? Maybe she knew him from up there."

"It would make more sense why she came to town."

"And how she was here for like two weeks with hardly anyone noticing her."

"Two weeks?" Connor looked surprised. "How do you know she was here for that long?"

Carolanne pulled receipts out of the pile. "Look. These are all local, and they span almost two weeks."

Connor picked up the phone. "Well, let's see." He dialed the number from the back of the card.

Someone answered on the first ring.

"Is this Derek Honeycutt?" Connor asked.

"Sure is. Who's callin'?"

"This is Connor Buckham."

"Hey, man. How'd you get this number?"

"You got a few minutes? I wanted to talk to you about that."

"Sure. I'm down at the bakery. I'll be here all night."

"I'll see you in a few minutes." Connor ended the call. "Our first lead."

Carolanne was relieved Connor wasn't going to sit and wait for Scott to get the time to look into it. She tried to hide her excitement, but it wasn't easy.

"I'll just ask Derek a few questions on my way to take this stuff down to Scott at the station." He went into his office and came out with a Piggly Wiggly bag.

"What's the plastic bag for?" Carolanne asked.

"I'm not carrying that girly pocketbook down Main Street. What would people think?" He stuffed the tote bag inside the Piggly Wiggly bag and headed for the door.

She started to call him back and tell him about Gina being at her dad's that night, but something stopped her. *I'm sorry I didn't tell you everything, Connor. Please find something that'll prove it doesn't even matter.*

# ❖ Chapter Eighteen ❖

Carolanne was kind of sorry she'd made the commitment to meet Anita at four o'clock today. Yoga seemed like the last thing she should be spending her time doing, but then again, if she ever needed some help relaxing, today was the day.

She changed into a pair of black yoga pants and a T-shirt, then grabbed a water bottle and headed down the block. Feeling a little nervous, she tried to imagine herself stretching into those poses Anita had done that afternoon. She'd made it look so easy, but Carolanne had a feeling it was going to be harder than it looked.

When Carolanne got to the bright-orange building, the doors were shut. Good. She hoped that meant Anita had cranked up the air-conditioning. The other day it had been hot when she'd stopped in. Hot yoga wasn't exactly her idea of a good time.

She reached for the door and pulled, but it was locked.

The gray paint bucket that had propped the door open the other day was just inside the door. Carolanne cupped her hands on either side of her face and peered into the space. She knocked on the door and waited.

She checked her watch, but she wasn't early. Maybe Anita was just running late, or maybe she was down at the bakery with Mac. Carolanne turned and headed for the bakery. She saw Connor coming up the block.

"Hey, wait for me." She ran to catch up with him. "I thought you'd have already come and gone from here by now."

"I got hung up talking to Teddy. When did you change clothes? Are you getting ready to work out?"

There was no mistaking her outfit for anything else. "Don't look so surprised."

"Sorry, but I am."

"I met Anita the other day. She's really sweet. I was supposed to meet her today at four down where she's opening the studio. She offered to teach me some yoga moves that I could practice until she starts classes in August."

"You?"

"Yeah, me. It was your idea. You said I needed to find some interests."

Connor looked skeptical. "But you never listen to what I say."

"That is not true."

"Did you already quit? Doesn't look like you even broke a sweat."

"No. She wasn't down there. I'm betting she lost track of time, and she's down here with Mac."

Connor opened the door to the bakery, and Carolanne stepped inside in front of him.

Derek wheeled a cake on a cart toward the back door. "Come on in. Good timing, Connor," he called out. "Come give me a hand. It's way easier with two people."

Connor handed the Piggly Wiggly bag off to Carolanne and stepped around the counter. He held the back door open for Derek to wheel out the cake. "Where's this cake headed?"

Carolanne hung back and waited as Derek moved the cart slowly on the bumpy pavement. "This one is for a guy up near Richmond. Dad absolutely hates the animated cakes, but I love making them. A perfect blend of carpentry and confectionery."

"Well, that cake you made for Garrett was pretty awesome. I want you to make my cake if I can ever snag a bride."

Derek rolled his eyes. "Don't think a guy like you would have much trouble in that area. But I'm ready whenever you are." He pulled a single key on a key chain from his pocket and unlocked the back doors of the van.

"A rental?"

"Yeah, had to rent a van. Dad and Anita took off in ours. They left me kind of high and dry. Not only do I have to deliver everything, but I had to finish the two cakes he hadn't completed when he left. Sure wish he'd give some notice when he's going to pull that crap."

"Where'd they go?"

Derek shook his head. "Heck if I know. He was supposed to open the store Saturday morning, and when I got here that afternoon as I'd promised, the place was locked up tight as a tick. I had no idea he'd gone out of town. It must have been last minute. Anita's always pulling stuff like that. She left a message on my voice mail."

Connor watched as Derek pumped the hydraulics pedal on the cart to line it up with the height of the back of the van. "I thought you two were close—you and Anita. Your dad was talking about that."

"Whatever. I'm just nice to her because Dad seems to like her and all the attention she gives him. She's a little loopy with all the yoga stuff. She keeps trying to get us to make gluten-free and sugar-free stuff. I'm like, it's a bakery, not a health-food store."

"I hear ya." Connor grabbed his end of the fabric-covered board and helped Derek slide it into the back. "You used to live in New York, right?"

Derek said, "Yeah." Then he moved the cart out of the way and positioned wax paper–covered foam blocks on each side of the cake board.

"Did you ever live on Flatbush Avenue?" Connor watched for a reaction. Sometimes just leaving enough quiet space would lead folks to say more than they should, but Derek didn't say anything.

"No. We lived in Bushwick. Nowhere near Flatbush Ave."

"Did you hear about that girl they found at the pond?"

"I did. Everyone is talking about it."

"I think it was a friend of yours."

Derek stopped and turned to face Connor. "Of mine? I don't have many friends around here. Who?"

"Gina Edwards."

Derek dropped the key. "Shut up. No way. She was just here the other day. Friday, I guess." He scooped up the key and closed the doors of the van.

"It was her."

"She was really nice. I didn't know her all that well. She'd been hanging around for a week or so, mostly asking questions about Dad and the town. That's messed up she wound up dead."

*You got that right.* Connor followed Derek back into the shop, where Carolanne was waiting. "I think you got stood up for yoga, Carolanne."

Derek said, "Don't feel bad. It's not personal. She's always doing stuff on the fly. They left Saturday. I have no idea when they'll even be back."

Carolanne looked disappointed. "Well, darn. I was really looking forward to it, too. I hope your dad gets back in time to do the cake for Jill's grand opening, if they're still going to have it."

"He's already got the decorations started. Don't worry about the cake. If he doesn't make it back, I'll finish it up," Derek said.

Connor took the bag from Carolanne. "Gina had your cell number in her bag."

"Yep. That's hers. She made that tote bag. Where'd you get it?"

Connor lifted the huge yellow-and-silver bag. "This? She made it?"

"Yeah. That was her thing. She'd sit and fold wrappers and turn them into those bags. They're pretty cool. She made me a case for my iPad out of Reese's Peanut Butter Cups wrappers. I always have a ton of them because I like to use them in the cupcakes. People love them. She asked me to save them for her. I thought she was a nut, but then she came back the next day with the iPad cover for me. It's really cool." He gazed off like he got lost in the memory for a moment.

"Sorry, man," Connor said.

"Me, too."

Carolanne saw the pain on the boy's face. "Any idea what could've happened to her? Was she afraid? Worried?"

"Mostly sad. Quiet. I can't imagine her being the type to make anyone mad. Like I said, she was nice."

Connor's phone rang. He gave Derek a nod. "I've got to get this. We'll catch you later," he said as he answered the phone.

Connor and Carolanne headed out of the bakery and down the block as Connor talked on the phone.

Carolanne spotted Scott getting out of his car and nudged Connor.

He ended his call and yelled out to Scott. "Hey, man. We were just coming to see you."

Scott held the front door open for them. "Come on back. There's a call I need to take, but come with me." He led the way and punched the speakerphone button on his desk.

A gravelly voice came on the line. "Medical examiner."

"It's Sheriff Calvin. What've you got?" he said into the phone.

"Got some information for you on your Jane Doe," said the medical examiner.

Scott winked at Carolanne. "Our Jane Doe has got a name now. Gina."

"That's good," said the medical examiner. "The cause of death was drowning."

"Ha," Connor laughed out loud, then whispered, "don't need a degree to figure that out."

Carolanne nudged and shushed him.

"Got anything useful? We found her floating in the pond with a turtle perched on her leg. That was sort of a dead giveaway," Scott said.

"Good one. Dead giveaway," said the ME with a booming laugh. "I'm going to use that."

Scott made a face. "The humor is free. What else did you learn?"

"Your girl was unconscious before she went in the water. She didn't fall in. She was dragged down to the water. The bruises tell that story pretty clearly."

"That changes things," Scott said. "Not an accident?"

The ME's voice lost the silly undertones. "The car hitting her may have been an accident, but her ending up in the pond and drowning—no, there was no accident about that."

Scott picked up the pen from his desk and rolled it between his fingers as he spoke. "So she was hurt and maybe unconscious before she got dragged to the pond?"

"Yes, she was alive when she went under. Probably unconscious, but the injuries she sustained could have been fatal, too, if she didn't get immediate care."

"What kind of damage are we talking?"

"Injuries to her rib and chest area that resulted in a torn aorta due to blunt force and some extremity injuries. It's not uncommon for pedestrians to sustain primary injuries from the impact of the vehicle. Secondary injuries occur when the impact with the vehicle forces the pedestrian into contact with the road or something else. Looks like she got it good, and she was facing the vehicle when it hit her. It broke her pelvis. Looks like she tried catching herself when she fell backward, which explains the bruising on her back and tailbone and the broken wrist, too."

Carolanne rubbed her wrist.

Scott glanced over his notes. "You're speculating that she was hit by a car or injured, but not dead? Then dumped there in the pond? Drowning was the cause of death."

"Injuries are consistent with that."

"Guess they weren't taking any chances." Scott tapped the pen against the wooden desktop. "It also means it could have happened anywhere."

Carolanne said, "Except that we know she was here in Adams Grove."

Connor spoke up. "It's dark on that part of Route 58. If she'd been walking, it could have been an accident, and if the initial injuries were sustained on Route 58, there's no telling where the driver is. Could have been anyone from any-where cruising down that stretch of road."

"True." Scott frowned. "Can you determine an approximate time of death?"

The ME answered, "You found her at about one thirty in the afternoon. I'd say that she was in the water about five and a half hours. Maybe around eight-o-five a.m."

"You can get that precise?"

He laughed. "No. Scientifically, I came to the conclusion of four to six hours, but honestly, her watch stopped at eight-o-five. Probably when the water seeped into the mechanism. I'm guessing it probably ran for a little while, but the water would have caused the battery to fail."

Scott put the phone on mute. "This guy drives me nuts. He's one weird dude, but he does know his stuff." He took the phone back off mute. "Had to have happened early that morning, then. Thanks, man. Keep me posted."

"I will," the medical examiner said. "Don't think there's much more I can tell you on this one."

Scott ended the call. "We're making progress."

"I think we've got something else that will help." Connor handed the bag over to Scott. "Carolanne found this. It belonged to Gina, and Derek Honeycutt knew the girl, too."

Scott pulled the items out of the tote one at a time. "Gina, what were you looking for? Who didn't want you to find it? Or was this really all one big accident?"

Carolanne folded her arms across her chest.

Connor wondered the same thing. Could it have just been some kind of random accident that she died right here in the same town, within a mile of the other tragedy her family had endured in the seventies?

It seemed a little too convenient, but somehow that seemed more comforting than thinking there was a killer among them.

# ❖ Chapter Nineteen ❖

Feeling a little zoned out, Connor wondered what Carolanne was feeling as they walked back to the office. It was unsettling to hear the details come together about the mystery woman with the turtle on her leg. When she was a mystery woman, the death hadn't seemed nearly as bad—now that she had a name and ties to the town, it felt personal.

They hadn't said a word the whole walk back, and Carolanne went upstairs to her apartment instead of back to work. Connor went to his office and forced himself to put his mind on work so that he might elevate his mood. He worked up the papers for Mac. It wasn't his place to make him wait, he'd decided.

Once that was done, Connor went and pulled the paperwork on the Dixon farm and reviewed it again. If Gina truly had been the daughter of Lindsey Dixon, then the decisions on the Dixon farm would have been in her hands. If there were no other heirs, that property would go to the town of Adams Grove. *Who stood to gain from that?* Just about anyone with the cash to buy the property. It was definitely prime real estate. Plus, if they logged the land, there'd be a heckuva windfall just from that.

He tucked the paperwork back in the folder and filed it away. He spent the rest of the afternoon responding to inquiries, but his mind kept going back to the cute redhead upstairs packing to move. For a tiny little gal, she clomped around like an elephant.

Nostalgia swept over him again. *What is it about weddings and accidents that make people reexamine their own lives?* Losing Mom this year hadn't helped, either. Connor opened his desk drawer and grabbed the keys to the lockbox area where they stored records. It didn't take him but a moment to find what he was looking for. He knew exactly where it was.

He pulled the original DVD from the file and walked back to his office. He dimmed the lights and stuck the disc in the DVD player built into his credenza.

Pearl Clemmons came into view. He fast-forwarded through most of the beginning of the video addendum to her will, then pressed the play button.

He laughed out loud when she accused him of calling her a pimp-granny. *I never said that!*

Although, in hindsight, it was probably a pretty accurate description. Once Pearl had a couple matched in her mind, she was like a pit bull about letting go of the idea. That old gal was a pistol. If Jill was even half as feisty as Pearl, Garrett would have his hands full.

Memories of the day Pearl Clemmons had spent in his office were crystal clear. The recording wasn't even ten minutes in total, but she'd spent nearly the whole day in his office. She'd even coerced him into buying her lunch on his dime. She must have started and restarted a hundred times. She was playing actress and producer, shouting "cut" and "roll 'em" like she knew what it meant.

*You gave me a run for my money, Pearl.*

Finally, once she'd said what she wanted to say—the *way* she wanted it to be said—she'd surprised him with that last little add-on. He hit play again and watched as she fussed into the camera. The video moved off Pearl, but only for a second. Then it came right back into focus on her.

Pearl had gone off on him for stopping the recording before she said she was done. He'd pressed the record button out of sheer exhaustion in hopes that the day would finally end.

"Jill, dear, tell sweet Carolanne that she needs to get her butt back to Adams Grove. She doesn't need to let that daddy of hers keep her from getting her a good man right here in town. Fact is, he's been doing pretty good staying on the wagon." Pearl hunched forward, leaning on her elbows. "I know she and Connor would make a great couple."

He winced at what was coming next. He remembered the way she shook her crooked finger at him.

"No, you cannot take that off. This is my last wish to my granddaughter. You just roll that 'til I'm done."

Turning back to the camera, Pearl smiled so sweetly that nobody would ever believe how bossy she could be. "I know Carolanne can wrangle this one. They're just alike. He's got that girl in Chicago or California, some big city somewhere, but God knows, if she ain't here yet, she never will be."

She'd been talking about Katherine, and Lord knows she was right. *Too bad I didn't realize it back then.*

"I love you, dear. You and Garrett find your happiness. The rest will all fall in place." She blew a final kiss into the camera. "Now I'm done, damn it. It's not like I was paying you by the inch of tape. You can shut it—"

The screen went blank in mid-sentence.

He skipped back to the beginning of that section and replayed it.

Pearl had been right about everything.

Right about Ben. *He's a good man. No crime falling apart after losing the love of your life.* Right about him and Carolanne being just alike. *We fell into an easy routine in no time. I think I was in love with her before the first week was out.*

Right about Katherine, too.

• • •

"Hellooo."

Connor turned off the television, dropped the remote on his desk, and went to the reception area of the office. Jill stood there in jeans and a T-shirt that had seen better days.

"Hi, Jill. You're a mess. Is this what happens to women after they get married?" Connor walked over to hug her but hesitated. "I was kidding, but I don't think I've ever seen you such a sight."

"I know. I've been unpacking pottery all day. It was a dusty mess, then Clyde's tail knocked my soda can off the table, and now I'm wearing dirty-soda tie-dye."

"Well," he tried to reason, "it looks crafty."

"That's a backhanded compliment, if I've ever heard one. Where's my partner in crime?"

"She's upstairs packing."

"Upstairs?" Jill pointed toward the second floor. "As in like she took off a day of work, upstairs?"

"Yep."

"That's a first."

"I know. I'm beginning to take her being so excited about this move personally."

"Maybe you should." Jill leaned against the desk. "So, how are things going with you two?"

"I figured you'd be in a better position to tell me that."

"No. Not really. I don't know anything. On a good day, she holds her cards close to the vest, but I have to admit I've been a little all about me lately with the wedding."

"You've got to be exhausted. I still can't believe you didn't move one of the dates—the grand opening or the wedding date. Two major life events in back-to-back weekends is crazy, even for you."

"I couldn't change the grand opening. It really has to be Memorial Day weekend at the latest, and we'd already picked the wedding date. You know Pearl always said changing dates is bad luck. I couldn't chance that."

*Of course you couldn't.*

"Remember when they moved the Fourth of July celebration to the weekend before, thinking it would be easier for the kids? Rained out. Remember when we moved our camping trip out a week so we could go to that concert? Poison ivy. Remember—"

"Yeah, yeah. I remember."

"Why tempt fate?" she said.

"I don't think even fate could come between you and Garrett now."

"Gosh, I hope not. That whole dead body thing has me pretty creeped out. I Googled it, but there's nothing on the Internet about what it means to have a dead body float up during your wedding reception. I think I'm a first."

"It's got to be better luck for you than it was for the girl. I guess you get to set the precedent for this one. You can start your own Wikipedia page."

"I think I'll pass on that golden opportunity."

Connor shook his head. "Could have been your fifteen minutes of fame."

"No, thanks. Have you talked to Scott? Has he figured out who she was yet?"

"As a matter of fact, I have and he has. Evidently, that girl had been in the library the other day. Same day Carolanne was in there. She was the daughter of Lindsey Dixon."

"From the Dixon farm? The Old Mill Pond Dixons?"

"The same."

"No one has been back to that place in years."

"I know. I manage the trust."

"It's so sad." Jill stood. "I hope they figure out what happened. You know once the *County Gazette* comes out with the story, other papers might pick it up. I hope we get past the grand opening before they do. This is when it's nice that the paper only comes out every other week."

"True," Connor agreed. "It could work to your favor and keep the bigger presses off your back."

"I'm praying for that," she admitted, but she looked worried. "Well, I'm going to go up and check in on Carolanne. I'll put a good word in for you."

*Am I that transparent?* Connor watched Jill go upstairs, then listened to the girly squeals come through the old ventilation system. Everything in this building echoed.

He shoved his hands in his pockets, wondering what next week was going to be like around here.

"You took a day off?" Jill stood with her hands on her hips.

"I know! Aren't you proud of me?"

"I think I am, but I'm not sure." Jill broke into a smile. "Is this my best friend, or did somebody body snatch you?"

"Stop." Carolanne grabbed Jill by the hand and dragged her over to the couch. Once she moved a stack of empty boxes out of the way, they sat down.

"Look at you whipping through this place like there's no tomorrow," Jill said. "You're almost as organized as I'd be."

"See how I even marked them with what the contents are? I'm having a ball with it."

"You'd said you were going to hire someone to do it for you."

"I changed my mind."

"I see that. I don't know what's gotten into you."

"It's all good. I've never been better. So, what are you doing here?"

"Garrett was running late for a meeting down here with the zoning guy, so I gave him a lift. He won't be long. I'm meeting him for lunch at the diner"—she flipped her wrist—"in about ten minutes. Since I was here, I wanted to ask you something. Your dad said you picked him up from the hospital. He said he's going to try to come back to work on Wednesday. Does that sound like what the doctor said?"

She nodded. "He'll have to take it easy, but they say he should be fine."

"OK. I just didn't want to take a chance."

"Thanks. I really appreciate that."

"Really? I mean, I just wasn't sure how you'd be feeling about everything. I know you were hesitant about me hiring him in the first place."

"I was, but you know, Milly was right the other day. Do you remember what she said?"

"That people don't swallow pins?"

"That, too, but no. She'd said, 'Your future will be as good as you let it be.'"

"So?"

"So, I've been hanging on to a lot of bad stuff for way too long. I realized that when I saw Dad's car wrapped around that post. Did you see it?"

"They'd cleared it by the time Garrett and I got out of there."

"It was awful. I can't believe he didn't get killed. I've been so mad at him for so long. I guess it just became habit. It's wrong."

"That wreck must've been bad."

"I can't even tell you how bad. Words can't describe what it looked like. I'm not sure how he got so lucky, but I'm not going to take the second chance lightly."

"Wow. OK. Now you're really freaking me out."

"That's OK. I'm freaking myself out a little, too. Jill, I feel so different. I don't know, but maybe it's letting all that anger finally go that's making me feel so alive. Whatever it is, I'm grateful for it. I feel like a lot of bad stuff that's been weighing me down has just been swept away."

"Well, that's good."

Carolanne took in a deep breath. "I'm going to miss this place."

"This place or living with Connor?"

"I'm not living *with* Connor. I'm only living here because you corralled all of your fiancé's time to finish the artisan center instead of my house!"

"True, but I kind of did you a favor."

"How do you figure that?"

"Because it gave you more time to realize that Pearl was right about you and Connor. Besides, now you can fill up all those extra bedrooms in that house with little redheaded babies. And before you start denying it"—Jill checked her watch—"I also need a little favor, but first let me say that Connor gets my vote."

"OK. I'm not sure you get a vote, but I've recorded it just in case. What is it you need from me?"

"Part of my grant requires we do some statistics

and stuff for the grand opening. I know you were going to come and be on hand in case we got too busy, but I was wondering if you'd help me with the numbers. You were always a much better math girl than me."

"No problem. I'm still planning to come over Thursday night and Friday night to help you get ready, too."

"That would be great." She got up and headed to the door. "Will Connor be coming with you Thursday?"

"Wait and see." Carolanne wasn't sure herself what the answer to that question was. "Now, you better leave, or you'll be the one who's late."

# ❖ Chapter Twenty ❖

Connor was shocked when he walked into Carolanne's apartment on Tuesday morning. The empty boxes that had been stacked all over the place now rested neatly in rows four boxes high, labels out, near the door. Not one picture hung on the wall, and nary a knickknack was left unpacked.

"Wow." He turned in a circle, flipping the daily crossword on his leg. "Is that my imagination? Do I smell coffee, or did you already pack the coffeepot?"

Carolanne walked up to him with a grin of amusement and a paper cup of coffee in each hand. "Hope you don't mind the disposable cups, but I was on a roll."

"I guess I should be flattered you thought to keep two cups out."

"You should," she agreed.

He took the cup of coffee. "Did you stay up all night?"

"Come sit. I don't have any stuff, but I still have furniture." She sat on the couch, and he sat down at the other end of it. She pulled her bare feet up onto the sofa and sipped her coffee. "I was up until about three, but I slept good knowing it was done."

"It couldn't wait until today?"

She shook her head.

He caught her uneasy glance.

"I've got something I have to do today. It's not going to be pleasant."

"What's going on?" he asked, placing his cup on the table in front of the sofa. "Anything I can help with?"

She groaned and took another sip of coffee. "I'm so dreading it, but I know I have to do it." She put the cup down on the table. "When I picked up Dad at the hospital, Scott was there talking to him about the . . ."

"Murder?"

"Don't call it that."

"I think it's clear now that's what it was." He hesitated, measuring her for a moment. Clearly she hadn't realized until just this minute that she was going to be living so close to where such a heinous crime was committed.

"I can't think of it that way." She shook her hands like that would shoo away the bad news. "Anyway, Scott showed Dad the picture of Gina, and he said he didn't recognize her."

He stared at her, baffled. "OK? No one in this whole town except you and Doris recognized her. Where's this going?"

She sat up as if preparing to make a speech. "I saw Gina at his house."

Connor cut his gaze to her.

"I know. It doesn't make sense. I was over that way the night after the rehearsal dinner, and she walked right out his front door and then drove away in his car."

Connor leaned back and sized her up. *How did Ben know Gina? He isn't the type to lie. There has to be something more to this.*

"I've got to tell Scott. I tried to yesterday, but then he got called away, and then I talked myself out of it."

"What did Ben say when you asked him about it?" He leaned his forearms on his legs.

She shrank back. "I didn't ask him about it, but he didn't offer up any information, either."

*You don't think . . . You couldn't . . .* "Do you think he did something to that girl?"

"I didn't say that."

"No," Connor said, unable to hold back the bitter feeling in his gut. "But you just said you were going to take the information to the sheriff without even talking to him. Carolanne, he's your father, for God's sake."

She jerked back like he'd just slapped her. "I'm not judging the situation. I'm passing along information."

"Listen to yourself. That's bull, and you know it. Your father would never so much as hurt a fly, much less a person."

She shrugged. "I'm not the bad guy here."

*You just might be.* "If you take that information to Scott, he'll have to check into it, and then he'll probably take your father in—and you and I both know that without any other suspects and probably no alibi, they are going to hold him. It's not going to look good. If you won't talk to him, I damn sure will."

"What would I say to him? I can't call my father a liar." She gave him a challenging look. "Seriously, you think I should just call him a flat-out liar?"

"But you can call him a murderer?" He slapped a hand on the arm of the couch. "You are unbelievable."

She got up and walked to the window. "I know. Or I don't. I really don't know what to think, Connor." With arms wrapped around herself, she turned to face Connor. "You don't understand. I was trying to make a positive move. I went over there, and instead of making a forward step, that girl walked out of his house." She closed her eyes. "It was like I'd been replaced."

"That's weak, Carolanne. Your relationship, or lack thereof one, was by your choice. You know that."

"It still hurt. She was using his phone, his car, sleeping at his house. It was like a regular little family over there."

"Did you see them together?"

Carolanne shook her head. "But it was at his house."

"Did you talk to her?"

"No, but I heard her talking on the phone to someone—her boyfriend back home, I guess—and she clearly said that Ben had let her stay there."

Connor felt like she was spinning figure eights around him. "Let me get this straight. You didn't talk to your dad. You didn't talk to the girl. But you saw her and overheard her whole conversation on what you say was your dad's cell phone."

"Right."

"How did you hear all that if you didn't even talk to them? None of this is making any sense at all."

She dropped her head back. "I was nervous about taking that first step, and as I walked up the sidewalk, the porch light came on. I jumped behind the bush at the end of his driveway. I saw her from there."

Connor couldn't help laughing. "Oh, this just gets better and better."

"I'm not proud of how I reacted, but I sure as heck don't know how I would have reacted if I'd been one minute earlier and she'd answered my dad's door!"

Ben had been his friend for a long time. He was a kind man, and if Gina was staying there, he had a good reason. Heck, she could have been one of the people he helped through AA. It was no secret he still went to those meetings. They could have met there, but talking to Carolanne when she was in this state of mind wasn't going to get him far. "If that's true, if that's the case, someone else saw Gina over there, and you can rest assured it's just a matter of time before Scott puts two and two together. You're not doing yourself, or your dad, any favors by not getting to the bottom of this."

"I can't."

"You're stubborn and selfish, Carolanne. He could wind up in jail."

"I'll trust the system."

A laugh of frustration belted out of him like a crazy man. "Carolanne, you and I have seen plenty of cases that have been won for the wrong reasons. I'm not taking that chance. He's my friend. If you won't help him, I will."

"Well, I guess it's good to know where your allegiance lies. You should probably leave."

Connor stood. "I was thinking exactly the same thing." He walked out the door and slammed it so hard that one of the boxes stacked near the door toppled to the floor.

# ❖ Chapter Twenty-One ❖

The next day, Carolanne stood in the middle of the living room in her new house. She hadn't seen or heard from Connor since the big blowup, but she'd successfully moved every single box out of the apartment without his help.

Even though there wasn't one piece of furniture here yet, it already felt like home—besides that the tension with Connor was too much. *This is where I belong.* She tried to picture her furniture and the pictures she'd picked out for each accent wall.

Three fast raps pounded on her front door.

*My first company!*

She jogged through the space, sliding to the door on the hardwood floors in her socks. Without even bothering to look through the peephole, she swung the door open, expecting to see Jill and Garrett since she'd called them earlier about using the trailer.

She froze for a two-count. "Dad? What are . . . ? Come in. How are you feeling today?" *Did Connor tell him?*

He looked like he was stuck in neutral, bobbing forward a little but not taking a step. "I saw your car. I hope you don't mind me stopping by. If it's not a good—"

"It's fine. Are you OK?"

"I'm fine. Fine." His mouth kept moving, but it was like he was on mute, because nothing was coming out.

"Come in. I'll show you around." She forced a smile and stepped aside so he could enter. "Garrett lent me his guys. They are bringing the furniture over later. I'm just waiting on them." It was good that Garrett had offered them up because there was no way she was going to ask for Connor's help after yesterday.

He looked nervous but not mad. How would she explain herself if Connor had already told him with his own personal slant on things, like she was a villainess?

"I brought something for you." He turned and walked back outside, and for a moment, she thought maybe the knock to the head had him totally wonked out and he was leaving, but instead, he squatted to lift something from the deacon's bench on the porch. The large box had been labeled at one time, but the years had faded the black marker past recognition. He carried the awkwardly wide box inside, turning sideways to fit through the front door.

"Is it heavy? I can help you with that."

"It's not heavy." Ben hoisted the box up with his knee to get a better grip.

She brushed a hand through her hair. "You didn't need to bring me anything."

"I know. It's something I wanted you to have, though, and now seemed like a good time. Something that seems perfect as you start another phase of your life."

She walked up behind him. "You can set it down back here on the kitchen counter."

He followed her through the living room to the kitchen and set the box down, glancing around the spacious open floor plan. "You've done real good for yourself, kiddo."

He walked over to the French doors. "You've got a great view of the pastures and the pond. You've worked really hard for this. I'm proud of you, Carolanne. I know I've never told you that enough."

"Thanks," she answered softly.

"Your mother—she'd have been proud of the woman you've become. You're so much like her. Strong."

The love showed in his green eyes when he spoke. *You still love her as much today as you did when I was a little girl.*

He must have been nervous, because he started talking faster and faster, but facing this overdue conflict scared the heck out of her, too. She could tell he was struggling to maintain control of his emotions. "I know I can't take any credit for the wonderful woman you are. I'll never get those years I wasted back. It's a tough pill to swallow. I'm glad you did so well in spite of me."

"Neither one of us should live in the past."

He looked relieved. "I'm glad to hear you say that."

"It's time we both tried to move forward." *I'm dying to ask you about Gina. How can I ask you without you knowing I was there? Maybe your vision just wasn't clear after the accident. That could be it.*

"Agreed. Won't keep me from thanking the good Lord for Pearl stepping in the way she did, though. Don't know what would've happened if she hadn't been there for the both of us all those years."

"I miss her."

"Me, too. You know, I worry about you being alone. With Jill and Garrett getting married, I've been thinking about that even more. Have you?"

"A little."

"You need more than just work in your life. You deserve someone special to share the good times with and to be there in the not-so-good ones."

"I've really never thought of myself as the marrying kind." *Until recently.* "I'm happy the way things are. I'm going to start taking yoga classes, and I'm going to be really busy decorating my house. I'll probably help Jill out with things at the artisan center. It's all good."

"That's not the kind of thing I was talking about. I know I didn't set a fine example of men, but don't hold that against the rest of the world.

The love I shared with your mother was more important to me than my own life. I'm sorry I let you down in the process. So, so sorry." Tears glistened in his eyes.

"Everyone mourns differently."

"I didn't go about it in too healthy a way. I'm sorry for that. I don't expect you to ever forgive me, but I hope you find a love like I had with your mother. It's true it tore me right out of the frame when I lost her, but I spent the best days of my life with her. I wouldn't trade a single one of them."

*It scares me to death to think how much that hurt.* "So what's in the box?"

Ben's voice softened. "It was your mother's. The wedding—it got me to thinking."

She stared at the box, then glanced up at him.

"Open it," Ben urged her.

Carolanne raised her hand, then hesitantly tugged on the tape. It had lost its stickiness over the years and pulled back easily. She lifted one of the cardboard flaps, and the top of the box sprung open. Tissue paper, folded neatly across the top, had yellowed from years of heat and dust.

She glanced at her dad, wondering what was in the box. She moved the paper gently to the side. A small gasp was all she could manage.

She laid her hands on the fine fabric. Unlike the tissue paper, the dress had remained white, and the intricate needlework was simple but elegant.

"I can still picture the first moment I laid eyes

on your mother in that dress." A smile and far-away look came across his face. "I'd never seen a more beautiful woman."

Carolanne lifted the dress out of the box. "It's lovely."

"There are a few other special things she'd put away for you in there, too." He shoved his hands into his pockets. "I know it's long overdue."

"This isn't about that stupid bouquet, is it? That's—"

"No, Carolanne. It's not about you catching the bouquet."

"But—"

"Your mother would've wanted you to have it a long time ago."

"She was about my size?"

"Yes. I think you're exactly the same height that she was, too."

Carolanne went to the hall closet and found a heavy wooden suit hanger. She carried it back over and slipped the hanger into the shoulders of the gown, then hung it from the top of the door. She stepped back and took in a long breath. "It's so pretty."

"Not real fancy. Your momma wasn't like that, but she looked absolutely stunning walking down the aisle in that dress."

"It's beautiful." She tugged the hem of the tea-length gown, pulling some of the wrinkles free. "Timeless, really. Dad, I can't take this from you."

"Don't be silly. She'd want you to have it, Carolanne. Our wedding day was the best day of our lives. I hope it brings you the same kind of joy we shared."

Tears welled, but she was maintaining control.

"You might never wear it. That's perfectly fine, but you should have it." He reached over and took her hand in his own.

His weathered hand looked tan and rough against her delicate skin.

A sob caught in her throat.

"It's OK, honey." He pulled her close and hugged her. "I never had one second thought about getting married to your mother. No cold feet. No desire for a crazy bachelor party. I knew how lucky I was to find my perfect match. But I didn't expect the impact of seeing her step around the corner in that dress. She took my breath away. Literally. If your Uncle Reggie hadn't been standing next to me, I'd have landed on the ground like one of them fainting goats. *Thunk.*"

She laughed though the tears still fell. "Look . . . My hands are sweating just thinking about it now."

"Don't be afraid of love. It's a good thing."

"It's a hassle."

"No. It's a blessing." Ben walked back over to the box. "These are pictures from our wedding day. I'd never even seen some of these pictures until the other day when I got this box out and went through it. They are of your mom and her girlfriends at the bridal shower and getting dressed the morning of the wedding. Some of them are funny."

He pulled one from the stack. "Look at this one. She has a garter on her head. Now, that's funny. I don't care who you are. That's funny."

Carolanne took the picture and held it in her hands. "Oh my gosh."

"I forgot how silly she could be."

She exchanged a smile with him. "We do look alike."

"Oh yeah. Very much so. You've always favored her."

Carolanne flipped through the crisp black pages of the photo album. The pictures had faded over time, but each was tucked between little corner mounts, and most had the dates and a caption under them. "Look how small the church was back then. Oh my goodness. It looks so little."

Ben shook his head. "The addition on the church didn't come for quite a while after we got married."

"Dad, are you sure you want to let go of all of this?"

"I want you to have it. You need to know, and remember, how happy our life was. You're hesitating about men and relationships. I know it. I can see it. You need to live your life without worrying about the what-ifs. A safe life can keep you from finding and living the real happiness you're meant to find."

She hugged the box of memorabilia to her chest. "Sometimes I have trouble remembering her. I don't want to forget. Especially the good things."

"You were young. It was hard. I wasn't there. I wish I had been."

"It's easier to remember the bad things, but don't." She raised a hand. "Don't, Dad. We need to just leave it in the past. You can't live your whole life being sorry. I can't live mine being mad at you. It's just wrong."

"I want to be there for you. I want to know you don't hate me."

"I don't hate you. I really don't. One step at a time."

"It'll be nice to have you so close. I mean, with me working right over at the artisan center and all, I could help you with your yard."

"That would be great. I don't know anything about that stuff."

"I could teach you. You even have room for a garden if you choose to go that route. Nothing like digging your hands in good rich soil to make you appreciate the bounty of nature, and what an awesome reward you get from a garden."

"I think for now I'd just like to have some grass."

"You see what I did with the artisan center grass."

"I know. That place looks like a golf course."

"Thanks. I can do that here, too."

"That would be amazing. Thanks."

"I know you want to get unpacked, and I don't want you to feel like you need to go through this stuff now. I just wanted you to have it. I love you, Carolanne."

"Thanks, Dad."

He headed toward the front door.

"Dad, wait."

He stopped a few feet from the door and turned.

At this moment, he looked ten years younger. Years of stress that had hung between them had lifted. *Do I dare take a chance on ruining this moment?* "I need to ask you something."

"Sure. Anything."

*Am I sabotaging the progress we just made? God, I hope not. Please have a good answer.* As casually as she could manage, she started, "The other morning, when I came to pick you up in the hospital, Scott was there."

"Yeah. You don't think I was drinking, do you?"

"No, no." Although she *had* been guilty of that, she really didn't need to go there now. "Um, this is about that girl who died in the pond, the one they found during the reception. I overheard you tell Scott you didn't know her, but Dad . . ."

She closed her eyes. It was too hard to look him in the eye and ask.

"I know you knew her. I saw her come out of your house the night before they found her."

There. She'd said it.

Tears streamed down her face, and there was no way she could stop them. Fear, hope, confusion— a mixture of emotion left her standing there wondering if she'd done the right thing by asking. *Do I really want to know?*

She leveled her gaze on him. He didn't look guilty, but he did look defeated.

He hesitated, seeming to measure her for a moment. "I shouldn't have lied to Scott. Don't even know why I did, except that it was such a shock."

He looked like he might pass out. His voice shook. "I need some air. Can we sit on the porch?"

She nodded and followed him out to the only piece of furniture she had, the deacon's bench.

He sat down and she sat next to him. He took her hand in his.

"I can promise you, Carolanne, I had nothing to do with that girl's death."

"Why was she at your house? What's the connection?" *Are you her father? Oh God, I can't ask if he cheated on Mom.*

"Well, none to start with."

"That doesn't make sense."

"I'd never met her. I knew her mom. When I

243

saw her, I knew instantly she was Lindsey's daughter. It was like the girl I knew in high school had shown up on my couch."

"On your couch?"

"Yeah. That's how I knew how to get into the back sliding door. Gina had been breaking into my house while I was at work. I had no idea until that week we had five days in row of ninety-plus heat. Remember?"

She nodded, wondering how it all connected.

"Jill sent me home. Told me I could split up my time between early mornings and late evenings to beat the heat. I came home to find Gina sleeping on my couch. With her boots on, no less."

Carolanne had to laugh at that. She knew it was one of his pet peeves—feet on the furniture. "Bet that struck a nerve."

"Not one you kill someone over. I shouldn't even joke about that, but I'd have never hurt that girl. She was fighting her own set of demons. I noticed it right off, and I figured if anyone in this town owed it to someone to extend an olive branch, it was me. I let her crash at my place while she figured out her life." He turned to her with tears in his eyes. "I struggled with it. I knew I'd been a disappointing father to you, and helping her felt good and so wrong, like a slap in the face to you, and that hurt me so much. I was afraid to risk you knowing."

Her tears matched his.

"A lot of damage I've done over the years." He rubbed the tears from his eyes. "Will I ever break the damn cycle?"

"It's OK. I get it. No, it was the right thing to do. I felt the connection to her immediately, too. She was a sweet, sweet girl. Why would anyone do that to her?"

He shook his head. "It's wrong. That girl deserved answers. Not more pain."

Carolanne nodded.

"You deserve answers, too. I'm trying like heck to give them to you."

"I know. I know."

They sat there on the porch. *My new house. New beginnings.*

His voice strained. "Should we call the sheriff?"

"No. I don't think so. We don't want to give him an easy way out on this." She studied her dad's face. "You're telling the truth. I know it. Not just as your daughter—and Lord knows I need it to be the truth—but my experience with criminals tells me you're telling me the truth."

"I am. I promise you."

"I can't lie if I'm asked, but for now . . . I'm not saying anything to anyone. Maybe we can figure out what happened and it won't matter and no one needs to know." Although, in her mind, she knew that wasn't the right thing to do.

"I'll follow your lead."

"We'll figure it out."

He stood and let out a sigh. "Not exactly how I meant this to go."

"I know."

He walked midway across the porch. "You know, since we're getting everything out in the open . . ."

All her nervousness slipped back to grip her.

"About that bouquet toss. Your mom caught the bouquet at her best friend's wedding the year before we got married. She didn't know she was ready to get married, either. It might not turn out so bad. Just let nature take its course."

He turned and left before she could even respond.

She watched as he walked down her driveway and jumped back on the artisan center golf cart. With a quick twist of the key, the electric cart tooled away on the only paved street in and out of Bridle Path Estates.

Carolanne stood watching until he was out of sight.

Old feelings and thoughts tried to push to the front, but she dared them to try to foil her new plan. *Thank you, Dad. This was very thoughtful. A good step.*

As she carried the photo album that was in the box with her mom's things to the bookshelf to put it away, a picture fluttered to the ground. She picked it up, then walked to the back of the house. From there, she could see Ben round the corner and head up the incline to the main building of the artisan center. He turned off and parked alongside the small barn next to it.

She glanced at the picture in her hand. In it, her dad stood holding her mom's hand and smiling a big toothy grin. He had beautiful teeth. Must be why she'd never needed braces. It was the same smile she'd seen on him earlier. It might have been the first time she'd seen that genuine smile on his face in . . . well, a really long time. She laid her hand on the pane of glass, dreaming of walking into church between her mom and dad. She hadn't even realized Mom was sick at the time. She knew now that Mom had fought that battle with breast cancer for over two years. She'd only known Mom to be sick for two weeks before she died. She'd had no idea there was something wrong. It was why she'd become so religious about mammograms and early detection.

Time. It's something you just don't get back. *Gina sure won't have any more.*

She wrapped her arms around herself. She'd been lucky to have the ladies of Adams Grove in her life after Mom was gone. Pearl. Milly. Jill.

Milly's voice, her message, was clear in her mind. *Your future will be as good as you let it be.*

Wise woman.

# ❖ Chapter Twenty-Two ❖

The next morning, Carolanne sat at the kitchen table sipping coffee and stretching out the kinks from the day of moving. Garrett's guys had not only moved the furniture, but placed each piece in its designated spot. When she'd walked downstairs, it looked and felt like a home. With no drapes on the windows, the morning sun had woken her much earlier than she'd have preferred, but even that couldn't dampen her mood today.

She glanced over at Mom's wedding dress, still hanging on the back of the door.

*You're probably the reason I dreamed of wedding cakes and flowers all night.*

Disoriented by her new surroundings the first night in her new house, she'd even jumped out of bed on a frantic search for baby's breath and daffodils before realizing it was just a dream. At least waking up in search of flowers was better than the frantic fear of floating in the pond like that girl with a turtle nibbling on her shirt, which was the thought she'd had to push from her mind to get to sleep in the first place after staring out at the pond shimmering in the moonlight.

Sipping a hot cup of coffee in her new kitchen was nice, but she already missed the morning routine of coffee with Connor and his crossword quizzes. The banter had been a nice way to start things for a person who wasn't normally that into mornings. It was just a little too quiet here, so after just one cup of coffee she got dressed and went into the office.

She'd already been sitting at her desk nearly an hour when Connor strolled in with coffee in a paper to-go cup.

"You're here early," he said, raising his cup. "I'd have brought you a cup if I'd known."

"That's OK," Carolanne said, although she could use another cup of coffee about now. "You didn't make any this morning?"

The tension between them was thick.

"Not worth making a whole pot for one person."

"You *can* make half a pot."

"It's never as good, and it's easier to just walk down the block."

"Maybe we could go back to making it here in the office."

He shrugged.

As Connor began to walk down the hall, she felt compelled to tell him about Ben's visit. "I talked to Dad."

Connor turned around. "OK?"

She pressed her lips together. Why had it taken him being disappointed for her to do the right thing?

"And?"

"And I told him that I saw Gina."

"I'm really glad to hear that. Your dad is a good guy. I really like him, and after Mom . . . Well, I just hate to see you waste any time that you could spend with your dad. You just don't know how precious it is until it's gone."

Sadness clouded his eyes.

*You'll never stop missing your mom. I know how hard it is.* "I've been thinking a lot about that lately."

"I think about it almost every day."

"I know you do." He didn't have to say the words. She knew. "I miss your mother, too. People think it's easier for adults to lose their parents, but I don't think that's true. Your mom is your mom no matter how old you are."

"You being there with me, through it all, it meant a lot to me."

"I'm glad. I wanted to be there for you. For her."

"Did you find out why Gina was at your dad's house?"

She nodded and told him about the whole conversation.

"So he was helping her. That makes sense. Still doesn't look good, but at least we can position it right before they make a witch hunt out of the only shred of evidence they've got."

"You're a good friend."

"We could be more—you and me."

She didn't respond at first. "I know we could, but it's not going to happen, Connor. Even coming here today, after our discussion . . . It's just too much pressure on us to even try and also work together. I can't do that."

"My mom really loved you. She lit up whenever you came with me. She'd have liked the idea of us being together."

"Don't think about coulda-beens. It'll make you crazy." She knew that better than anyone. "Your momma was a special lady. Probably why you're such a great guy." She sat back in her chair. "Connor?" *I want to tell you there could be more . . .*

She stalled, taking a breath as he stared at her. "I'm going to the artisan center to help Jill tonight if you want to come along."

The Adams Grove Artisan Center looked like it was ready to be open for business by the time Carolanne and Connor strolled in that evening. Shelves were stocked and the place no longer had the echo of a new building now that the artwork covered the walls and the final pieces filled in the smaller spaces and nooks.

Everyone was starting to run out of energy and had congregated around the jewelry counter at the front entrance. Jill had opened a bottle of local Virginia wine that the store would be selling.

"Looks like we came at just the right time," Carolanne said as she and Connor took in the scene.

Jill motioned them over. "Y'all come over here and let's toast to being ready on time for the grand opening—that is, as long as Mac comes through on the cake. He's my only loose end right now."

Just as they raised their glasses, headlights cast a glow through the front windows.

"Someone's here," Connor said.

"Are you expecting anyone else?" Garrett asked Jill.

"No," Jill said, trying to see out into the parking lot. "Anyone recognize the car?"

Connor walked over to the front door and looked out the window. "It's a van."

"Is it Mac?" Carolanne asked.

Connor unlocked the front door and let Mac in. "Sure is. Look what the cat dragged in. We were just talking about you."

"You're back," Jill said. "I was beginning to wonder if I was going to have a cake!"

"Have I ever let anyone down?" Mac spoke as slowly as he walked. He never did seem to be in a hurry.

"Never, but I didn't want to be the first. Although that son of yours has your talent. Everyone is still talking about that silly cake—"

"Silly?" Garrett chimed in. "That was a kick-ass cake."

"Sorry. I meant to say groom's cake." Jill batted her eyelashes and tried to look innocent. "You missed it, Mac. When that cake started making noise and chugging smoke, Garrett's eyes lit up like a kid on Christmas morning."

"Hey, all the guys loved it," Connor admitted. "That was an awesome cake."

"The kid was professionally trained up at the culinary institute in New York. I never had any training at all. I guess he could probably teach me a thing or two. But I have to tell you, when it comes to adding motors and mechanics to a cake, that just doesn't even make sense to me. Whoever heard of needing a workshop to build parts for a cake?"

"That cake was the highlight of the day for some of us," Connor said.

Carolanne elbowed him.

"Except for the wedding cake and how pretty Carolanne looked. That dead body floating up was right memorable, too."

"Connor!" Carolanne slapped his arm.

"What?"

Mac looked surprised. "What's this about a dead body?"

"Derek didn't fill you in?"

"I guess not." Mac looked pale. "We just got back in town."

Connor went into graphic detail about the young girl floating up in the middle of the reception. "Those Johnson boys may never be the same."

"Holy hell." Mac wiped his brow. "What's happening to our town?"

"I'm pretty sure Scott'll be wanting to talk to you. They've been talking to everyone. Seems the girl's mom was Lindsey Dixon."

"Lindsey's daughter?" Mac swallowed, clearly shaken. "Lindsey and I go way back. We were best friends all through school." He wrung his hands. "Dead?"

"Yes. It's been a shock for us all." Jill got up from her chair. "Sit down."

Mac took her seat. Sweat beaded on his forehead.

Jill tried to lighten the moment. "See what happens when you leave town? The whole place falls apart."

"Yeah. Makes me feel a little squeamish."

"Sorry. Well, on a brighter subject," Garrett piped up, "I'm already planning a pretty cool idea for the grand opening of Bridle Path Estates once we sell all the lots. A neighborhood-warming celebration with the most amazing animated cake ever. I can't wait to run it by Derek."

"He'll be thrilled. I think that kid might even get up early in the morning to make those things." Mac rolled his eyes. "That's saying a lot, by the way."

"We missed you at the wedding," Jill said. "But thanks for getting everything set up. It was all perfect."

"Glad to hear that," Mac said absently. "Where'd you go?"

"Anita needed a little getaway. She surprised me at the last minute with an interview for another cake competition show. Only, it fell through when we were already halfway up there, so we ended up just visiting some folks up in Northern Virginia that she knows. Hope we didn't worry you none."

"Is she in the truck?"

"No. She ended up staying behind. She's going to visit her sister. She's not doing so well, but Anita'll be back in a couple days."

"Oh dear. Is it serious?"

Mac waved a hand dismissively. "I don't know. Woman stuff. I didn't get into it."

Connor nodded. "Hear ya on that."

"I wanted to stop by and confirm the delivery for your cake Saturday morning. I'd like to deliver it early so I won't be in the way while I put the last touches in place."

"You still have the code from last weekend, don't you?"

Mac's brow wrinkled. "Not sure. I think it was in the van, but we traded that old clunker in for the new one out there. You better give it to me again."

Jill jumped up and got a slip of paper from behind the counter and wrote down the code for him. "Here. You can come as early as you like. I'd like to have everything set up and ready to go no later than nine, though."

"I'll have it ready for you." Mac turned and started heading to the door, then turned back. "Real sorry to hear about Gina. I'll see you Saturday."

After Mac left, everyone was quiet.

"Y'all ready to call it a night?" Garrett asked. "If we leave it to Jill, she'll have us work through it."

"I would not."

"You might," Carolanne agreed.

"Then let's go. Just leave everything where it is. Shoo. Y'all can go now. Garrett and I will lock up and be out right behind you."

Connor walked Carolanne out to her car. "I'm sorry I was so hard on you the other day."

"I deserved it."

"I could have been kinder about it." He waved to the Malloys as they backed out of the parking lot. "I guess you'll be sleeping in your place tonight. You know I still would have helped move your furniture."

"It worked out fine."

"Are you going to show me your place?"

She nodded. "Sure. When do you want to come by?"

"How about now? It's still kind of early, since all that talk about Gina kind of plummeted the party mood in there."

"I know. He seemed pretty upset about it, too."

"So, what do you say?"

She shrugged her shoulders. "Sure. Follow me over. I don't think you'll get lost. It's the only house in the neighborhood."

She got into her car and took the back exit from the artisan center toward home. *Home.* That felt good.

Connor followed behind her.

There weren't any streetlights. She was thankful for the bright moon; otherwise it would have been pitch-black.

All of the lights were on timers, so once they got to her driveway, things were well illuminated. Even though she didn't have much in the way of landscaping, the lighting around the garden areas and the pathways had already been installed, too.

Connor stepped up behind her on the porch.

When Carolanne twisted her key in the front door, Connor surprised her by handing her a bottle of wine.

She took the bottle and then looked up at his playful grin. "Aw, that was sweet."

"I'm not sweet. I'm charming. Remember?" Then he scooped her up and carried her through the doorway.

Carolanne squealed as he whipped her through the air like a sack of potatoes. "What do you think you're doing?"

"I'm giving your house good luck."

"That's not how it works. Put me down."

"Are you sure that's not how it works?"

"Yes! Put me down."

He tossed her on her couch. "Well, since you're determined to be an old maid, I figured someone should carry you through the threshold at least once in your life."

"You could have given me a heart attack. Thanks for almost giving me the last thrill of my life."

"You're made of tougher stuff than that." He shoved his hands in his pockets and looked around. "Man, this place already looks like a home. You have pictures up and everything."

She was proud of what she'd gotten done so quickly; of course, she'd been waiting for this day for months. She'd placed the furniture in her mind a hundred times.

"Want a glass of wine?"

He followed her into the kitchen. "Sure."

She took two wine glasses down from the corner glass-front cabinet and handed him the wine opener.

He opened the bottle and poured. He lifted his glass. "A toast to my very dear friend."

She touched her glass to his. "Special friends." She took a sip and felt a warm glow. "That's good."

He looked at her intently, then strode to the door that led to the patio. "Are you going to give me the nickel tour?"

"You have to pay up front. I know how you lawyers can be. You'll talk me out of charging you later."

He jingled the change in his pocket, but instead of a nickel, he dumped his whole pocketful of coins out onto the granite kitchen counter.

*What the heck are you doing?* She lifted her gaze to meet his light-blue eyes.

"If a nickel gets the tour, what can I get for that?"

She poured a little more wine in each of their glasses. "Well, I guess you get to see the whole darn place."

He followed her through each room downstairs and then out onto the back deck. "It's nice out here," he said.

She tilted her glass in the direction of the pond. "Except for the fact that someone died right over there, it couldn't be more perfect. But I'm trying not to think about that."

"You're safe here. Scott wouldn't have let you move in if it weren't."

"I know. It's just a little creepy." She shivered, though the air outside was warm.

His finger stroked her arm sensuously. The hairs on her arm stood to attention at his caress. She knew she should stop him, but she didn't really want to, and it was innocent enough. He stepped behind her and set his chin on top of her head. "It's a nice view from here. With the moon so full, you can see the tree line, and the lights from the cars traveling down Route 58 are kind of nice."

"Like giant fireflies. I wondered if it was going to be noisy, but really, it's rather soothing."

"You'll be happy out here?"

She nodded, causing his chin to bounce up and down as she did. "That hurts," she teased, stooping down and spinning out from in front of him. "Come on. I'll show you the rest of the place."

He followed her inside, locking the door behind them. "You want more wine?"

She placed her glass on the counter. "No. I think I've had enough."

He put his glass down beside hers and followed her back into the living room.

"Wait a second," he said. He looked up at the raised ceiling in that part of the room.

"What are you looking at?" She stepped closer to him and looked straight up, following his line of sight.

He swept her up in his arms again and started carrying her right upstairs.

"This is not funny!"

"It kind of is," he said, laughing with every step.

At one point, he even tipped her toward the handrail.

"You better not drop me!" She was laughing so hard she could barely breathe.

He took the last step onto the landing and then

walked into the master bedroom straight ahead. He tossed her on the bed and belly flopped on it right beside her.

"That was fun," she said between breaths. "I might even give you a refund."

"Cool." He rolled over in a push-up position over top of her, then lowered slowly, catching her lip between his teeth and then softly covering her mouth.

She didn't know if it was the wine or her heart taking over, but she relaxed into his cushioning embrace.

The kisses he pressed to her neck sent volts of passion through her that threatened to steal her ability to think, and she couldn't imagine a better place to be. His breathing was heavy, but his touch was featherlight as it slid from her shoulder to her hand.

She lifted her mouth to meet his.

Connor's phone chirped.

Carolanne groaned.

"You know I have to get that, right?"

She nodded.

"Don't you move." He turned to the side and took the phone from his hip as he stood next to the bed. "Connor Buckham." He held up a finger.

She watched, wide-eyed and feeling less than patient.

A serious look washed over Connor's face. Then he turned his back and walked into the hallway.

"Yeah. No. I can do that. Sure." Connor was steadily nodding his head. "Sit tight. Don't say a word. I'll be right there."

He turned around and stood in the doorway.

Carolanne was propped up on one elbow. "You've got to leave?"

He nodded. "I really don't want to."

"Can I get one more of those sexy kisses before you go?"

"Nope." He crawled onto the bed and slowly kissed her. "You can have two."

# ❖ Chapter Twenty-Three ❖

Connor rushed into the police station in a personal tug-of-war over not telling Carolanne who had called and even more so over answering the call to begin with.

The schedule board was just inside the door. One glance confirmed that Scott wasn't in. Not many were. He wished Scott were around so he could get some details from him first, but this late at night, he wouldn't be at the station, and Connor couldn't bother him at home without some concrete information. *Damn if this isn't awkward. What am I supposed to say to the poor guy? Sorry I took so long. I had to peel myself off your daughter.*

A deputy walked up to the front desk.

"I'm here to see Ben Baxter," Connor said.

The deputy escorted him down the hall from the holding cells.

A few minutes later, Ben was brought in and seated across the table from Connor.

"What's going on?" Connor asked.

Ben let out a breath. "I lied, and now it's got me in trouble, but I swear I didn't do anything. You've got to help me." He sighed. His voice was full of anguish. "I know this puts you in a bad position—me asking you not to tell Carolanne."

*If you knew what position I was in when you called . . .* "Puts me in a very awkward position."

"I know, but I wanted to talk to you first."

Connor had his doubts that keeping it from Carolanne was a good idea under any circumstances, but he figured he best hear the whole story first. "Start at the beginning." He tugged his pen out of his shirt and wrote the date and time at the top of a clean sheet of paper.

Ben filled Connor in on the details of the day he'd come home to find Gina in his house. "She'd broken in and apparently had been doing it for a couple days."

"But you were aware she was staying there for at least some period of the time, right?"

"Yes. I was." Ben scrubbed his hands through his hair. "I can't believe this. You'd think somewhere along the line I could catch a break."

Connor wrote down notes as Ben detailed the events leading up to the day of the wedding and his car accident.

"I didn't even know about Gina being dead until that Monday when Scott came to the hospital."

Connor knew most of this from Carolanne already, but maybe Ben would say something helpful that Carolanne hadn't relayed. "Do you remember what time that was when you left the reception?"

"I guess it was around one, because I went to grab something to eat. Penny's was crowded with a late lunch crowd."

"Sounds about right. I'll check with the folks over at Penny's. She might even be able to pull the ticket and give us an exact time."

"Penny was there. They were packed, but she should remember."

"Good. At least she can attest to whether you were acting like something was wrong."

"Well, that's not going to work to my favor. I was feeling five kinds of blue. That whole wedding had my heart tied up in knots. It's why I left. It was just too big a temptation for me to stick around. I've worked too hard to get this far to slip back."

"Let's see what she has to say."

"When Scott showed me that picture of Gina and asked me if I recognized her, I just wasn't thinking. All I could think of was that I didn't want Carolanne to be upset with me for trying to help that girl after I'd been such a piss-poor father to her. I lied. It was stupid, but I did. The words were out of my mouth before I knew it, and I didn't think it would turn into a big deal."

"But it has."

"Hell yeah, it has. Dead is some kind of bad trouble."

"The worst."

Ben went on. "Someone must have seen her coming and going from my house. They haven't told me who, but when they showed up, it wasn't just to ask some questions—they already had a search warrant."

"What did they find?"

"Some journals were stuffed under my couch. I didn't know they were there. I have no idea what's in them. I think that's all they found."

"Any idea where she got those journals? Did she have them with her when she showed up?"

"I have no idea."

"When was the last time you saw her?"

"Friday night before the wedding. She was asleep on my couch when I went to bed that night, and she was gone early the next morning."

Connor tapped the pen on the table. "That's the morning of the wedding, when your car wouldn't start?"

"Yes. She was already gone when you stopped by the house."

"That was early." Connor wrote eight thirty and a question mark down on the piece of paper. "Are you sure she was there all night?"

"I guess she could have left during the night, but I'd have thought I would've heard her. She was asleep on the couch when I went to bed. I don't know when she got up."

Connor looked Ben square in the eye. "We know why she didn't come back."

266

"Because she was dead."

"At least we know now that she was alive the night before. What time did you go to bed?"

"Around ten?"

"That's a start. That gives us a time frame. Let me go find out what they've got."

"Connor, the deputy insinuated I wrecked my car last Saturday on purpose. Something about covering up some kind of evidence."

Connor laid his pen down. "Ben, Carolanne said she saw Gina drive off in your car that night at your house. Did she tell you that?"

Ben looked confused. "No. I didn't let her use my car."

"Well, according to Carolanne, she drove off in it that night."

"But my car was right where I'd left it when I got up in the morning, but Gina wasn't there. That doesn't make sense."

Connor shook his head. "No. It doesn't. Look, if there's anything you're not telling me, tell me now. I can't help you if you're not straight with me."

"I know."

"Was she ever at the artisan center that you know of?"

"Yes," Ben said. "I took her with me one night. She helped me with some raking and cleanup. She was a good help, too."

Connor winced.

"This doesn't look good, does it? You've got to believe me. I'm a champ at self-destruction, but I'd never harm anyone else."

"I know," Connor said. "I believe you. No, it doesn't look good, but I'm glad you're telling me this. It could be important. The more I know, the more I can help."

"I swear, Connor, I didn't do anything to Gina. She's a nice kid. I wouldn't have called you if I'd done something wrong. You've got to believe me."

"I do, Ben. Completely. But I don't think I can keep this from Carolanne. Adams Grove is a small town. I don't know how long it'll stay quiet."

"Here's the thing. Carolanne knows about Gina being at my house. We talked about that, but I can't ask her to fight this for me. It's not fair. I've put that girl through too much already. It's why I called you."

"I'm not bailing you out yet. You sit tight in here."

"Not like it's the first time I've slept here."

"I know, and I'm sure it's not a pleasant memory, but we're better off if you're here with an airtight alibi. If there's anything you can think of that might give us a clue as to what happened, get them to contact me. I'll see what I can find out, and I'll be back."

Connor signaled for the deputy, who came in and led Ben out of the room.

# ❖ Chapter Twenty-Four ❖

It wasn't unusual for Route 58 to be busy on a holiday weekend, but this Friday morning before Memorial Day, the little piece of it where the new Adams Grove Artisan Center sat was as busy as a beehive.

Carolanne could have walked to the artisan center from her new house, but expecting it to be a long day since she'd agreed to help Jill with the stats, she'd driven so she wouldn't have to walk home in the dark. She pulled into the back lot and parked next to Jill's car.

There was already a flurry of activity out front. Two news vans were setting up, and people were already starting to mingle in anticipation of the big event.

Carolanne went in through the back entrance and headed for the front counter to see how she could help. She stopped mid-stride as she realized a television crew was filming.

"This is Steffi Zimmer coming to you live from Adams Grove for the ribbon cutting and grand opening of the new Adams Grove Artisan Center. Stay tuned to News Channel 3 for the full report."

"Got it," said the cameraman.

They filmed one more bumper, and then Steffi,

the field reporter from the CBS affiliate in Virginia Beach, waited for her cue from the morning show anchors for the ten-minutes-after-the-hour slot.

Carolanne waved to Jill, who stood to the left of the reporter, looking much more comfortable in her sundress than that poor Steffi Zimmer did in her business suit.

Outside, the temperature was already pushing record-breaking numbers for a May morning, and the air-conditioning was working overtime trying to cool the large building.

Carolanne resisted the temptation to run over and sweep away a little bead of sweat from Steffi's temple before they started the interview with Jill.

One of the guys helping folks park walked by, looking sharp in his crisp brown uniform with the artisan center logo embroidered in white over the left pocket. The simple logo—a lowercase "a" with a capital "C" wrapped around—was a nice blend of art and simplicity that matched the architecture to the letter—in this case, "a." Garrett had designed the building in the shape of a lowercase "a." The part of the building that was the sweeping oval of the bottom gave visitors an endless loop of displays, and the top arch was where the apartment studios would be for the artists-in-residence program.

"How's it going out there?" Jill asked.

"Glad we had the guys from the Ruritan Club come help with the parking. The front lot is full. We're starting to park them in the grass."

Milly stormed through the space like she owned the place. "Can you believe this turnout?"

Carolanne gave her a welcome hug. "I know. I'm so thrilled."

Milly hitched her straw purse up on her elbow and held it tight to her body. "The old geezer out front tried to keep me from coming in. I told him I was family and nothing would keep me from coming inside. I'm so happy for Jill." Milly put an arm around Carolanne and gave her a quick squeeze. "Her grandmother would be proud of her today."

Jill waved from across the room.

Milly waved back and then turned to Carolanne again. "Thank goodness that storm skirted us last night. If all of these cars were driving on soggy grass, they'd have ruined months of Ben's land-scaping."

Garrett stepped up next to Milly. "Ben really turned these grounds into something impressive, didn't he?"

"He did an amazing job," Milly said. "Where is he, anyway?"

Carolanne looked around. "You know, I haven't seen him, but then, I haven't seen Connor yet this morning, either. It's already so crowded it's hard to track down anybody."

"We won't complain about that," Garrett said. "Besides, Ben's work is done for now. The place looks nicer than most golf courses. Everyone has commented on it. He deserves the chance to just enjoy the day."

Nervous excitement built in the room as the seconds clicked off to airtime. Even though the Kase Foundation may have ended up being a big fat scam, Jill's position there had garnered her valuable experience in handling the media, and that was coming in handy with all the attention the artisan center was getting. She looked cool as a rock star.

Just like someone had flipped a switch, Steffi Zimmer exploded into motion.

Steffi's unexpected burst of energy caught Jill by surprise, causing her to hiccup.

Jill flashed a look of panic toward Carolanne and Garrett.

*Can you believe this?* She mouthed the words, then slung her hand over her mouth as another hiccup escaped.

Garrett shrugged and turned away, then spun around, swept Jill into his arms, and planted a big kiss smack-dab on her lips.

When Garrett released her, Jill staggered back, blinking, but the hiccups seemed to be gone.

Carolanne gave him a high five. "Perfect timing."

Jill stepped back in place next to Steffi, who hadn't missed a beat.

"Steffi Zimmer coming to you live this morning from Adams Grove, Virginia, where later this morning they'll begin the ribbon-cutting ceremony here at the Adams Grove Artisan Center. They've got an amazing schedule of festivities today."

The cameraman widened the angle, and Steffi stepped closer to Jill.

Steffi continued. "I've got the founder, Jill Clemmons, right here with me."

"Good morning. Thank you so much for joining us."

Steffi focused on the camera. "Jill took us on a tour of the facility this morning. Let me tell you firsthand, this place is filled with amazing artwork from talented artists from all over the state. You can find everything from pottery, painting, photography, furniture to quilts and even one-of-a-kind handcrafted jewelry here. I've got my eye on a couple special pieces!" Steffi turned to Jill. "Words can't do it justice. Let's cut to some footage of our tour."

Steffi held a finger to Jill, then put her hand to her ear, listening for the cues.

When Steffi burst back into character, Jill flinched, but thank goodness she didn't get the hiccups this time.

"Before we wrap up and get ready for the big ceremony, Jenn and Greg, I just had to share this other piece of exciting news from Adams Grove this morning." She waved to the cameraman. "Can you pan over here?"

Steffi moved to the side of an elegantly set table with a huge cake in the center. "Perfect. Can you see this cake?"

From the newsroom feed: "It's huge!"

"Right, Jenn. Do you remember Mac Honeycutt from the Food Network cake show last fall?"

"Yes! He was my favorite contestant," Jenn said. "I knew he was from Virginia, but not from so nearby."

"Yep, from right here in Adams Grove. He made it all the way to the final three, but then his cake fell just a quarter of an inch short in the finale of the Extremely Amazing Monster-Size Celebration Cake Bake-Off. Well, no missteps today. We've measured this one. This creation is the full four feet of towering sugar inferno."

Steffi motioned the cameraman to the detail. "Zoom in here on this sugar bubble. There are tiny pieces of edible artwork inside each bubble. Truly a masterpiece."

The cameraman pulled back. "We'll be chatting with Mac and a few of the artists at the noon hour."

"That's great. Thanks for the live report," Jenn said.

"Bring us a piece of cake," Greg added.

"I'll see what I can do about that. Coming to

you live from Adams Grove, Virginia—I'm Steffi Zimmer."

The cameraman counted down on his fingers in 3-2-1 and then made a fist. Steffi dropped back into a casual Southern drawl and gave Jill a hug.

# ❖ Chapter Twenty-Five ❖

Carolanne's responsibility of keeping folks out of the way during the taping of the news pieces was done, and she had some time to mingle since doing the stats for Jill wouldn't start until the end of the day. It was fun to play a supporting role in something rather than running it for a change. Maybe she *would* eventually get used to the slower pace of Adams Grove.

Pearl's death shook this whole town, but it had been pivotal in her returning home to help Jill through it, and that was just like Pearl to have her way with all of them even when she was gone. She'd been right about Jill and Garrett all along, and now that their nuptials were official, only she and Connor stood in the way of a perfect record for Pearl Clemmons in the matchmaking arena.

*Never doubt Pearl's wisdom.*

She'd given that advice to many over the years. Why hadn't she believed it herself? *Because I'm more complicated than all that.*

Carolanne pulled in a quick breath as a warm rush teased her senses at the memories of Connor's touch. He wasn't one of those guys who worked with his hands all day like those she was usually attracted to. There wasn't one callus on his manicured hands—and she and Jill had given him plenty of grief over that—but what Carolanne hadn't expected was the power and strength in his hands. They'd awakened her in ways she'd never imagined. She'd also never noticed the tiny golden flecks that danced in his blue eyes or the way his normally booming voice could quiet to a tingling whisper on her neck.

People crowded the front lawn. A bright-yellow ribbon spanned the porch, keeping visitors from entering the building until after the ceremony, so she took the side door and bypassed all the hype.

She walked to her car and sat in the driver's seat to change into nicer heels from her practical flats. She tossed her purse back in the car and locked it up. No sense dealing with her purse on her shoulder all day long in this crowd. She didn't need anything in it.

Around front, she hiked up the slope toward where all the ribbon-cutting festivities would take place. She had to admit Dad had done a pretty amazing job whipping the grounds into a nice-looking array of colors and greenery. Who knew he had such a green thumb? She was proud of him, something new in the dad department for her. The thought of her and Dad working on the yard at her house together brought a smile to her lips.

Carolanne exchanged waves with a few of the locals as she got closer to the front of the building.

She rose on her toes as she walked to keep her high heels from sinking into the soft soil.

A warm glow flowed through her when she caught the light dancing off strawberry-blonde hair in the distance. The ginger tone wasn't too hard to pick out in a crowd, even with his back to her. Her heart danced a little jig as she headed in his direction to join him for the ceremony.

Then she stopped.

About five yards beyond Connor, a woman dressed to the nines in all black and big baubles at her throat and wrists stood with her arms outstretched and a huge too-white smile. And that woman seemed to be looking straight at Connor. The voices around Carolanne seemed to merge into a low hum as she stopped, standing their frozen for a two-count. Carolanne watched Connor begin to walk toward that woman.

For every step he drew closer to the other woman, Carolanne took one backward. The crowd around her may as well have disappeared. Uncertainties threatened to bring her to her knees. She spun around, trying to keep from watching, but dying to at the same time.

With her back to Connor, she took a second to make herself breathe. *It has to be Katherine.* She'd never met her, but that girl had rich Chicago girl written all over her. She was out of the picture. Hadn't he said that? Or maybe it was that he'd said nothing about her. What else didn't she know about Connor? She'd never considered herself the jealous kind, but what she was feeling right now . . . It wasn't good.

What if she talked him into going back to practice in Chicago? A partnership in a big firm could mean big things for him, and his mom was gone—nothing to tie him to Adams Grove now.

She took a careful step forward, not sure for a moment if she could even walk. She turned back for a second look, but they were gone. She scanned the groups of people making their way from the extended parking area to the center. Doing a full pirouette, she didn't see Connor or that lady in black anywhere.

The last thing she wanted was to bump into them now. She spun and went back toward her car.

"Hi, Carolanne," Patsy Malloy called out.

"Forgot something." Carolanne pasted a fake smile on her face and waved as she passed Garrett's mom and dad. "I'll be back."

"We'll save you a spot," Mrs. Malloy said with a nod.

*I'll never be missed in this crowd.* A single tear escaped as she finally rounded the corner and could see her car. She jogged the rest of the way and brushed the tear from her cheek as she grabbed for the door handle and lifted. Locked. Realization struck.

"Doggone it." Carolanne smacked the car and leaned against the door with her eyes closed.

*How could I have locked my purse and keys in the car? No escaping now. Pull it together, girl. There could be an explanation. No, there's not. Who am I fooling? Only myself. Men. They're all the same. They can't be trusted—any of them. Ever.*

Well, if there was any good news about the last week being hectic, it was that she hadn't told anyone, not even Jill, about what she'd thought was news in her and Connor's relationship. It had been up, down, sideways, and hopeful again, but no one would be the wiser to what a fool she'd been.

She smoothed her blouse and ran her fingers under her eyes to tame any mascara runs, then plastered her old cheerleader smile back on her face and headed back to the ribbon cutting. If there was one thing she'd mastered over the years after Momma died and Daddy went drunk-nuts, it was looking cool and nonchalant, no matter what was going on in her heart.

Carolanne ran back inside the artisan center through the back door to escape the feelings that threatened to make her scream in the middle of the crowd out front.

Jill nearly bumped into her. "Have you seen Garrett? We're almost ready for the ceremony, and he's conveniently disappeared."

Carolanne had to laugh, although she knew Jill didn't think it was funny. "That man's superpower is being able to disappear when a camera comes within shooting distance."

"I think you're right."

Carolanne noticed Jill's left eyebrow rise—her tell sign that Jill was stressing out.

"Calm down. We'll find him. Come on."

She and Jill speed-walked past each of the named rooms. Just as they passed the Dogwood Room, something caught Carolanne's eye just outside the window.

"Keep going. I'm going to backtrack." Only, she didn't. Instead, she took two steps back. Someone was standing at the side of the building. There was no reason for anyone to be out there. Carolanne stepped inside the room, next to a display near the window, to take a closer look.

Connor's face was redder than his hair, and he looked flustered by more than just the humidity. His voice rose to a level that she could hear from inside the building, but she couldn't quite make out what he was saying. Whatever it was, it didn't seem pleasant.

Across from him, the woman in all black with lots of blingy jewelry had her arms crossed and her stare leveled on Connor. Her tight lips had that crinkly look. *Probably a smoker.* She bit back the catty thought. OK, so Pearl had predisposed her to not like Katherine.

Connor seemed to be the only one doing any talking, and he looked a bit like a giant pterodactyl the way his arms were flapping around as he spoke. Katherine glanced up toward the window.

Carolanne stepped out of view. *Why is she even here?* Just then, Anita walked up, and Connor threw his hands up and left. Anita and the woman in black embraced. Maybe it wasn't Connor who had invited Katherine, after all, or maybe the woman wasn't Katherine.

She leaned forward to take another look, feeling like a fool for reacting so badly without even giving Connor a chance to explain.

"There you are."

Carolanne spun around at the sound of Garrett's voice.

Garrett stood at the edge of the display area. "Jill and I were looking for you. We're headed out front for the ribbon cutting. Come on."

Carolanne glanced to the window and then back at Garrett.

"Are you OK?" he asked.

"Yeah. OK. Yeah. I'm fine." She ran her hand through her bangs.

Jill stood next to the front door, waving Garrett to hurry up.

"This is your moment," Carolanne said to Garrett. "Go on. I'm going to slip out the side door and watch from out front."

Carolanne watched Garrett leave through the huge hand-carved doors that led to the front porch of the artisan center where he and Jill would cut the ribbon. She went out the side door and walked around to the front. Her heart swelled as she scanned the crowd for familiar faces. Everyone she knew was here showing their support, and there were lots of people she'd never seen before, too. She spotted Connor, and he waved for her to join him with the Malloys.

"Excuse me. Sorry," Carolanne said as she maneuvered through the crowd toward Connor. She looked around for the lady in black, but didn't see her.

"Where were you?" he whispered.

"Where were *you* and with *who* is a better question!" Her words bit, and she wasn't proud of it, but she couldn't masquerade as if everything were OK. It just wasn't her nature.

He leaned in. "What?"

Someone behind them shushed them.

Carolanne glared at him.

"I saw you." Clenching her teeth, she was even madder now that he was playing all coy. "Don't deny it. I saw *her*."

The look on his face confirmed he knew exactly what she was talking about.

She lifted her chin and forced herself to pay attention to the ceremony.

Jill stood between Garrett and the mayor behind the supersize ribbon that stretched from post to post across the entryway of the new Adams Grove Artisan Center.

Mayor Winnberg began his speech. The light-colored plaid suit jacket he was wearing strained from one too many Southern meals, and the bright sunshine glistened off his balding head.

Carolanne resisted looking over at Connor, although she could feel his eyes on her.

The mayor would drone on too long like he always did. Pearl used to call him "Mayor Windbag," and she'd never made it any secret that she hadn't cast her vote for him. Carolanne loved that about Pearl.

Carolanne tipped her chin to the bright sun. Despite the clear blue sky, her day felt cloudy and gloomy. She watched Garrett give Jill's hand a squeeze. The pride he felt for Jill's accomplishment was very telling. Those two seemed to be able to communicate without even saying a word—soul mates.

She'd let herself believe that she and Connor might be like that. *I know better than to get caught up in that.*

The mayor continued his speech. His enthusiasm was as high as his hopes that the attraction would slow tourists down for a visit on their way east to Virginia Beach. As nice as that was, she wished he'd wrap it up before she fell over from the heat or made a scene in front of all these people and ruined Jill and Garrett's big day.

Carolanne recognized Jack from the *County Gazette* front and center but was delighted to see they weren't the only ones pressing forward for a good camera angle. There were several press types up front and at least three TV crew vans with their huge live-broadcast satellites stretched into the sky. *All the more reason not to make a scene today. I'd be front-page news, and not in a good way.*

Mayor Winnberg picked up the giant scissors and held them out toward Jill and Garrett. "You ready to do this thing?"

They stepped up next to the mayor and held the monster-size bright-red scissors over the ribbon like a gator getting ready to bite its prey. Cameras flashed and someone whistled. Then, with a snip, the ribbon fell and everyone cheered. Carolanne let herself get swept into the stream of people moving toward the building as Garrett shook the mayor's hand and announced, "I present to you—the Adams Grove Artisan Center."

# ❖ Chapter Twenty-Six ❖

Carolanne edged her way between the visitors who filed from the left and right to the center hall to join in the festivities as Jill and Garrett sliced into the beautiful cake. People mingled, sharing their opinions on the artwork, noting their favorite displays, and making new friends.

Steffi Zimmer had already pulled Mac to the side for an interview.

Garrett nudged Jill and motioned Carolanne closer. "Did y'all hear that?"

"What?"

Garrett said, "I just heard Anita tell that woman in black that she and Mac are going to move to Chicago."

"He's lived here his whole life," Jill said. "He wouldn't even move out of the state for his wife. That's why they split up when she wanted to move home to New York."

Carolanne shook her head. "I don't believe it for a second."

Jill looked dumbfounded. "How'd he keep that a secret around here? Do you think he's just planning to let Derek run the store? The guy is talented—he could probably do it."

Milly weaved through the crowd and put her arms out wide for a hug. "How are my girls?"

"Hi, Aunt Milly," Jill said.

The three of them hugged, and Jill reached back and passed a piece of cake to Milly.

"Thanks, dear," Milly said. "This is almost perfect. If that Chicago woman hadn't shown up, it'd have been a perfect ten. That woman needs to just stay up there in Chicago with her fancy-pants people. I guess this seemed like a hoity-toity enough event for her to grace us with her presence."

"Milly. That's not nice. We don't even really know her," Jill said.

"My point exactly," Milly said with a sneer. "I know her kind. She hasn't been around in months. One big shindig and here she is." Milly wagged a bony finger in Carolanne's direction. "Don't let her get in your way."

"I'm not the least bit worried about her. She is none of my business," Carolanne said, hopefully sounding convincing.

"Good afternoon, ladies." Izzy Markham stepped into the small group. "Good to see you."

Carolanne was relieved for the diversion. Izzy was always a great distraction. She couldn't help but end up being the center of attention. She'd always been like that, even back in school.

Milly grasped her hand. "Hello, Izzy, dear. You look absolutely lovely. Too bad Pearl isn't here to get you hooked up. We were just talking about Connor's mismatch showing up."

"We weren't talking about it. Mostly Milly was talking about it," said Carolanne. "Katherine has other friends besides Connor in this town."

Izzy gave Milly a hug. "You could step right in to fill Pearl's shoes, couldn't you? You two always were a heck of a team." Izzy turned her attention to Carolanne and Jill. "She's staying at the inn."

"Who?" Carolanne asked.

"Katherine?" Jill asked.

*Can we forget about her already?*

Izzy nodded. "Yep. She and that weird brother of hers are both staying there. Mac's girlfriend, too. All of 'em are staying at Markham House. They're driving Momma nearly batshit crazy with all their demands."

"Is that who is with Katherine? I was wondering who that man was," Milly added. "He looks like a weasel."

"Uh-huh. Prickly, too," Izzy said. "When Mom introduced him to me as Richard, I asked if I could call him Rich, and he didn't only say no, he said"—she stood tall and stiff and spoke in a nasally asinine accent—"'my name is Richard. Please use it appropriately.'"

"Just like her, probably." Milly pursed her lips and looked for agreement. "Don't see anyone calling her Kathy or Kate, do you?"

"Snooty booties, if you ask me." Izzy leaned in to not be overheard. "He complained that he needed to know the ingredients in the handcrafted soaps because he had sensitive skin. When Becky told him that it was all natural and made from goat's milk, he almost heaved on her shoes. She responded with something like, 'If you think that's bad, imagine what's in the well water.' I don't think he's had anything to drink except bottled products since."

"Sometimes you have to love Becky's snarky ways," Carolanne said.

"Yeah, as long as they aren't being thrown in your direction!" Jill chimed in.

"I hear that," Izzy agreed. "I swear Momma and Daddy just might raise the prices at the inn after those guests. Momma says either that Richard jerk isn't sleeping in his paid-for room or he's one heckuva housekeeper because there hasn't been a thing out of place, and yet he's complained more than any other guest. Those people are giving Momma and Daddy a run for their money. I heard Katherine trying to talk Momma into cooking them some of Spratt's famous rib-eye steaks for dinner tonight, too."

Milly pursed her lips. "I thought she only cooked breakfast for the guests. Isn't that why it's called a bed-and-*breakfast?* She's not going to do it, is she?"

"Who knows? You know Momma. She loves to please."

Carolanne chimed in. "Be nice. I love your momma."

"I know. I know. Me, too. And she does love to cook."

"Well, she sure outdid herself for the rehearsal dinner. It was the best meal I'd ever had," Carolanne said.

Jill nodded. "And it wasn't even just the meal—it was the setting and service. It was perfect." Jill leaned in and lowered her voice. "Why wasn't this Mac-girlfriend thing news to all of us until recently? Don't y'all think that's kind of weird?"

Carolanne said, "Mac's never been much of a talker."

Jill didn't look convinced. "Yeah, but the kudzu telegraph in these parts usually doesn't miss much. I bet if Pearl had been around, we'd have known."

"True that," Izzy said and lifted a glass. "To Pearl."

"To Pearl," echoed Milly. "And putting the boots on Northern girls who don't belong."

"Well, maybe she'll spend some of that Northern money to show off. I'd be fine with that," Jill said. "Have you checked out the jewelry? I have my eye on a couple pieces. Hopefully Garrett will pick up on my subtle hints."

Carolanne felt Connor ease up behind her. She knew it was him without even looking.

"Having fun?" he whispered into her ear.

"I was, until your ex-girlfriend became the topic of the town with all the girls. Everyone's making quite a big deal out of it."

He stepped around to face her. "You're not thinking anything crazy, are you? You know I didn't invite her, right?"

"I'm fine, unless you plan to leave Adams Grove for a job back in Chicago."

"That's not how I operate. These people, this county, they're part of me. People here count on me to make sure they make good decisions, and my gut has paid off for plenty of them over the years. I have no intention of leaving Adams Grove for Katherine—or anyone, for that matter."

"Then I'm fine." She wouldn't have been if she hadn't seen the big argument, but she had no intention of telling him that. He didn't need to know that her self-confidence was sabotaging her again. She'd become quite a pro at that kind of thing—a habit she hoped to break once and for all.

"I guess she's in town to spend time with Anita, not to see me, and I have no idea why that good-for-nothing brother of hers is with her. The loser got disbarred for some sketchy practices, including fraudulent activities, and Katherine knows I don't have two words to say to that punk. I'd sooner punch him than look at him."

Mac swept through the crowd and excused himself as he stepped between Carolanne and Connor. "Hey, man. I need to talk to you. It's kind of important." Mac turned to Carolanne. "Sorry to hear about Ben being arrested. You know he'd never hurt anyone. Everyone knows that. There's got to be some other explanation."

Carolanne looked at Connor, whose face drained of all its color.

"What did you just say?" She tried to stay calm, hoping like all heck that she'd heard him wrong. "Connor? Mac? OK, one of you needs to tell me what the heck is going on here."

"Sorry. I put my foot in my mouth, didn't I? I was just talking to Sheriff Calvin about Lindsey Dixon's daughter. He told me that Connor had been in to talk to Ben about it."

She spun toward Connor. "When? My father's been arrested? Why didn't I hear about it until just now?"

"Calm down. I can explain."

Crestfallen, she folded her arms across her chest and stood there, knowing there was no good response he could give. "I'm waiting here. So, what do you have to say?"

"It's true. The phone call when I was at your house—it was your dad."

Carolanne couldn't believe her ears. She knew exactly when that phone call had come. "I was *right* there, and you didn't tell me?" She turned to Mac. "And he's still in jail?"

Mac gave a resigned shrug. "I think that's what Scott said. I haven't seen him here today. Might be." He looked like he wished he could die. "I could have it all mixed up."

"But he doesn't have it mixed up, does he, Connor?"

"I can explain."

"I doubt that. What kind of lawyer are you that you couldn't get Dad out of jail? They don't have anything on him. He's innocent. They can't get away with this. I'm going to go file against the county for this. I'm not letting them railroad him. Not happening." Her heart was beating so hard she could barely hear her own words over the pounding.

"Slow down, Carolanne. I know he's innocent. We're letting the DA have this little temporary win to buy some time to figure out what really happened. Your father is fine."

His voice, all calm and quiet, was about to drive her insane. *It's fine to you because it's not your father.*

"Trust me. I know how to handle these folks in Adams Grove. We're fine."

"Little win? Oh, heck no. I'm not having this, and for the record, *we* are not fine. You have no right keeping things from me about my father."

Connor grabbed her arm. "Hold on. This isn't New York. We have two DAs. Two. That's it. You can't just go pissing them off. We need them on our side."

"Do not try to tell me how to practice law." She tugged her arm away from him and marched out of the building. *Dad, how am I going to help you?*

# ❖ Chapter Twenty-Seven ❖

Although the artisan center officially closed at six, it took nearly forty minutes to clear everyone out and finalize the sales. Connor sat by wondering what the heck Carolanne was up to. He hadn't laid eyes on her since their blowup earlier. He glanced at his watch, anxious to get out of there and see what else he could find out to help Ben. Keeping Carolanne from stirring up more trouble was top of mind, too.

Jill plopped down in a bright-blue folk art–style chair carved and painted to look like a glitzy mermaid. She kicked her shoes off and pulled her feet up into the chair. Patsy and Jim sat in the pink flamingo love seat next to her. Garrett stepped up behind Jill and rubbed her shoulder as they recapped the highlights of the day with his parents.

Elsie walked out of the office waving a tablet in the air. "Ready for the official numbers, Boss?"

Carolanne followed at her heels.

*When did she get back?* It was a relief to see her, but he still had his worries.

"Yes." Jill scooched to the edge of her seat. "I know it's good."

Elsie leaped into the air. "It's awesome!"

Carolanne took in a long breath and then started

running through the stats. Her jaw was set and her voice tight. "I'm going to have to run after this, so I'm going to make it quick, but all the details are in the report. We had a total of four hundred and five people at the ribbon cutting. People came from nine different counties. By the end of the day, one thousand two hundred and sixty-two people had visited from eleven states."

"That means we had vacationers, don't you think?" Elsie said, then started drumming on the counter. "We sold an average of . . . Drumroll, please . . ."

Carolanne was still mad, but more than that, she was upset. He could tell by her clipped sentences and the fact that she was acting like he was invisible spoke pretty loudly, too. *I'm sorry, Carolanne.* She was here out of duty and friendship to Jill. He should've known she'd never let Jill down.

Jill, Garrett, and Elsie started slapping their hands against their thighs in a faux drumroll.

"Twenty-three dollars per visitor."

Connor could tell Garrett was doing the math in his head.

"I see smoke coming out of your ears," Elsie chimed in. "That's over twenty-nine thousand dollars."

"You're kidding!" Jill raised her hand to her heart and glanced to Pearl's portrait. "Lordy goodness, I never would have dreamed that many people, let alone that much money, coming through these doors on day one."

Elsie pulled a slip of paper from her back pocket. "I was keeping track of some of the repeat sales. Mary Claire's note cards were a big hit. I don't think we have but a couple left, and those are the Christmas ones. We had a lot of lookers at the western pottery, but I think it was a little high-priced for impulse buyers. I bet some people come back for it, though. You know what we sold out of? Those gum wrapper purses."

Connor noticed Carolanne straighten when Elsie mentioned the gum wrapper purses.

"I'm not even sure when they came in. Elsie must have checked them in," Jill admitted.

Mrs. Malloy piped in. "You're right. Lara from the diner bought the very last one. She was showing it to me. She helped the girl collect the wrappers to make them."

"Ben dropped them off during the reception. I saw him put them back here. I didn't get a chance to talk to him, so I'm not sure where he got them, but they were really popular," Elsie said.

"I know who made them. It was Gina Edwards." Carolanne straightened. "When did my dad drop them off?"

Connor knew what she was thinking. He was thinking the same thing. This could help clear Ben. Only, no one else in the room had any idea just how important this piece of trivia was.

Elsie looked like she was searching the ceiling tiles for the answer. "At the wedding reception. Yes, I remember now. He said she wanted to sell them on consignment."

"Whoever made them did an amazing job," Jill said.

"Jill, it was Gina who made them," Carolanne said, stressing the girl's name.

Clarity registered on Jill's face. "That Gina?"

Elsie rambled on. "They're great. I'd hoped to buy one for myself. Wish I'd done it now. We'll definitely need more of those. We also sold a bunch of those cute little wine stoppers with the funny faces on them, too." Elsie folded up the paper.

Carolanne walked over to Elsie. "Are you a hundred percent certain that Ben dropped those handbags off for you on the afternoon of the wedding reception?"

"Yes. A hundred percent certain. In fact, hang on." She ran over to the cash register and brought back an envelope. "Here's who we're supposed to make the check out to. Gina Edwards. Just like you said."

"I've got to run," Carolanne said. "I'm sorry, Jill. I'll explain later."

Carolanne headed out the door to her car.

Connor caught up with her. "Carolanne, wait!"

"I'm in a hurry." She stomped her foot. "I forgot I locked my keys in my car this morning."

"You don't have a spare?"

"Yes. Just not with me. I have one at the house."

"I can take you to get it, or I can drive. You know Ben wouldn't have brought those purses in if he'd killed Gina. That would have been flat-out stupid. He was trying to help her," he said.

"Exactly."

# ❖ Chapter Twenty-Eight ❖

Connor drove Carolanne to the sheriff's station, but Carolanne wasn't in an appreciative mood. "I'm sorry I didn't tell you about the arrest."

"Let's just fix it, OK?" She messed with her seat belt and avoided his look.

"He asked me not to tell you. I was caught. I wanted to help, and I didn't want you to worry."

She held up her hand. "Don't. Not now, OK?"

"I'm on your side on this."

She stared out the window, although there wasn't much to see now that the sun had set.

Connor hated to ask, but he needed to know where they stood. "You didn't file any—"

"No. I didn't. I was mad and feeling protective of my dad. You're right about small-town law being totally different than practicing in New York."

He laid his hand on her knee. "Thanks for listening."

She pushed his hand off her leg. "I did it for my dad. If we get this solved, then we'll talk about forgiveness. Right now, I don't have the capacity to process anything else."

"Deal."

But she was mad as a hundred angry bees, and she was even going to be more pissed when she found out he had more information that she didn't. He wished he could tell her, but his hands were tied.

Connor could not wait to get down to the station to bring Scott up-to-date on the details, but between Mac's information and the fact that he himself had seen and could account for Ben's whereabouts between the narrowed timeline, Ben was surely in the clear. He just hoped Carolanne wouldn't act all crazy when they got there.

Connor led the way back to Scott's office without even checking in at the front desk. "Knock, knock," Connor said as they walked into his office. "Hey."

Scott looked at Carolanne. His face showed the guilt and stress of having her dad there behind bars. "I feel awful, Carolanne."

"You're just doing your job."

"I'm trying to get the evidence I need to make this right. I'm sorry. The information came through from the mayor's office. I didn't have a choice."

"I understand. Let's just figure this out."

Connor closed the door. "I've got more information." He looked to Carolanne. "You better sit down, too. You don't know all of this yet, either."

Carolanne's jaw pulsed. "You're going to be the death of me, Connor Buckham."

Scott looked away.

Connor shrugged. "Don't sweat it, Scott. I'm used to her redhead fuse."

"Look who's talking," she said. "Can we just get my dad out of jail, please?"

Connor ran down the information he had timelined out on Ben's activities and what Ben had shared about Gina.

Scott added, "Well, the journals we found at Ben's house belonged to Gina's mother. We think she probably got them from the old farmhouse. I'm going to check that out myself."

"That would explain the chain being down that day," Connor reasoned.

"Possibly. We didn't find anything in Ben's house that pointed to foul play."

"Of course not," Carolanne said.

Connor sat on the edge of Scott's desk. "Mac came to me with some information. You know he and Anita were out of town when all this happened."

Scott and Carolanne both nodded.

Carolanne spoke up. "He showed up at the artisan center to check in with Jill. That's when he first heard about it, and . . ." Carolanne's eyes lit up. "Connor, why didn't I realize it before? Did you?"

"What?" he asked.

"When Mac left that night, do you remember what he said? He knew her name. We'd never said it, but he said he was sorry about Gina!"

Connor nodded. "Before you go jumping to conclusions and throwing around accusations, let me tell you what he told me. You see, Mac talked to Gina the morning of the wedding. He told me that himself."

"He was the last one to see her alive?" Carolanne looked like she was more confused now than before.

"How did this girl get around this town in stealth mode?" Scott looked confused by all the details. "I've gone from a big fat nothing to more details than I could wish for."

Scott's phone rang.

"Hang on a second." He took the call, then stood up and started putting on his coat. Gesturing for them to follow him, he whispered, "Come on. We'll talk on the way."

They piled into Scott's car.

"Keep talking, Buckham," he said after hanging up the phone.

Connor leaned forward between Carolanne and Scott from the backseat. "The short version is Gina was at the artisan center talking to him when he was there to deliver the cake."

"He told you that?" Carolanne said.

"Yep. It was early, like seven thirty in the morning. She was alive when he last saw her, but he's worried—real worried—and he needs your help, Scott."

"I'm listening."

Connor told them how Mac had pulled him aside and told him that he remembered seeing Gina the morning of the wedding. He'd even talked to her, but he was in a hurry and she was gone before he'd gotten the chance to finish their conversation. He'd assumed that she'd just gotten tired of waiting, but now he knew it wasn't looking good, and he was right. He doesn't know what happened, but he knew he needed to clear Ben, even if it was going to make himself look guilty.

"Hold that thought," Scott said as he turned onto Route 58.

"Where are we going?" Carolanne asked.

"To the Dixon farm."

A few minutes later, they pulled in front of the path that led back to the Dixon property.

"The chain's back down," Connor said.

Scott drove down the overgrown path. The branches seemed to reach and tap out a warning on the windows as they drove to the back of the property.

Connor felt badly about Gina Edwards. This was a nice property. She'd died before she'd known it was her birthright. He wondered if she was the one who had been taking down the chain. "I wonder if she came out here that night." It might have been when she'd gotten her mother's journals. *Would've been nice to have something happy here to replace those old tales.*

Scott pulled his car tight to the right edge of the dirt path to avoid a deep mud gully. Someone had been back here and not that long ago. It was overgrown, but the path was easy to follow because the grass was packed down, leading the way to the old farmhouse and pond.

As they made it to the clearing, he pulled in front of the house. The front door was wide open. Apparently, someone had been doing more than just four-wheeling or swimming back here recently.

Scott called in his location, then turned off the car and grabbed his floodlight.

He flashed the light across the front of the house. He'd boarded up those front windows himself. Only, now, the window next to the door had been shimmied up.

"It would have taken some tools to get that open. I screwed the boards in myself to keep folks out," Scott said, handing a floodlight to Connor.

Connor swept the light across the space and stepped inside. He could see at least a couple different sets of shoe prints in the dust. The handrail going up the stairs had clear spots where someone had gripped it as they made their way up or down the stairs.

Wouldn't matter if they took something—there wasn't anyone left to care if it was missing. Maybe Gina had been here, or maybe someone else had and didn't want Gina to come back.

Connor walked back outside, where Carolanne was standing.

Scott walked toward them from around back. "Y'all follow me. You're not going to believe what I've just found."

"What?" Carolanne ran to catch up with Connor and Scott.

"Let me get some things from my car, and I'll take you back to see for yourself."

They followed Scott to the backyard. As they walked, Scott called in to dispatch from his radio. "Dispatch, I need Deputy Taylor out here at the Dixon farm."

Scott's radio crackled. Then dispatch made the call and confirmed the connection as they walked. When they got around back, they walked to the far end of the house, near the old garage.

When Scott flashed his light, something reflected back. "See that?"

"I saw something, but what is it? Some kind of a reflection. A mirror?" Carolanne said.

"That's what caught my attention, too." He started pacing forward. "Follow me."

They walked toward the garage, and when they got close enough, a vehicle came into view. Not just any vehicle, though. Mac's old bakery van.

"I don't understand."

Connor turned off his light. "Mac said they traded in his old van. He and Anita traded it while they were up North."

Scott nodded. "And when he told me about it, he said that Anita had talked him into doing it and she handled the whole thing."

"Why would she do that and then put the van back here?" Carolanne looked at Connor for an answer.

Scott walked to the front driver's side of the van. "Look." He waved Carolanne over. "Here. Hold this, but don't y'all touch anything."

Carolanne held the light. Connor looked at the damage while Scott ran back to the cruiser.

Scott came back with some supplies, including a digital camera. He took several pictures of the van.

Carolanne shifted the light to just below the headlight.

Connor squatted and examined it closer. "Look at the damage to the front quarter panel."

"Looks new," Carolanne said. "And is that blood?"

Scott took more pictures. "When the forensics team gets here, they'll take the official photos, but I always like to be able to prove that nothing changed between when I found the site and when they start, just in case something goes awry."

Then he snapped on a pair of gloves and handed Connor a paper sack.

"Hold this," Scott said as he lifted the door handle to the van. "The key is still in the ignition."

"Look how far the seat is pulled up," Carolanne

said. "Mac could never fit behind the wheel with the seat that close."

Lights washed over the overgrowth as a car idled down the path to the house.

"That should be Deputy Taylor," Scott said. "Come on."

Dan stepped out of the car just as they walked back out front. "What do we have?"

"Couple things. Someone has been in the house. Not sure there'll be anything worth spending a lot of time on in there, but there's a vehicle out back. I've got the forensics team on the way. Just need you to sit tight here and be sure nothing gets disturbed before they arrive."

"No problem."

Scott turned off his floodlight and placed it inside his trunk. "Did you hear anything back from the team that was looking at Ben Baxter's car?"

"I did. No trace evidence. Hard to say if he'd hit a person if they'd been in the same spot he'd hit that tree, but the fenders were clean."

"That's good." Scott looked to Carolanne. "We'll be releasing your dad. Any circumstantial evidence we thought we had has been explained now."

"While you're waiting, you might go ahead and collect anything out here on the grounds. It was pretty clear last time I was out here," Scott said to his deputy. "Could be something new now. See what you find."

"Will do. What time is the team supposed to be here?"

"Around eight. You've got all night."

"Won't be the first time," Deputy Taylor said.

# ❖ Chapter Twenty-Nine ❖

Connor escorted Ben to his car to give him a ride home.

"I can't thank you enough." Ben reached for Connor's hand and shook it.

"If Mac hadn't come to me with what he knew when he heard you'd been arrested, no telling how this would be going right now." Connor clicked his key fob to unlock the car doors. "You know what we have to do first, don't you?"

"Oh yeah. Tell Carolanne that I told you to keep the information from her to get your ass out of a sling." Ben pulled his seat belt into place.

"I'd appreciate that."

"You're a good man. Thanks for everything. I promise I won't put you in that kind of a position again."

"I'm glad to hear you say that, because if I have it my way, I'll be asking her to marry me. I'm not going to putz around and take a chance on losing her. With that fiery temper of hers, we could be up and down a million times, but one thing I know is that I want that little redhead by my side."

"I know exactly how you feel," Ben said. "Her momma was the same way. You'll have my blessing, but good luck. She can be a little stubborn."

Connor gave him a sideways glance. "I'll count on you to help me out, then."

"Well, I do owe you."

"And Mac—you owe him, too. If he hadn't come to us with that information, you could still be in a heap of circumstantial trouble. Trust me— even circumstantial evidence is still no picnic. You'd be surprised how many convictions get made on that."

Ben traced his hand on the door handle. "Do they know what happened to her yet?"

"Scott has a theory. He's going to try to prove it today. That's all I can tell you for now."

"That'll have to be good enough, then."

Connor pulled into Ben's driveway. "I'll keep you posted."

"You'll keep me posted on the case *and* on my daughter, right?"

"You got it," Connor said.

"Before you leave, do you have a minute?"

"Sure. What's up?"

Ben opened the car door. "Wait here. I have something I want to give you."

When Connor got back to the office, Carolanne was filing. He watched her for a minute before walking over to her. "I'm sorry," he said, reaching for her hand.

She let him take her hand, but she kept her gaze on the file drawer.

"Look at me." He tipped her face toward him.

Carolanne lifted her eyes to his.

"I love you. I will never let you down, I will never hurt you, and I will never keep anything from you again. I know I've disappointed you, but trust me on this. Please."

Her lips parted. "Don't make promises you can't keep. You don't know what the future holds."

"I do know."

She was keenly aware of his determination. "Why are you making this impossible?"

"Because I can't be without you, and I'm afraid you're going to walk away from what we could have together."

Carolanne wiggled out of his hold. "I can't do this."

"Please let me in. I promise you the worst thing that can happen is you decide you don't love me, and you can leave. No harm. No foul. I'm not asking you to give up anything. Please. Just try."

The door to the office slammed open, and Derek Honeycutt came running inside. "I need your help."

Connor jumped up and ran out to the lobby. "Derek, what's the matter?"

"They've just arrested my dad." The twenty-something man had the fear of a fourteen-year-old boy in his eyes.

"This can't be happening." Carolanne ran out to the lobby. "Come on. Let's go."

Derek was already sprinting toward the bakery. Carolanne and Connor ran to catch up with him in a mad dash to help Mac.

By the time the three of them got there, Mac was in handcuffs.

Carolanne's heart dropped. "No."

Connor pulled out his phone.

"Who are you calling?"

"Anita." He hit send. "Anita? This is Connor. They've just arrested Mac. You've got to get down here."

Derek stood frozen, watching the arrest go down. Carolanne ran to his side, wishing something comforting would pop into her head to say to make him feel better, but she knew what he was feeling. Embarrassed. Helpless. She'd been there a million times herself.

Connor ran over to Scott. "What's going on here? There's got to be a mistake."

Scott had never looked so serious. "Mac's old van was found behind the Dixon farmhouse. Forensics just confirmed the blood and material on the damaged fender of the van match Gina Edwards."

Derek's eyes went wide. "No. My dad would never . . ."

Carolanne knew that they'd found that van last night, but Mac had already talked to Connor.

Something wasn't right. This arrest seemed a little over-the-top. She put her arm around Derek. "Connor will sort this out. There's got to be an explanation."

Derek ran a nervous hand through his hair. "He didn't like Gina hanging around. He'd seen her talking to me. He told her not to hang around anymore. Do you think . . . ?"

"No. No, I don't." Carolanne pulled him to the side. "This isn't the time to speculate. Let's be calm, and don't say anything like that aloud. That's a totally innocent remark, but the police will hang on to it like a life raft if it helps their case."

Derek nodded.

"Let's lock up the shop, and I'll give you a ride home."

"I can't sit at home. I'm working on a cake in the back. I think I'd rather do that than go home."

"OK." Carolanne's heart was breaking. She led him back inside. "That's a good idea. You keep busy, and I promise I'll be back as soon as I have information."

Carolanne flipped the sign on the door from OPEN to CLOSED and locked it behind her. She rushed down the street to catch up with Connor at the police station.

She was glad the focus wasn't on her dad, but there was no way Mac was guilty. She felt it strongly. Connor stepped outside just as she walked up the steps.

Out of breath, Carolanne prayed he'd have good news. "What's the deal?"

"Come on. I'll fill you in on the way back to the office." Connor took her hand, and they walked up the block in silence.

When they walked into the office, he sat in a chair in the waiting area, and Carolanne sat across from him.

"So?"

Connor smiled. "Everything is OK."

She looked at him like he was crazy. "It's not OK if we just traded Dad for Mac. Mac isn't any more guilty than my dad in this. There's no way. I don't believe it."

"That Scott Calvin is one slick dude." Connor leaned back in his chair and laughed.

"Why are you so giddy?" *This is not the time to joke around.* "Would you please be serious?"

"That whole thing with Mac just now, the arrest—it was a total setup."

"What?" It took a moment to process. She leveled a stare. "You knew the whole time?"

He nodded.

She picked up a magazine from the coffee table and flung it at him. "I could kill you. I was worried to death! What happened to no more secrets?"

"Well, I didn't know all the details until a few

minutes ago." Connor ran down the chain of events, blow by blow.

"I know all that, Connor. I was there, although I did think it was weird that you had Anita's phone number in your phone."

"She gave it to me to give to Katherine that day I met her in the bakery. When all this started coming together, I called Katherine to ask her a few things about Anita, and that's when I found out that Anita was not friends with Katherine, but with Katherine's brother."

"That Richard guy?"

"Yes. He's bad news, but that's another story. Scott had me put Anita's number in my phone as part of the plan to get her back to Adams Grove."

"If I wasn't still so stunned, I'd be laughing. This kind of thing only happens on television."

"Not anymore." Connor leaned forward. "But here's the other thing you didn't know. Mac told Scott that Gina Edwards had shown up late Friday night at the bakery while he was finishing up the cake for Jill and Garrett's wedding. She was asking about her mother and what had happened at the Old Mill Pond all those years ago."

"So she didn't know about the drowning before she came to town?"

"Nope, and at first, Mac thought he might have been her father. He'd even said as much to Anita after Gina left that night."

"Is he?"

"No. Mac said when Gina showed up again in the morning, he asked her specifically about her birth date. Gina knew that he wasn't her father all along anyway."

"But Anita didn't know that?"

"No, she didn't. The connection between Mac and Gina's mom was high school. They were sweethearts. Mac and Lindsey were supposed to have been watching her brother that day. They'd been swimming in the pond, and then Mac and Lindsey had scooted off to make out. They heard Jimmy yelling, but they thought he was just playing because he knew what they were up to. Only, Jimmy hadn't been fooling around, and when they went back to the pond to round up Jimmy, he was gone."

"That's when her brother drowned?" Carolanne shivered. "That's so sad."

"He was fourteen. I imagine the guilt they lived with factored into Gina's mother's depression. Mac said that Gina told him it was her mother's suicide that had made her come looking for answers."

"That's kind of what she'd indicated to me, too. I can understand that."

"That morning at the artisan center, Mac told her about the secret pact between he and Lindsey, but then he asked her to wait because he had to get the cakes set up. When he came out of the artisan center, Anita had come up with the spurof-the-moment trip for the two of them, and Gina was already gone."

"Did Anita say why Gina had left? That doesn't make sense. Why would Gina go to all that trouble to find out that information and then not stick around?"

"Anita told Mac that Gina had gotten a call from her father and had to leave. In Anita's mind, she'd just convinced Mac he wasn't the father, but that was something Mac knew already. So it made sense to him."

"So, Anita hit Gina with the van?"

"That's the theory. This whole setup today, with Derek not knowing and all, is to draw Anita out and get to the bottom of it."

"Mac really loves Anita. If Scott's theory proves out, I feel sorry for the old guy."

# ❖ Chapter Thirty ❖

Connor was with Scott in his office when Anita showed up at the Sheriff's Department demanding answers.

"That didn't take long," Scott said to Connor. Scott gave the deputy the go to let Anita see Mac. "Come on. This should be interesting."

Connor followed Scott into the office that backed up to the interrogation room. They stood next to the mirrored glass and waited.

The deputy led Mac in first. They left him hand-cuffed.

"He looks distraught," Connor said.

"He is." Scott gestured back to the window. "Here she comes."

Anita was dressed in black slacks and a flowing colorful blouse. She glanced at the window, like she was looking right at them.

Connor nudged Scott. "You sure she can't see us?"

"Positive."

The deputy stepped back against the door.

Anita rushed to Mac's side. "What is going on? Connor Buckham called me and said you'd been arrested. What did you do?"

Scott snickered. "Guess she's going to throw him right under the bus."

She gasped when she saw his wrists in the handcuffs. "Mac, this is serious."

Connor felt uncertainty creep in. "Hope this works out the way you think it's going to."

"It will. We practiced," Scott said.

Mac paled. "I didn't do anything." He looked unsteady as he ran down the details just as Scott had coached him. Leaving out things like the fact that they'd already located the van. "That girl who had been hanging around Derek, then showed up the morning of the wedding—she's dead."

"You knew she was trouble. You told Derek to stay away from her the first time you saw her." Anita leaned forward and whispered, "I hope Derek doesn't tell them about how you yelled at him about keeping her away from the bakery. It wouldn't look good."

"That was before I knew who she was." Mac lifted his cuffed wrists and scratched his nose with one of his hands. He glanced over at the deputy and then back at Anita. "I wouldn't kill anyone. You know that."

Anita tensed. "I'm here for you, Mac. I love you. I'll be by your side no matter what."

Mac softened visibly at her words—her clear commitment. He didn't even seem to notice that she didn't agree with him.

"I hope he can stick to the plan," Scott said.

"See why I'm worried?" Connor shifted and let out a sigh. "Hang in there, buddy."

"You saw her that morning at the wedding reception. Your alibi should clear me."

She paused. "I think we better act carefully. I've got a friend that can help us. He was a lawyer up in Chicago. He'll know how to handle this. I wouldn't want to make more trouble for you by saying the wrong thing."

"Talk to Connor," Mac said. "You know that he's always handled all my legal stuff."

She shook her head. "Oh no, you need a real lawyer. Let me take care of this for you, dear. I'll need your power of attorney to get things going and to pay for it and all, but don't you worry. I will take care of everything. We will have you out of here in no time, and we'll be back together."

Mac blinked.

"I can't wait for us to do all the things we've talked about. You know how much I care for you. I'd do anything for you."

"Stick with the plan, man," Scott coached quietly.

"He's not going to be able to do this," Connor said. "He's eaten up with it. He loves her. Look. It's all over his face."

"I know I can trust you. Thank you, Anita."

She stood and walked to the door. "I'll be back in just a little while."

The deputy opened the door and led her down the hall.

Mac laid his head on the table.

"Now what?" Connor asked.

"She'll be back."

Scott's radio crackled.

Connor couldn't make out the garbled message.

"She's sitting in her car in the parking lot," Scott said. "I'm going to go check on Mac."

Connor watched through the glass as Scott talked to Mac. It was sad to see the poor guy go through this. Anita had no intention of helping Mac. It was easy to see from this side. It was too hard to watch. He turned and started answering e-mails on his phone.

Scott came back in the room.

"How is he?"

Scott shrugged. "You're right. He's struggling with it. If I'm wrong, he's liable to kill me for it, but I don't think I am."

"Where's Anita?"

"The guys just checked in. She's still sitting in the parking lot."

Connor checked his watch. "She's been sitting out there for nearly an hour. What is she waiting for?"

"Maybe she's waiting for her lawyer friend to show up."

Scott's phone rang. It was a quick call.

"She's on her way back in."

"This should be interesting," Connor said.

Anita walked back into the room to see Mac with a folder in her hand.

She sat across the table from him with her hands in front of her, then swept at tears.

Mac lifted his wrists onto the table. "I'm sorry, honey. I didn't mean to upset you."

Anita laid her hands on top of his. "I love you. Everything is going to be just fine. I talked to my guy. He faxed me these papers for you to sign so that I can act on your behalf. Don't you worry about a thing."

Connor couldn't believe the performance she was giving. "That woman is one heck of a liar. I'd believe her if I didn't know for a fact that she was just sitting in the parking lot out front for the last hour."

Mac glanced at the window, then turned the paper around. "What is it?"

"Power of attorney, like I said."

His jaw clenched and his eyes narrowed slightly as he stared at the woman seated across from him.

"I'll handle everything. Don't you worry."

Mac shook his head. "I'm innocent. I'd never hurt anyone. You know that, right?"

She patted his hand. "Of course."

"You were there that morning. You saw Gina. She was very much alive. You said she'd made contact with her real father and that she'd rushed off to see him."

"You just relax." She patted his hand. "I've got this. My guy is flying in this afternoon. It might take a day or two, but we'll get you out of here. So, don't worry."

"She's not going to incriminate herself. She's going to let him take the fall," Connor said in disbelief.

"Just sign the papers, Mac," she said. "I'll take care of everything."

He took the pen and signed his name. Then Anita picked up the pen in her left hand and signed them. "There. We're all set."

Connor nudged Scott. "Signing that piece of paper doesn't mean squat without a notary. You and I both know that."

Scott watched intently. "She's up to something."

"When will you be back?" Mac looked defeated.

Connor felt badly for the guy. He knew she was taking him for a ride. That had to hurt.

Anita stood up and turned to the deputy. "Can I give him a hug?"

The deputy nodded.

She stepped close to him and wrapped her arms around him.

Mac stared at the two-way glass. He looked like he had about a hundred things he'd like to say to that woman right now, but he held his tongue.

"I'll be back tomorrow afternoon." She gave the deputy a nod as she walked out of the room.

Connor turned to Scott. "What now?"

"We wait. Hardest part." Scott opened the door and went back into his office. Connor followed behind him. "We've got all his accounts monitored. As soon as things start happening, we'll know."

Late that afternoon, a man met with Anita in her yoga studio building. Connor identified him as Katherine's brother, Richard. When he'd contacted Katherine to ask her about her friendship with Anita and her brother's tie-in, Katherine admitted that she barely knew Anita. It was her brother who was friendly with her.

It didn't take long for Scott to pull all the information on the sketchy background of Richard, and by nine thirty the next morning Anita and Richard had cleared Mac's accounts under the watchful eye of Scott and his men.

By ten o'clock Scott had his men arrest her for the murder of Gina Edwards and the fraudulent activities she committed once she'd decided to steal Mac's money. Richard's arrest followed, and by noon Mac was back in his bakery making a batch of fresh bear claws to thank everyone who'd helped him.

Connor sat in Jacob's Diner with Carolanne and Scott. "You told me you had one piece of evidence that you'd withheld from any records that would help you confirm that you had the real murderer?" Connor asked.

Scott smiled. "I did say that, didn't I?"

"Once I started looking into Anita's past, the

two husbands that she'd outlived had both been rather wealthy up until the time Anita met them."

"She seemed so nice," Carolanne said. "It's hard to believe we're talking about the same person."

"I guess that's why she was staying under the radar," Connor said. "Mac said that he thought she was just a very private person."

Scott took a sip of his sweet tea. "It'd be nice if there were a device that would let us know when people were being sincere. That Anita put on one good act for Mac. It's too bad, really. I could tell he was really crazy about her."

"I'm glad Dad and Mac are cleared, but I'm so sad that Gina ended up in the middle of all that," Carolanne said. "All she wanted was some answers."

# ❖ Chapter Thirty-One ❖

Connor stood on the porch of Carolanne's new house with a handful of contraband begonias—the peach ones—in one hand and two cups of coffee balanced one on top of the other in the other.

He took in a deep breath, prayed for the right words, then pushed the doorbell with his knuckle. A laugh soothed his nerves when he heard her heavy footsteps coming down the stairs.

Carolanne swung the door open. "I thought that was your car. What are you doing here?" She caught the glimpse of color in his other hand. "Oh no, you're not stealing flowers again?"

"Pruning. Doing my part to keep Main Street looking nice."

"You've got an answer for everything. Maybe you should be a lawyer."

*Or more than that.* "It's tradition."

"It's a crime," she said. "And I think you just became a habitual offender."

He stepped closer, as close as he could without spilling the coffee on her. "Are you going to let me in?"

"No. I don't think so." She took the cup on top and smiled. "OK, I guess I can let you in since you brought me presents."

"Good, because this is serious business."

Her smile faded. "Oh no? Is something wrong?"

"Very." He motioned for her to sit down. "You better sit down for this." He closed the door.

She sat down and hunched forward. "Connor, after all that we've been through lately, I don't think I can go through anything else. Please tell me everyone is alive and well."

"Calm down. Not that kind of serious. Everyone is fine."

"Thank goodness."

He saw the relief wash over her, and he felt a little badly for making her feel that tension, even if only for a moment. She pulled the plastic lid off the coffee cup and blew into it before taking a sip. "OK, so, what's the problem?"

He patted her leg. "I can't start my mornings without you." He shrugged. "I've tried. I've run. I've tried coffee at Mac's, the diner. I've even tried truck-stop coffee. It's not the same, and it's too quiet around there without you."

She turned to face him. "I kind of miss the old routine, too, but we'll make a new one."

"I'm glad you said that because that's exactly what I was thinking."

"Oh no. I know that look. What did you have in mind?"

"I don't just miss the routine. Carolanne, I miss you." He took her warm hands into his own and held them. "I've fallen in love with you, Carolanne Baxter. The last thing I'd want to ever do is hurt you, and I know sometimes I bumble around in ways that drive you crazy, but I'd never do anything to make you sad."

"I believe you, but—"

He put his finger over her lips. "Let me finish."

She nodded.

"I want you more than anything. Do you know what I'm saying, here?"

Her mouth opened slightly. "Do *you* know what you're trying to say?"

He nodded. "I love you. I want you in my life. Forever. Your dad and all. The baggage. The grumpy mornings. I'll even eat your cooking."

A tear slipped down her cheek. "That's serious."

"Well, maybe I can do some of the cooking. You're the best thing that ever happened to me. Pearl was right. We're a perfect couple."

"You really think so? Baggage and all?"

"I do."

He knelt down, and Carolanne sucked in a breath. "What are—?"

"Carolanne Baxter. Will you be my bride?"

She swallowed hard. "If I say yes, you better not break my heart."

"I won't. I promise you." Connor dug into his pocket. "I talked to your dad about my intentions, too. He gave me these to give to you." He opened his hand. "They were your mom's."

"My mother's wedding rings?" She pulled her

hands to her face. "Oh. My. Gosh. How could I say no?"

"I was hoping you couldn't." He pulled her hands away from her face and replaced them with a soft kiss on the velvet warmth of her lips. "I'm hoping you won't."

Carolanne leaned forward into his arms, and he held her close. He felt his whole future wrapped up in this feisty redhead, and he was eager to see just how much chaos she could bring into their happy lives.

She pulled back, and the serious look on her face scared him. *Please don't fight me on this.*

"Yes. Yes, Connor, I will marry you, but"—she paused—"under one condition."

"Anything."

"We have to move quickly and keep it small, else Jill is going to want me to use that big wedding planner binder of hers. I'm just not the big-white-gown kind of girl."

"Can't I get a cool cake like Garrett got?"

"Fine. A cake and a cookout at the house to celebrate with friends, but that's as far as I'll go."

"How about in the morning?"

"What in the morning?"

"We can get married tomorrow morning. Why not? You said you didn't want a big wedding. So, what's stopping us?"

She seemed to stumble for words. "Your fancy cake?"

Connor pressed a couple of buttons on his phone. "Hey, Derek. It's Connor Buckham. Yeah, man. I'm good. I need a favor."

Connor whispered across the room to her. "I love you like crazy." He loved the way her eyes sparkled when he made her laugh.

He turned his attention back to the phone. "Yeah, Derek, I need one of those fancy groom cakes . . . by tomorrow night. Can you swing it?"

"Just fifty or so people," Connor said.

"Fifty! I said small." Carolanne put her hands on her hips.

"Make that enough for just forty-five people." Connor put his hand over the speaker. "You and I have a date, baby."

"Yeah. Yeah, Derek. We're here. The cake? Uh, yeah. How about in the shape of a coffeepot? Only, I want that coffee decanter to be filled with chocolate. And throw in a crossword puzzle, too. Oh, and I've got it. Make the crossword puzzle with four words on it. You writing this down?"

Connor paused. "Yes. The four words are 'You Were Right' and 'Pearl.'"

He nodded as he listened. "Yes, you've got it. Can you do it? And plan to stay for the party. It'll need to be delivered here to Carolanne's place at Bridle Path Estates by, say, five o'clock. We're having a celebration."

Connor tossed his phone on the table next to the couch and pulled her into his arms. "Done."

"Just like that?" She threw her hands in the air. "We'll need witnesses."

"You said small. We'll do it at the courthouse. We'll call Jill and Garrett to witness it."

"And my dad."

Connor broke out into a wide grin. "Definitely your dad. We're all set except for the flowers, but I can handle those."

"Oh no, you don't. We aren't going to have a flower left on Main Street if you keep that up. How about we start a new tradition? Alstroemeria— my mom's favorite."

"Anything you want. So, we're all set then."

"Are you mistaking me for someone spontaneous?"

He pulled her close against him and kissed her on the neck. "There's no mistake about this. We have a date."

# Acknowledgments

Thank you to my writer girls who, knowingly or otherwise, keep me inspired to keep writing through the emotional journey of making up a story and bringing it to the page and ultimately to the reader. Without y'all—it wouldn't be nearly as fun.

My Montlake team, Kelli Martin, Krista Stoever, Jessica Poore, and the whole gang over at Montlake Romance, y'all make a girl feel like she can do anything. Thank you for helping me become a better writer and for making my dreams a reality.

As always, for their enthusiasm and support, I thank my family. The emotion and love in my stories is a direct result of the blessings from my loving extended family. And to Hunter, my black Lab, who sits faithfully with me, hour after hour no matter what, through every single draft.

# About the Author

Nancy Naigle was born and raised in Virginia Beach. She balances her career in the financial industry with a lifelong passion for books and storytelling. When she isn't writing or wrangling goats on the family farm, she enjoys antiquing and cooking. She lives with her husband in Drewryville, Virginia.